This was the ideal time to move, Jenny thought. Say goodbye to Henry, who is already looking at something far away I cannot see, have a good, therapeutic clearing out of junk, then on with a fresh start in a new home without him. It's almost like waiting for someone to die, she thought, waiting for him to go, not wanting him to, but not being able to stand much more of this waiting. He's not going for another week, yet already he is receding. I must be seen to be busy, she thought, must not give him the idea that things will grind to a halt when he's gone. I am going to show him that I can have just as interesting a time, in a different way, as he can. I shall have a happy face on when he leaves.

Anna Yeomans is an Oxford graduate and mother of two daughters. She is temporarily living in New Zealand where she writes full-time. *Where Are You, Henry?* is her first novel.

Where Are You, Henry?

ANNA YEOMANS

PHŒNIX

A PHOENIX PAPERBACK

First published in Great Britain by Orion in 1996
This paperback edition published in 1997 by Phoenix,
a division of Orion Books Ltd,
Orion House, 5 Upper St Martin's Lane, London WC2H 9EA

A CIP catalogue record for this book is available
from the British Library.

ISBN: 1 85799 843 X

Printed and bound in Great Britain
by The Guernsey Press Co. Ltd,
Guernsey, Channel Islands.

For Isobel Joan

CHAPTER I

Henry had dedicated his life to Arctic Char. This fascination had not been a sudden thing; Henry did not go in for sudden things. It gradually dawned on him during his years at sea, studying the patterns of the ocean floor on survey ships, staring at the grey horizon day after day, that he had built up a strong and lasting bond with this elusive fish. He used to glimpse the shoals occasionally, shimmering beneath the dark green surface of the water, the only living creatures as far as the eye could see. He felt a lonely companionship with them as they, like him, travelled the seas, nomads of the icy rivers and ocean. Not that he would have dreamed of speaking of this to any of his fellow workers. They were not on the whole a reflective, sensitive crowd (although some were deeply sentimental) and this was not the stuff of their conversation. But then, Henry was not ever really part of their cohesive little group. He was pleasant and friendly and always got on with everyone on board, but he was always a little separate. People liked him, but they generally tended to leave him alone with his books. With a degree in marine biology he had become, by luck and a convoluted route, a seismic surveyor for a series of international oil companies. He had worked in the North Sea, the Atlantic, the Persian Gulf and off the coast of Africa. This nomadic life, combined with Henry's natural reticence, had meant that he had avoided any kind of emotional attachment during these years. He had been a dedicated and competent seismic surveyor, he had seen the world, and with no one to help him spend his money, he had become moderately rich. Yet secretly, all along, he had really wanted to study fish. When Henry was thirty-four his father had died and left Henry seriously wealthy, so he had decided to give up the long months on survey ships and go back to what he liked best, which was studying. Now a second degree and an MSc later, he had at last been granted the opportunity to do a PhD on the subject of Arctic Char and he could not imagine doing anything else. This, he thought, was the opportunity of a lifetime.

People often asked him, what is the fascination of this little-known and rather ordinary looking fish? Is it good to eat? How big is it? Will it solve the problems of the ailing British fishing industry? Does it have a particularly exotic life style? Henry was always more than happy to explain. You see, the strange thing about the Arctic Char was this. You may see small Arctic Char, you may see large Arctic Char. But you never, no really, never, he insisted every time – usually to middle-aged women at university dinners – see any middle-sized ones. (This was also true of lecturers' wives, Henry noticed, but he added this joke only if he happened to be talking to one of the small ones, or to someone who was not a wife.) You may find that hard to believe, he would say – Henry did himself at first – but after years of studying these fish at sea, he knew it to be true. So where, Henry would wonder aloud to his companion, who was invariably leaning forward at this point, fulsome chest bulging with flattering eagerness to know the answer, where were all the middle-sized Arctic Char? This was what he was going to Greenland in the hope of finding out. It seemed extraordinary to Henry that no one had ever thought to ask this question before. His companion would agree with him in breathy fascination and gaze into his eyes long enough to decide that, however good-looking he was (and he was undoubtedly very attractive), this was not enough to compensate for having to compete for his attention with a little-known cold water fish, even if it was the only one of its kind that migrated to the sea. At this point his companion would usually disappear rather speedily to find another drink.

He had it all planned, flights booked, he had even sold the car. In Henry's life, nothing was left to chance. He had given up his dark-panelled room at York University, situated in one of the rambling Victorian terraces owned by the university just outside the city walls, put all his precious books in boxes and deposited them with various friends. This perhaps was the hardest wrench, for his

2

library was an extension of himself. But his eyes were resolutely fixed on his coming adventure. He knew, obscurely, that he would come back a changed man. How could he not? Six months at a scientific study centre in Greenland, with frequent and quite long trips around the Arctic Ocean to catch up with the shoals and follow them as far as possible. This would be the really interesting bit, for no one knew where the shoals would take him, where the breeding grounds were, and of course, the crucial question, where do the fish go for the year or so while they are maturing? Henry was really looking forward to this part. He was setting off in June, the best time as it was the Arctic summer. Then, by the time it was unbearably cold in December, he would be spending three months at the University of Illinois, writing up his findings. If all went well for this first academic year and he managed to produce results (he would have to give a paper at a conference in California in March) then he would receive funding for the second year of his studies. He would be back in Britain from April to June, then the whole process, rather like the annual cycle of the Arctic Char, would begin again. By the end of this, Henry would not only be Doctor Henry Proctor, which he considered a rather unfortunate name but it could not be helped, he would also be the world expert on Arctic Char. He was off in three weeks' time.

The only fly in the ointment, although Henry did not like to think of her as that, was Jenny. Jenny was warm, solid, smiley, thirty-five, and very fond of Henry. He loved her dearly, in a deep and painful way he found impossible to articulate, so he took her out for meals a lot and made silent, vigorous love to her to show his feelings. Jenny had seen life in a way that Henry, despite his years of travelling, had not. Shielded by his work and his fastidious intellect, Henry had passed through and observed life in its widest and most varied forms. Jenny had touched the sides. She was blunt, colourful, down-to-earth, especially about sex, which he found immensely refreshing; and of course, she had Josh.

Josh was one of Jenny's main attractions as far as Henry was concerned. Never having known his own mother, he loved to see Jenny being a mother to Josh. He had never told her this, of course, it fell into the category of things that Henry felt strongly but never articulated. He had perhaps a larger store of these things than most people. He liked the direct way Jenny spoke to Josh, whether she was joking or serious, as if he were an equal and a friend. Even when she was reprimanding him, she did it in such a way that they both recovered quickly with no loss of face. She always said, 'Come on, let's have a hug, it's over now,' and things continued much the same as before, with Josh taking it all in good part, then carrying on grubbily doing whatever it was he had been doing before. That was quite unlike the brutalising humiliation that Henry's own father had dished out for any misdemeanour. Correcting the young Henry, a mild but mischievous boy, had been undertaken with a zeal and regularity that had often left Henry feeling battered and drained. His father had had no sense of proportion, no idea of matching the punishment to the crime, so whether Henry had spent the newspaper money on a chocolate bar, or climbed up on the high, steeply sloping roof of the local primary school, endangering life and limb with a boy called Clive to throw eggs on passers-by, or just stuck his tongue out at the old woman in the corner house who waved her stick at them from the window, the punishment was the same – a five-minute harangue, a cane on the hand, and an instruction to Mrs Pickford, the elderly home help, not to leave Henry any tea the next day. As a result, much of Henry's childhood had been accompanied by a great and gnawing hunger. However, this was only in school holidays. During term Henry was entrusted to the care of an energetic and definitely unintrospective boarding school, where a long cross-country run and a cold shower was the cure for most things. Henry thought that for boys of twelve to sixteen, it probably was. At school the food was basic, stodgy and plentiful. So Henry grew into a muscular, athletic and handsome young man equipped for life with a fistful of good exam results and a standard, regulation issue set of hang-ups. His father felt the money had been well spent.

Jenny and Josh probably got on so well because they had always had only each other. This was what Jenny said. Henry loved the idea of a ready-made family. His inner loneliness, so familiar he was hardly aware of it, disappeared when he, Jenny and Josh were all in a pile on the sofa, eating chips and watching television, or when he joined in with Josh to tease Jenny, or took him to the off-licence to get beer. These activities fulfilled his idea of a simple, normal family, and he could bask in these comforts. Yet because they had existed before him and without him, he felt that he could participate in them whenever he liked, that none of this domestic harmony was dependent on him. Jenny had managed perfectly well, he considered, before he had come along, so he felt absolved of any responsibility in this small family. Jenny ran the show, and he considered himself simply an appreciative observer, sometimes a participant. He was still free to be Henry Proctor the explorer, the solitary man. He was still able to walk away.

Jenny was less warm and smiley now that Henry was leaving. Naturally she could not come with him; they had not even discussed it. There would be no place for her and Josh in Greenland and anyway she had her job as an occupational therapist at Bootham, the psychiatric hospital, and she had just bought a house. He had told her, with great effort, for these things did not come easily to Henry, that he cared for her, that if he could study Arctic Char in York, he would. He told her also that he was planning to come back.

'Hmm,' she said, 'we'll see. Don't make promises you might not be able to keep. Anyway, who says I'll still be waiting?'

He never knew whether this was just a taunt to make him feel even worse about leaving her, or whether she meant it. Of course, she intends me not to know, he thought, feeling very wise and perceptive. She is just trying to keep me on my toes. Of course she will still be here; where else could she be?

'Well, I do intend to come back,' he insisted, but this just seemed to annoy her more. He couldn't see that it was his choice of words that hurt her. To intend to come back was not enough. She would have liked (but would never have dreamed of asking him for) a promise that he would be back. It was no good, whatever he said, and he found it hard to say the right things, she took it as a rejection.

'Let's enjoy the time we still have left,' he said, several times.

'I can't, I keep thinking how I'll feel when you're gone, and what's the point?'

'You could come and join me in Illinois,' he said. 'That would be great, wouldn't it? For a couple of weeks?' He tried to sound enthusiastic. It was not easy in the face of her (as he perceived it) determined self-pity.

'Where would I get the money for the air fares?'

Henry markedly did not offer to pay for her ticket. It did not even occur to him.

'And Josh miss all that school? And mum's becoming more of a tie, you know what she's like. Anyway, you'll be busy with your studenty friends.'

'What studenty friends?' he said. 'I haven't got any. And I don't want any, either.'

'You will have. Women will be falling over themselves. You're so naive, Henry, it's just as well it's only fish you're studying. You know more about Arctic Char than you do about people, otherwise you'd have some idea of how I'm feeling.'

And so it developed into another argument. Well, not an argument exactly, he preferred to think of it as a frank exchange of views, but whatever you called it this was not how he wanted to spend his last few weeks with Jenny, as he really did love her. They had been together for four years now, ever since he had first arrived in York. This was the longest Henry had been with anyone, and the entire time he had been doing his second degree and MSc as a mature student. He could not envisage life without Jenny in the background (background, perhaps, being the operative word) supporting and encouraging him. He knew she was the stronger of the two. He knew also that this was what he needed. His motherless upbringing had been coloured by the warm, powdery presence of Matron at boarding school. Then, two weeks before he had to leave for Greenland, he had an idea.

Jenny called in to see her mother most days on her way home from work. Today she fitted it into the lunch hour in case Henry called in the evening.

'You've got to do it, Jen. Grandma Phipps didn't do anything with her life. My mother didn't do anything with hers. I haven't done anything – you've got to do it. It all hangs on you. You've got to do it for all of us.'

These words of her mother's were a constant refrain, and had been for as long as she could remember. It was not at all clear to Jenny exactly what she was expected to do to rescue them all from this history of terminal uselessness. She doubted whether her mother knew what she was saying any more, the phrases just came out because her mouth was so used to framing the same, familiar patterns of sound. She had her cardigan on inside out, the label stuck up at a rakish angle. It gave her a falsely jaunty appearance.

'You've got your cardigan on inside out.'

'What's that, dear? This hair,' complained her mother, patting the sparse and harshly frizzled fluff that still clung to her head. 'It's terrible. That Sylvia, I don't know what she was thinking of, I can't do a thing with it. Stuffed full of nonsense, that's what she is, doesn't have her mind on the job. Give me a hand with this, will you?'

Her mother was clearing some black, foul-smelling jellyish substance out of the u-bend under the sink. It was mostly kipper skins, Jenny thought, as she tipped it into the bin, but it may be that after a certain stage of decomposition everything resembled kipper skins. Cleaning out the u-bend seemed to Jenny the epitome of unfulfilled female existence. If you had made anything of your life, she thought, you had someone else to clean out the u-bend in the sink.

'But you've brought us up,' she reassured her mother, not entirely with conviction.

Her mother snorted. Her legs were getting thinner, her tights were wrinkled around the ankles.

'Brought you up so your sister lands herself up gutting fish in a supermarket' (it was turning out rather a fishy day) 'living in a bedsit with some long-haired sponger – '

'That was months ago, Mother,' Jenny put in, unheard.

' – Brought you up? Animals can do that. Rabbits can do that.'

'Fish don't do it.' This must be Henry's influence, she thought, I've got fish on the brain. She felt a familiar stab when she remembered he was leaving in two weeks' time. She was getting so used to this sickening feeling of not knowing what was going to happen, it was becoming almost normal to feel this way. She understood him though, better than he knew, and certainly better than anyone else did. Most people were dazzled and attracted by his fair good looks, his freckled skin, browned and roughened by years of sun and ocean winds, his broad, athletic body, his air of remote and rugged independence. His blond hair was crisp and crinkly, cut short so that the curls got smaller and smaller down the nape of his neck, like the fair, fine wool on a sheep's legs. It was rough and dry to the touch. These looks acted like a magnet to the type of woman who sees it as a challenge to tame a man. Many women who approached him could not believe their luck when they discovered he was not married and were undeterred by a shadowy girlfriend in the background. Girlfriends were easily disposed of. But after ten minutes in his company they would back off, bewildered by those kindly eyes that did not focus on them properly, that certainly did not give the look of predatory assessment they expected from a man. They were confused by his obscure conversation, his naive assumption that they were interested in his research just because they said they were, his inability to conduct the kind of coded conversation that signals availability and the possibility of sexual adventure. They saw it as a defect that he was more interested in ideas than people. These sophisticated women, whose position in society rested on their ability to charm, quickly retreated when they realised Henry did not play the games they played. He did not take up the well-used cues they offered him. Perhaps he's gay, they thought, limited by their own terms of reference, for everything came down to sexual attraction, didn't it? They did not know how else to make contact.

But Jenny, with her kindliness, her warmth that enveloped everything, her refusal to judge, understood him. She realised that the very qualities she loved in him were the reasons she would never really have him – his single-minded pursuit of one consuming interest, his abstracted kindness, his ability, need even, to walk alone through life. She knew the reasons for his benevolent detachment. He would always be a solitary figure with his eyes on the horizon. She, with her eyes firmly focused on the demands of every day, and her feet bound in the rich and fertile soil of the Vale of York, admired that in him. He represented and claimed for himself the freedom she desired. Her mind was like a cluttered junk room. His was a tidy, neatly catalogued office. With an effort she tuned back into her mother's constant voice.

'Fish?' her mother was saying. 'Who wants to be compared to a fish? "You shall have a fishy, on a little dishy, You shall have a bloater, when the boat comes in,"' she sang, then said, "Have you ever had a bloater? I don't think I have. Don't fancy the sound of them. Sound like they've been dead in the water too long, type of thing. All puffed up, like. Give me a nice bit of herring any time. Your father likes a rollmop. Never takes his slippers off the radiator though. Is that a new jumper? Purple's not your colour, dear. Sylvia says I should wear more mauve, what do you think?'

There was a pause while her mother's mind floated out into the yard.

'Anyway,' Jenny went on doggedly, determined to say what she had come to say, 'I just came round to tell you I'm moving, not far, just into Hazel Terrace, here's the phone number. I'll still pop in most days.'

'Moving? Again?' Her mother had the irritating habit of repeating back to you what you had just said. She was only sixty-three, too young for this elderly childishness and too old for child-like behaviour to be endearing. 'You've not long been in your last place. Fallen out with Janice, have you? Now there's a nice sensible girl, you could do worse than be a nurse like her. A proper job. A nice tidy uniform. That's the only way they'll take you seriously.'

Ah yes, thought Jenny. The mysterious, ubiquitous 'they' who always had an opinion on anything you did, and it was usually a critical opinion. Like some invisible Greek chorus, 'they' featured highly in her mother's life.

'I've got a proper job.'

'And what about Josh? He's only just got used to the last place. And what about that young man of yours? When's he going to get round to making you an offer?'

'The flat was much too small, as you'd have seen, if you'd ever come to visit. Anyway, it's not like that with Henry, Mum, I've told you before. He's going away. He's been offered something in

Greenland. It's a brilliant chance for him.'

And the only offer he's ever likely to make is a visit to the takeaway, Jenny added to herself.

'Greenland? What's there, for heaven's sake? Why is he going to Greenland?'

Jenny sighed. It was always like this. 'To study fish, Mother, I've told you that's what he does. Now let me put the kettle on.'

'Studying fish is no sort of career for a man. Herring, I hope they are. I like a nice bit of herring.'

She's getting worse, thought Jenny. When will I know that she's really going ga-ga and it's not just the old cooking sherry talking? Will I be able to tell the difference?

'The house is mine. I've bought it, Mother. Janice is going to be my lodger to help with the mortage. And Josh is pleased, anyway – he'll have a room of his own.'

It's always the way, Jenny thought. Achievement to men means adventure, flying high, leaving responsibility and mundanity behind, going away. Achievement for women means succeeding in tying yourself, rooting yourself to the ground with chains made of love, then being the one to clear up the mess left behind by your loved ones. Her mother creaked to her feet and wiped her hands on her apron, leaving black streaks from the sink.

'Oh well, that's different, your own place.' She sniffed. 'Can I smell cabbage? Have I left a pan on?'

'It's the bin, Mother. You wouldn't be cooking cabbage this early, would you? It's only just gone twelve.'

'Is that all it is?' said her mother in amazement, as if Jenny had told her the moon was only twenty miles away. 'Wait 'til I tell your father.' Her mother carried on the same love-hate relationship with Jenny's father and kept him up to date with all the news, as she had when he was alive. He had been dead three years.

'Your own place, that's lovely. You'll never be any man's plaything with your own place. Your father and I will come round for a housewarming.' Presumably she meant she would bring him in his urn. Most of the time he sat on the bookcase in the dining room, faithfully dusted on Mondays and Thursdays.

Jenny hoped that owning her own house and being financially

independent would not exclude the possibility of her being some man's plaything once in a while. It was just the sock retrieval from under the bed and the having to use the bathroom just after a man that she intended to avoid.

'Oh, Maggie's left that black man,' her mother was saying, 'that – what do you call them? Reminds me of raffia – Rastafarian, that's it, what was his name? Gone to Brighton, God knows what for, or was it Bognor? "Bugger Bognor" – who said that? Did I read it in one of my books?' She used the word 'book' to describe the floppy magazines that formed the bulk of her literary diet. 'Left that bedsit,' she went on, 'Not that that's any great loss, looking right over the gasworks like that and so close to the Council tip, I never did think it was very healthy. Gave her a black eye, so she said, not that she doesn't ask for it sometimes the way she carries on. Pity your father didn't put her across his knee more often, things might have turned out different then.'

Jenny said nothing. It is so much easier to pile blame onto the heads of the uncomplaining dead.

'Well, I'd best be off now,' Jenny said, after watching her mother down two tumblers of cooking sherry in celebration of the new house. She did not look very celebratory as she did it. Jenny had declined a drink, but her mother was not ready to let her go. She sloshed gin with the barest splash of orange juice into her empty glass – 'that's for me vitamin C,' she said virtuously – and warmed to her subject.

'Well, I mean, you don't meet someone in the street and ask them to live with you, for God's sake, what do you expect? I knew she should have finished that typing course.'

'Mother, the typing course was three years ago. She works in the supermarket, remember? To get the money for drama college?'

'Drama? I'll give her drama. There's enough bloody drama round here as it is, with that Cheryl whatsername at number eight. The starlings have only got to twitter, she thinks they're whistling at her. Sleep with a man as soon as look at him. That gas man was in there two hours yesterday. Her meter must be in a funny place if it takes two hours to read it. The things I could tell you go on in this street.'

'I bet you never get a chance to stop twitching the net curtain all day.'

'Running off at seventeen, your father was livid. And when are you going to fix that light for me?'

But really there was no point in arguing. Roles had been allocated, positions taken years ago. Wishing she hadn't bothered to call in, but knowing she had to, Jenny just let her mother's tirade wear on until something distracted her. She had an amazing capacity to keep a topic going long after everything had been said that could be said, and a lot that didn't need saying, several times.

'There was that Iti, what was his name, Mario, or Marco, anyway, he seemed all right, bit greasy but what do you expect for a waiter, at least he didn't beat her up, but was he good enough for her ladyship? Oh no, she had to go on to that married one that ran the shoe shop – at least she got a few pairs of shoes out of him,' (and an abortion, reflected Jenny, but her mother didn't know). 'Anyone could have told her that would end in tears.'

'And I expect you probably did.'

'Then there was Peter, he was a nice lad, clean and decent. At least he looked as if he'd been to the barber's in the last two years, even if his motorcycle did leave oil all over the road.'

'He's in prison, Mum, for stealing from old ladies, posing as a window cleaner.'

'Well, yes. He did have a good set of teeth though,' she added, as if it made any difference. Which, to the old ladies who trusted him, it probably did.

Her mother sighed and sipped – or rather gulped – her gin. Any excuse for a drink, even at one o'clock in the afternoon. It seemed to blacken her mood into maudlin sentimentality.

'She was such a beautiful little thing. Much prettier than you – you were always the brainy one – so sweet she was, those eyes would turn you to butter, even when she'd done something really naughty. She still is beautiful, mind. Could have been a model. That's the trouble. Men can't leave her alone.'

Jenny felt that whatever she had done, even before, when her mother knew what was what and told the world so, it was never quite good enough for her exacting standards. You could eat your dinner off the floor in that house when Jenny was a child, as her mother was fond of saying at the time (it would be a health hazard to try it now), but hugs were as rare as gold dust. Love was not a commodity her mother found easy to come by, so she kept it to herself, never shared it around. Even her children had been made to feel you had to earn love, it was never freely given, and this had set them against each other in a joyless competition to earn their mother's love. Maggie, being a more physically attractive child, had always fared the better of the two.

'You shouldn't drink so much, Mother. Try not to start till six o'clock, at least.'

Her mother brushed her words aside with a wave of her hand.

'Nag, nag, nag, that's all you do. You've got to give yourself a bit of pleasure in this life, Jenny Burdge. If you did that you'd have less of a sour face on you yourself, lady.'

Jenny wondered what pleasure her mother had managed to extract from her life. What, if any, satisfactions had she had? She would have made an excellent nurse when she was younger, Jenny sometimes thought. She would have plumped up pillows with admirable briskness and would never have been in danger of becoming too kind or involved. As a child she had often been told the story of how her mother had wanted to be a nurse, but 'they' had thwarted her. That was why she was always telling Jenny to be more like Janice, she supposed.

'Try and be a bit less of a misery-guts. Now Maggie always cheers me up when she comes.'

The conversation was becoming pointless. This was Jenny's cue to leave.

'I'm off, Mother. See you on Saturday.'

'The woman in the supermarket was very off with me the other day. You know, that one you can't tell which eye to look at, they both point different ways. Very off she was, you wouldn't think they wanted people's custom, would you? I swear there's a nasty smell, can you look dear, has Snowy done something behind the sofa? I didn't put him out last night. There's cat thieves around.'

Jenny had a sudden mental picture of the bad-tempered Snowy turned into a very fine white fluffy waistcoat. Dutifully she peered behind the sofa. There was nothing, only a furry apple core and a five pence piece among a lot of cat hairs.

'Let me give you a hand with this, Mother. When I come on Saturday I'll give it all a good clean out.'

'All right, love.' She hadn't taken it in, Jenny could tell. 'Can you take the rubbish out on your way out? What *is* that smell?'

Jenny left her wandering around the kitchen and sitting room, sniffing loudly into the corners of the sofa.

When she got home Janice had the bleach out again. She was a nurse, and treated every domestic surface as if a diseased corpse had just been dissected on it. She also had the quality Jenny thought essential in a house-sharing arrangement – she couldn't bear to leave the washing up. It made Janice positively ill to see a sink full of greasy dishes. In fact, so eager was she to pursue this favourite hobby of washing up, that she sometimes had the plate you were eating off plunged into the bubbles before you had put in your last mouthful. Thus, by frequently depriving Jenny of her last few mouthfuls of food, Janice played her part in the valiant battle against the hidden enemy – fat. This enemy was not at all in evidence around Josh or Janice, and it only lurked furtively around the stocky figure of Jenny, but Janice thought you could never be too careful. Fat was, of course, the second most lethal enemy, the chief one being dirt. In this battle Janice was indomitable.

Neat and trim in person, Janice was an amiable, unobtrusive (except for the smell of bleach) presence in the house. She was regular in her habits, entertaining Roger, an accounts clerk who drove an enormous car for one so young, by means of equally quiet, unobtrusive dinner and sex once a week. Jenny didn't know this because of intimate chats, or by being awakened by noisy romps around the house. It was just that Janice left her diaphragm, freshly washed (she would have bleached it, only it tells you not to in the leaflet) on the bathroom windowsill to dry.

'So it doesn't perish,' she told Jenny a little sheepishly, after Jenny had thought she had left it there by accident. Josh, aged nine going on twenty-seven, had read the leaflet on a sneak foray into Janice's room (forbidden territory, therefore irresistible) so he knew all about it and didn't need to ask. Jenny just fondly assumed that in his childish innocence he had never noticed it.

Apart from this mild eccentricity, or lack of delicacy – Jenny knew that working in a hospital you get inured to anything – Janice was the ideal flatmate. The same could not be said of Geoffrey the cat, whose sanitary arrangements left something to be desired. But in putting up with Geoffrey and giving him a plated dinner twice a day, Jenny was making a private pact with Fate, trusting that when she too was old, crabby and toothless, someone would do the same for her. So Geoffrey would be coming to the new house too.

Maggie was beautiful, her mother was right. Her beautiful, unreliable sister, that was the role she had been allocated so that her mother could feed her fantasy that one of her daughters could have been a model. Then she could have shown her friends a painted face on the cover of a magazine and say, 'That's my daughter'. Then they would have envied her. Mrs Burdge had never been envied for anything in her life, so she made up for it by envying everybody else and letting it come out as spite and petty gossip. However, Maggie did her best to live up to the image. She may not have the career of a model, but she had the necessary level of self-absorption. Jenny had noticed that people tolerate selfishness and bad behaviour from beautiful people, much more than they do from the average lumpy, cheerful individual, as though beauty was an excuse for anything you like. Men for Maggie were just tools, toys in an elaborate game. Each one was a challenge, like a mountain for a climber, or a wave for a surfer – something to be mastered, overcome, then forgotten, eyes on the horizon for the next, better one. The next one would always be the best. She collected them like shark's teeth on the necklace of a mating costume. She was like a handmade silver pistol – beautifully crafted, lightweight but capable of inflicting plenty of damage. With a hard, smooth body and a mind to match, she was a dangerous chameleon. She would be whatever a man wanted her to be. He could paint his fantasy onto those beautiful features, empty of expression except what he put there, empty of the lines and creases that are the outward signs of personality. Unthreatening, she laughed at his jokes, didn't make her own. She gave the impression of being as lithe as a whippet, and as loyal, as eager and willing to be trained. Yet with this very quality – her unthreatening, apparent adoration – she mastered any unsuspecting man before he knew it, and all the while she let him think he was the masterful one, in control. Then, just when the particular fish she had her eye on at any one time was really hooked, the game would go out of it for Maggie, the exciting challenge was over. She would catch sight of the next one and she would be off, her disappearance just adding to her elusive air of mystery and charm. The sort of men who were susceptible to girls like Maggie could look after themselves on the whole, Jenny thought, most of them got what they deserved – burnt fingers for playing near the fire. It was the women, usually wives, Jenny felt for. The real women, whose stomachs have sagged as their personalities have blossomed, whose lives and confidence are broken by the skimming games of girlie women. Women like Maggie, who touch the surface, paint a fantasy with a few light brushstrokes that a man can turn into anything he wishes to see, then vanish like a gazelle into the trees, leaving just an air of misty fragility to yearn for.

Jenny had only once made the mistake of introducing Maggie to Henry. It had been just before Christmas two years ago, in the flat. She had not planned it, although perhaps Maggie had, out of curiosity (or some less honourable motive). Henry had come round for supper and Maggie had just happened to call in on her way to a social function. She was seeing some middle-aged barrister (married, naturally) at the time. She was wearing a tight black dress of stretch velvet that fitted like a sheath. Her dark hair was twisted into a silky knot, the odd strand escaping flirtatiously to caress her neck. She had done something clever with make-up to make her dark eyes look enormous. She was brimming with the juiciness of expectation and promise before a new, romantic date. Her long, firm limbs were golden in the mellow lamplight that Jenny had put on to create a romantic atmosphere. The effect had been only too successful. Henry had been bowled over.

'I hope these stockings are OK,' Maggie had said with touching self-doubt, stroking her slender thighs, letting her skimpy dress slip up. Outrageously, a slice of creamy skin was momentarily visible. 'Should I have got charcoal instead of black, do you think?

They're the sort that stay up by themselves.' This was accompanied by a darting glance at Henry. 'Oh, I hope you don't mind girls' talk,' she giggled coyly. Henry was agog. With no mother, no sisters, and only fleeting (and increasingly infrequent) liaisons with women in foreign cities – 'getting rid of dirty bilge water' they had called it amongst themselves, with no emotion attached to it – his real, as opposed to mechanical, knowledge of women was minimal. He had never been party to this kind of clean but naughty girlie talk, which was, of course, purely for his benefit. Jenny ran her eye over him with matronly protectiveness. Maggie could not possibly be attracted to him, she went for much more obvious charms. She just found it impossible not to make a conquest, even against her own sister. An old ghost reared up in front of her. She pushed it aside. She would deal with that later. At this moment she was concerned for Henry. She hoped the front of his trousers were only ruckled up, not filled out, then reproached herself for coarseness – not at his age, surely. His hand was fiddling in his pocket. Stop fiddling, she wanted to snap. She's only winding you up. She's winding me up, too, so much I want to slap her. I haven't done that since she was eight and I was seventeen, she thought, when she put lipstick all over my bedroom walls, just for spite. About time someone did it again.

'Henry's not interested in the details of your clothing,' she said icily, the expression and colour on Henry's face proving the opposite. He was alert and absorbed, all the animal in him to the fore. Between them, Jenny, in her soft viyella dress and warm woolly tights, felt about as sexy as an old sheep. Jealousy lay like a hard, sour lump in her chest. She knew her face was looking sour and pinched, because jealousy makes you hunch yourself and swallow your pain like a bitter nut. All your warmth and power to give out love is shut off. She felt invisible. There was such a syrupy sweetness emanating from her sister and Henry was lapping it up with such eagerness, she wanted to be sick. She had never seen him lit up like this before. All his vague benevolence and distant gaze were gone. He was entirely awake and focused.

'How are you getting to the party?' Henry had asked.

'Well, I was going to ring for a taxi if Jenny will let me use the phone,' Maggie had said, with all the soft appeal of a much wronged but loyal younger sister, towards an older, bossier one.

'Oh no,' Henry had darted forward, the besotted courtier. 'I can take you. We haven't started yet, the meal will wait twenty minutes, won't it?' He made the word 'meal' sound so much duller to Jenny's jealous ears than the exciting, fun word, 'party'.

Jenny picked up the phone. 'Maggie will be perfectly all right with a taxi. Won't you?' she said with gritted teeth. 'And I'm sure your boyfriend' – said with emphasis – 'will bring you home.'

Maggie brushed her fingers lightly across Henry's shoulder as she passed behind his chair. 'She's very strict, you know. Is she strict with you?' Henry could only laugh at this, in what he intended to pass for a nonchalant way. Maggie leaned towards him, the front of her dress giving him an intentional glimpse of the small, pert breasts. 'Thank you *so* much for offering, though,' she breathed. 'It was really sweet of you.' She made it sound like the kindest thing anyone had ever offered to do for her. Henry was enchanted.

Then she left Jenny and Henry to have an argument – well, not strictly an argument, for only Jenny talked – on why it was that men could never see what some women were up to, and how they always put other women in the wrong for pointing it out. Jenny reminded herself never again to put this theory to the test.

This was the ideal time to move, Jenny thought. Say goodbye to Henry, who is already looking at something far away I cannot see, have a good, therapeutic clearing out of junk, then on with a fresh start in a new home without him. It's almost like waiting for someone to die, she thought, waiting for him to go, not wanting him to, but not being able to stand much more of this waiting. He's not going for another week, yet already he is receding. I must be seen to be busy, she thought, must not give him the idea that things will grind to a halt when he is gone. I am going to show him that I can have just as interesting a time, in a different way, as he can. I shall have a happy face on when he leaves.

The new house in Hazel Terrace was waiting for them with an air of expectancy. It was one of a red-brick row in a small street close to Rowntree's. It was not a smart part of the town, but quiet and respectable. Some people had put hanging baskets outside their houses, so that splashes of colour brightened the brick and shade. One house had been rendered and painted green so that it stuck out from the rest of the row. The massive, angular shape of the chocolate factory dominated the street, dwarfing the houses still further. There was a shop on the corner, run by the Patels. All the front doors opened directly onto the street, some still with the original thick panelled wood painted in different colours, others replaced by modern, often incongruous, plastic alternatives. Some salesman in replacement windows and doors had made a killing in Hazel Terrace. Jenny was pleased that her house had one of the original doors. Hers was number six, in the middle of the row. Its two downstairs rooms, one behind the other, were grey with age and tired wallpaper and the kitchen crouched grubbily behind the back room. A small bathroom lay beyond. The basin had a large chunk out of it, as though someone had dropped a hammer into it in a failed attempt to get a new one paid for by a bogus insurance claim. Upstairs, there were two large bedrooms with high ceilings which were a lovely, airy surprise. The tall windows looked out onto the small street in front, and a yard at the back, which had the potential to be a really nice garden (quite a sun trap, the agent had said). At present the yard was full of rubble and it backed onto an alleyway full of bin liners and stray cats. Geoffrey will have his paws full here, supervising the patch, thought Jenny. Josh claimed the back bedroom, so Janice had the front one, and Jenny decided to have the front room downstairs as her bedroom. She painted the walls turquoise and dabbed small, meticulous gold stars on the ceiling to make the room her own.

'Reminds me of the morgue at work,' said Janice, sniffing, when she first saw the kitchen. The walls were greasy and grey paint flaked off. 'Only dirtier.'

So it was gutted, some wooden-fronted units put in and the whole thing painted terracotta red. Vaguely Etruscan, Jenny thought, pleased.

'That's better,' Janice said approvingly. 'More like the inside of a uterus. And much easier to keep clean.'

Two days after they moved in, their next door neighbour introduced herself. She peered over the wall between the yards as Jenny was picking her way over the rubble to hang out some washing.

'You can use my washing line if you like. It's easier to get to.'

'Thanks, but you wouldn't want the neighbours thinking my leopard skin knickers were yours, would you?'

The woman crowed delightedly. 'Oh, I wouldn't worry, love, I've been scandalising them for years. They'd have nothing to get steamed up about if it wasn't for me.'

She was a small lady, she could only just see over the wall on tiptoe, her head was surrounded by a thick cloud of dark pink fluff. This improbable hair was all whipped up round the sides, but when she turned away for a second Jenny saw that the back was greasy and flat, stuck to her head, so that the effect was like that of a Red Indian's feathered head-dress. There seemed to be little white bits in it, which fascinated Josh, who had come out at the sound of voices, because he couldn't tell if they were nits, dandruff, or the sticky residue of hair lacquer. They introduced themselves.

'I'm Astrid,' said the woman, who looked in her sixties, but could have been ten years either side of that, for her cheeks had the plumped out, highly rouged, shiny look of a Victorian baby doll. Her eyes were incredibly blue, as bright as the blue eye shadow that was painted on up to her thickly pencilled eyebrows, whose jaunty line bore little resemblance to the modest curve nature had intended. She didn't just smile, she absolutely beamed and her voice was high and sparky, every sentence ending on a trailing, upward crow, like a seagull's cry. She sounded as if she came from the southwest of England originally, for there was a definite roll to her speech which was overlaid by a veneer of exaggerated refinement that slipped on certain words.

'It's nice to have a boy next door,' she said, 'I like boys. You can meet my Gavin when he comes for lunch. He comes every day, he's very good. I hope you're good to your mum,' she said to Josh in a coaxing, flirty way. 'Boys should always be good to their mums, shouldn't they? My Gavin's very good to me.'

'What are they like round here, the neighbours?' asked Jenny.

Astrid's eyes went as round as boiled sweets. This was obviously a pet subject. 'Well,' she said, folding her arms and preparing for a saga. 'Them on that side of you is all right, I never see them, both out at work. Their cat's a bloody nuisance, though, peeing in my geraniums. I shoos 'im off, I does, shakes pepper at 'im, that does it. I says, "Ooh, get on out of it, peeing on my tubs," but apart from that I never has no dealings with 'em. The one on *my* side, mind you, that's a different story. They're only young, he looks much too young to be married, he looks about twelve he does. Honest, you'd think he was a boy, but he's like a bloody miserable old man. He bangs on the wall about me telly, he does – I'm a bit deaf, only a bit, mind – but he hammers away like the place was burning down. And she's a skinny little thing, tiny, like a little plucked chicken she is, all skin and bone, no meat on her at all. Sunbathes topless in the garden she does – it's embarrassing, honestly.'

'Can you see her boobs?' asked Josh, perking up momentarily. This was more interesting than the usual adult conversation he was forced to listen to. Boobs were a topic of great and unending hilarity in the playground at the moment. Tessa in the top class had some.

'Boobs? That's what's embarrassing. I'm not averse to a nice pair of tits – refreshing, it is, to see a nice pair when your own are round your knees. But poor girl, she's got nothing. *Nothing*. Honest, they're like a couple of press studs. I feel mortified for her, how can she show them, they're so pathetic? It's sad, it really is. Bet you haven't got press studs,' she nodded approvingly at Jenny's more generous shape. Jenny was glad Janice was indoors. Josh thought he had never met such an embarrassing grown-up in his entire life. They weren't supposed to talk about things like that, it was disgusting.

'So what have you done to Muriel's old house? I hope you've given it a good clean out, her eyesight wasn't too good, poor old thing. Mind, I better be careful, that might be me soon.'

'Come round and see for yourself. I'll put the kettle on.'

The bright mask beamed and disappeared.

'Mum, did you have to? She's awful.'

'Shut up and get the biscuits out.'

Astrid was very interested in everything. 'I haven't been in here for years, it hasn't changed a bit. Hope you're going to get rid of that terrible fireplace.'

'I was going to restore it.'

'Oh no, dreadful. So old fashioned. You want a nice gas fire with pretend coals like mine. So clean, no fuss.'

When it emerged that Jenny was an occupational therapist, the bright blue eyes twinkled a little less for a moment. Jenny was used to this response. But it wasn't the usual.

'Oh good,' Astrid said, 'I can tell you about my Gavin, then. People are funny about him, but you wouldn't know it, honest, not unless I said. He's completely fine now. Well, mostly. He's schizophrenic, you see. But you really wouldn't know it, he's on medication.'

This was quite common for Jenny; it was rather like a GP endlessly having people come up on social occasions to discuss their bad backs.

'They told me it was partly my fault, said I smothered 'im when 'e was little. Well, there wasn't no one else to give 'im no love, was there? Anyway, it's in the genes, isn't it?'

Jenny understood how, even years later, Astrid needed the reassurance of a total stranger that her son's condition was not her fault. 'Yes, they do say it has something to do with that,' she said carefully. 'So, what was your job before you retired?' she asked her, to get her onto something else.

She cheered up immediately, like a puppet whose strings have been tweaked. 'Me?' she twinkled mischievously. 'I haven't retired. As long as me old faithfuls are still alive, I'll be working.'

'As what?' Perhaps she was a housekeeper or home help.

'A tart, dear. A lady of the night. Or of the lunch time, the elevenses, or whenever you like. That's my job. I've got my few regulars who I've been seeing for years – see, nobody thinks you still do it when you're old, do they? But I can tell you, they do.' She burst into gales of laughter. 'That took you by surprise, didn't it? How do you like having a tart for your next door neighbour?'

'What's a tart?' asked Josh, but nobody chose to hear.

'You can stuff chickens for a living for all I care,' said Jenny. 'If you'd be prepared to do a spot of babysitting now and then.'

Henry was leaving on Friday. Today was Tuesday. Jenny asked him round to see the new house. He was very busy, he said, but he would try to call round as soon as he could.

'A last farewell,' Jenny said, and as she said them the words filled her with a terrible pain.

'No, not that,' he said.

Work in the hospital continued much as usual. On Wednesday Jenny arrived to find Margaret putting a memo on everyone's desk. Margaret was one of the old breed of occupational therapists. She was definitely in the 'Get them all doing macramé and they'll forget their troubles' mould. She preferred wiping bottoms – which she wasn't supposed to do, but there were never enough nurses around – to discussing problems of the psyche. She had only got into mental health because of a reshuffle at the General which had meant she had to relocate or lose her job. She was really much more interested in weaving and hand injuries. She liked people to 'brace up' and frequently told them to 'put a good face on it, dear, we've all got our crosses to bear'. The nature of Margaret's particular crosses was never made clear. One of them appeared to be all the other occupational therapists. Today's memo was one of a series along similar lines.

FROM: MARGARET
TO: EVERYONE

PLEASE NOTE THE COFFEE, MILK AND SUGAR IS NOW COLOUR CODED.
BLUE = KATE
RED = JENNY
YELLOW = JOE
GREEN = MARGARET
THIS IS TO AVOID THE POSSIBILITY OF ERROR WHEN MAKING COFFEE. THIS IS FELT TO BE A NECESSARY MOVE AFTER THE RECENT SPATE OF 'BORROWING' WHICH HAS RESULTED IN MY HAVING TO PURCHASE 3(!!) JARS OF COFFEE IN 2 WEEKS.

Jenny's eyes met Kate's over their cluttered desks.

'Nothing wrong with her, is there?' commented Joe as he chucked his copy in the bin. 'Think I'll start a "Save the Rain Forests" campaign – starting with recycling Margaret into a toilet roll.' Joe was tall and thin with long, sardonic features. He was in his fifties, but with a grubby, relaxed trendiness, and from the side his posture gave him the shape of a question mark.

Just then Margaret entered, scared mouse's eyes darting around the room. 'Dr Baljekar's on his way down, let's try and make a good impression for once,' she twittered.

Joe flung himself to the floor as if a sniper had started firing in from the window ledge.

'What on earth are you doing?' she shrieked. 'He'll be here any minute!'

'I'm just getting ready to lick his boots – isn't that what you wanted?'

Jenny and Kate smothered their laughter. Just then the small, rotund Indian doctor came in and Margaret started pirouetting and gavotting around him like a ruffled, scraggy hen trying to mother an aloof pug that is intent on taking no notice of it.

'Are we ready, Jenny?'

Scooping her papers together Jenny gave a twinkling glance at the others and followed the glossy, bad-tempered little man.

On the ward round, Jenny had to interpret what many of the disturbed patients were trying to say to Dr Baljekar (or Bulgy, as he was known) as he gave them a blank stare. This type of conversation was a common occurrence:

Dr B: 'What are you telling me? You feel that you are on another planet? No, (pause to peer at name on notes) no Miss – er – Bains, I can assure you there is no other planet you can be on.'

Jenny: 'No, Doctor, what Susan means is that she *feels* she is on another planet. She knows there are no other planets she can be on, that this to our knowledge is the only one that supports human life –'

Dr B: 'Then how can she say such a stupid thing?' (Patient begins to cry.)

Jenny: 'Doctor, this is a psychiatric hospital. You are a psychiatrist. Susan is deeply depressed (and this is doing nothing to cheer her up, she added silently). Shall we move on? Susan, I'll be back to see you later.' (Susan sinks down by the bedside in tears.)

No Henry on Wednesday.

Thursday. Ward round completed by 10 am. Jenny was giving an Art Therapy class at eleven, so she went down to start putting out the materials. When she came back up to make her coffee (she picked up the green jar without noticing) there was someone standing by her desk. First she thought he must be a patient, as they often came in search of her when they felt like a chat. It was usually Damien, who was forbidden to talk about sex as he was obsessed, and often insisted on telling her all he had done (or thought he had done) with various women before he came in here. On any other subject he was quite pleasant and rather quiet. But it was not Damien.

'Can I help you?'

He turned. He was a very beautiful Indian man in a very beautiful suit. He smiled. His teeth were a dentist's joy. Don't be stupid, Jenny, he's ten years younger than you. No harm in appreciating perfection, though. He's bound to be a disappointment when he opens his mouth – people usually are, thought Jenny, and beautiful people even more so, because your expectations and hopes of them are so much higher. The better the shop window, the more full of good things you expect the shop to be. But that smile really is something.

'I'm looking for my father, Dr Baljekar.'

There, she knew it would be a disappointment. How could this creature of beauty, this god, be the progeny of that fat, arrogant little man who was so lacking in warmth and understanding? Perhaps Dr Baljekar had looked like this twenty-odd years ago. Perhaps that was why he was so crabby now. Anyone would be bad-tempered at having undergone such a depressing transformation. No. Dr Baljekar had never looked like this. He must have a beautiful wife.

'He's upstairs. Let me show you.'

'No, it's all right. I know the way, thank you.'

What thick lashes he had, curling up from his deep brown eyes. He was like a young bull – a silky, muscle-rippling, warm-skinned young bull. He was looking at her in concern.

'Are you OK? You've gone rather flushed.'

'Me? I'm fine, actually. Yes, honestly, quite fine,' she gushed. 'Absolutely.' Except I'm getting to the age when I lust pathetically over young boys who are practically still in nappies, she thought. Absolutely fine. He turned to go.

'I'm Jenny, by the way,' she said unnecessarily, hoping to detain him. He smiled again. That smile. Her stomach turned to water.

'Sanjay. Pleased to meet you, Jenny. Again sometime, I hope.'

Impeccable manners, but then what would you expect, she could hear her mother's voice. With those shiny shoes.

'Damn.' She had knocked her coffee over her desk.

When Jenny got home Josh was eating pizza and watching television.

'Hey, that was meant to do for three of us!'

Josh answered without taking his eyes off the screen. 'I was starving, Mum. We had rugby practice.'

'How did it go?'

Josh grimaced. 'Matthew Stokes twisted my ear. *On purpose*. It really hurt. I'm going to kick his head in tomorrow.'

'Mm,' murmured Jenny, ruffling his hair abstractedly, thinking, where did that sweet, angelic child go? When was it swapped for this thug? 'What am I going to eat?' she asked. Josh shrugged with his mouth full. 'Anything you like,' he said generously.

'Thanks a lot, buddy. There's three of us in this house, you know. Team work, remember?'

Josh remained glued to the screen. 'Sorry. Can you write a note saying I'm too ill for rugby?'

'No I cannot. Turn the telly down a bit, can't you?' Irritably she went through to rifle the fridge. She knew there was nothing but an old lettuce and two cold potatoes in there, she hadn't had time to get to the supermarket after work. Henry never saw these bits, she thought crossly. He'd be put right off if he did. Then she remembered a bottle of wine she had got in just in case he came round. She cheered up at the thought. She was surprised to find Janice standing in the middle of the kitchen, still and strange, a knife in her hand, like a character in a low-budget horror movie.

'You gave me a fright,' said Jenny, 'I thought you were on lates.'

Speaking to her was like breaking a skin she had grown. She burst into tears. 'I changed my shifts –'

It was a Roger night, Jenny had forgotten. Some large mushrooms and kidneys lay on the bench. The kidneys were rather bloody and a dark red trickle was running down a cupboard door.

Silently she put her arms round her friend and let her cry. Eventually, cried out and emptied by huge gusting sighs, Janice fumbled for a tissue. She noticed the trickle of blood down the unit and absently wiped it instead of her nose.

'The bastard,' she managed. She snorted into the bloody tissue which left a streak of glutinous purplish black on her face.

'Can't he make it? What's he done to upset you?'

This set off a fresh bout of sobbing. 'No he bloody can't. Not tonight, not ever. That's it. Finished.'

'But why? You didn't have a row?' He never communicated enough to have a row, Jenny thought. Couldn't muster enough energy.

'He's been – seeing someone else. The slimy bastard. You know that Serena, the one he works with, the one he said was really frumpy and old-fashioned? Well, she's not, apparently. So bloody calculating. Said I "didn't have the intellect he was looking for"' – she mimicked his pompous tone so effectively, Jenny almost asked if she had thought of going on the stage. Another time, perhaps. 'As if he'd been test driving me like a bloody car.'

'Well, let's hope the frumpy Serena is more than he can handle. She even *sounds* like a car,' said Jenny kindly. 'If you want to know the truth, I never thought he was up to your standard anyway. So boring and dull. He never took you anywhere, did he?'

'Probably in case we saw Her,' Janice wailed afresh. 'And I got kidneys in specially.'

Perhaps the prospect of the kidneys was more than he could take, thought Jenny.

'*And* she's got better pelvic floor muscles.'

'He told you that? You mean he's tried them out? The absolute bastard. I'm sure yours are lovely,' said Jenny, patting her and somehow feeling this wasn't quite the right thing to say. 'Well, let's have the kidneys anyway, as Josh has eaten the pizza. They're nobody's we know, are they? Good. I'll get that bottle of wine. We'll have a celebration. Good riddance to Roger the Dodger.'

Chopping the kidneys appeared to be good therapy for Janice. Drinking deeply, she sliced the purple, rounded ends with relish.

'He did have some good points, though.'

It must be the wine talking, thought Jenny. They had downed the first bottle with great speed and were into the second, the one Janice had bought for Roger. The best thing about Roger, she imagined, was his car.

'He was nice and clean. You know – personal hygiene.'

Jenny didn't know. 'This is the Man In Your Life we're talking about – sorry, ex-man-in-your-life – not a domestic pet.'

Janice looked thoughtfully at the kitchen cupboards in a hazy, alcoholic way while her hands worked automatically on the vegetables. 'No, I mean circumcised. Nice and clean.' Out came an aubergine to meet the blade. 'Nowhere for – you know – germs to lurk. Very nice.'

A carrot got sliced with such fast precision Jenny feared for her friend's fingers.

'Bet he didn't know what to do with it, though,' she smirked.

Janice laughed for the first time today. 'No, he didn't really. He thought he did.'

'Don't they all?'

By now they were hooting loudly so that Josh came and pointed the television remote control at them to make them be quiet. As that failed, he shut the door pointedly and turned the volume up.

'This is Roger,' Jenny held up a stick of celery that had been forgotten for a fortnight in the bottom of the fridge.

Janice sloshed the remainder of the second bottle into Jenny's glass. 'And guess what,' she gasped. Jenny was laughing hysterically before Janice even said anything. 'He always brought his wet wipes with him.'

They collapsed at this.

'What for – before or after?'

'Both!'

They were sitting on the floor now with their backs against the kitchen cupboards, the kidneys sizzling above them. When Jenny could speak, she said, 'Obsessive potty training', which set them off again. Half an hour and a trip to the off-licence later, they tried to eat the kidneys pretending they were Roger's, discovered they were far too cremated and threw them away.

'You two are barmy,' said Josh, prodding his mother with a disapproving foot. 'You're embarrassing, Mum. It's gross. Why can't you behave like a proper mother? What can I write in my journal in school tomorrow – "Last night my Mum got drunk and sat laughing on the kitchen floor"?'

'They'll have the Social round,' giggled Janice.

'Yeah, that's it, get your only son taken into care,' said Josh. 'Perhaps they'll give me to a *normal* mother.'

Jenny grabbed Josh and pulled him down next to her. 'Don't you be a shit when you grow up, you hear me? You be my nice boy. Treat women nicely, don't be one of those bastards, OK?'

'*Mum*,' Josh was outraged. 'You're *swearing*.' He stood up. '*I'm* going to bed,' he said primly, 'And I think *you* should do the same.' As he walked up the stairs they could hear him murmuring, 'Really gross.'

So Josh discovered, at an early age, how dull it is to be in the company of drunks when you yourself are stone cold sober.

Josh lay on his bed admiring his curtains. They were navy and white stripes, wide stripes, straight at the top then getting wavier as they went down, with the large white outlines of fish swimming along the bottom. Henry had helped him choose them; Jenny had sent them out together a few weeks ago. He liked Henry. They were allies. They had chosen a fish mobile to go with the curtains, seven beautiful wooden fish painted in brilliant colours, that swam round slowly on their nylon thread. Josh watched them as he lay on his bed, trying as he always did, to decide which one he liked best. He never could decide. The curtains made him think of the sea, of diving deeper and deeper into the depths, past the waves, past the fish, past the forests of seaweed where the starfish grazed, down and down to where the colours stopped. Just think, there was no weather down there, no night and day. The fish could sleep whenever they liked. But they could not close their eyes. This fact fascinated Josh. He lay there trying to imagine what it would be like never to shut your eyes. He tried to keep his eyes open as long as he could, not even blinking until they began to water. It was a kind of torture.

He had come to bed but he couldn't sleep, his mother and Janice were making too much noise. Besides, it was June, midsummer, not yet ten o'clock, and light was still filtering through the curtains. He thought about his real father. He had been killed in a car crash but there were no pictures of him round the house. A couple of years ago his mother had asked if he could remember him and Josh had said no, so she had dug out an old photo which he kept in his underpants drawer. It showed a dark man with a moustache sitting in a deck chair. He had a very hairy chest. This fact disturbed Josh. Somehow he couldn't imagine anybody dead ever having had a hairy chest. It seemed too – alive and manly. Josh could not feel that this stranger had anything to do with him, yet looking at the photo gave him a dragging feeling in his chest. It made him feel sad, so he hardly ever looked at it.

The dusk was creeping in now. He liked that phrase, he'd read it in a book. Creeping, like an animal. Like a burglar. The colours were fading in the room. The fish were becoming indistinct. Downstairs they had put some music on. It was playing only quietly, but he could hear the dull thump of the bass notes. He sighed and gave up on trying not to blink. He'd hated seeing his mother drunk. She wasn't like herself, she was loud and red, her eyes had a funny, shiny look. He had found it frightening, as if another person was inside his mother's body, looking out through her eyes, a person he did not like. It didn't seem like her, it was creepy. Couldn't they see how gross they looked? And all over that stupid Roger, who was such a dork no one would want him for their boyfriend. Grown-ups. He never would understand them. He reckoned he had more sense than most of the ones he met. He turned his mind to more interesting matters. He'd met a boy today, who seemed OK. He was called James and he lived up the street. They had met in the stone alleyway behind the houses, on bikes. James's bike was bigger and better, but Josh was two months older. He put his hands behind his head and thought about the basketball net he was going to have on the end of the house when they had sorted out the yard. Eventually he fell asleep.

At ten o'clock in a drunken haze, Jenny picked up the phone. No Henry. She tried again at midnight, by which time the walls were spinning and she knew she would not sleep. Janice, for some reason best known to herself, had decided to clean the bath. She was swaying precariously over it, waving the bleach bottle. Jenny let the phone ring and ring. Still no Henry. He had not been in touch all week. Where on earth could he be? There would be no final fond farewell after all, not even a sensible, casual 'Cheerio, send us a postcard', which of course he would much prefer. Tomorrow he would be far away.

On Friday morning Josh was the only member of the household who awoke fresh and bright. He was pleased that horrible Roger had gone. He thought about it while he hunted for clean pants and socks. He couldn't find any, so he quietly put on yesterday's dirty ones before his mother could say anything. Horrible, smelly Roger who smelt funny, like perfume, only not, and made heavy jokes that were supposed to be funny, and which Josh always had a sneaking feeling were at his expense. He knew they were meant to be funny only because Roger laughed. Nobody else did.

He hadn't minded Roger at first – after all, it was nothing to him who Janice went out with – only they didn't go out, they just monopolised the television and hinted that he, Josh, should go to his room. What a cheek. It was his house. It was OK in the flat. The bathroom had been between his room and Janice's. But here it had been awful. Roger had come only once since they'd moved. Josh had heard a funny noise – a rhythmic thumping noise and some horrible grunting – it sounded like an animal. It must have been Roger. Josh had crept out in his pyjamas. It was quite late and the bedroom door was ajar. He couldn't see Janice, just a mountain of bedclothes, and Roger, shoving and grunting. shoving and grunting, it was the most disgusting thing he'd ever seen – worse than that dead pickled thing their old doctor had in a jar on his mantelpiece. Of course, he knew what they were doing, the boys

31

talked about it in school – having sex, they called it. If that was what sex was, he didn't want it, no thank you very much. Not even for a computer and a bike twice as big as James's. How could Janice stand it? Some of the boys said girls liked it, but he couldn't believe it. It was revolting – rough and horrible. He knew his mother and Henry didn't do that, Henry wasn't like that, and his mother was much too sensible – except when she got silly, like last night. Even then, she wouldn't do a thing like *that*. His mother must have done it once though, with his father, or he, Josh, would not be here. That was an extraordinary thought. He could not understand it, it was so crazy. That two people – his mother and his father – could grunt and grapple like that and that he was the result. Worse, that if they had not done it, he would not exist. What a near miss. He might never have lived on earth at all. But if he wasn't here, where would he have been? Where was he before?

All this was too much to think about, and his mind drifted back to Roger and Janice in the bedroom as he went downstairs and got himself a bowl of cornflakes. He slopped some milk on the bench without noticing. He was shocked by the movement, he remembered, the way Roger shunted back and forth. He'd read the little book his mother had given him a while ago, and he knew exactly what happened – that was bad enough – but he somehow had imagined that it was a static process. Nothing had prepared him for that rough shoving. Just like animals, only it was natural for them, they didn't know any better. Just like dogs in the park. Or on your leg, if you weren't careful. They hadn't known he was there. So he'd watched, transfixed, until that foul beast Roger slumped onto poor Janice, then he'd pulled the door to and returned frozen to bed.

He ate his breakfast standing up in the kitchen. His mother didn't allow this, saying it was bad for your digestion to eat standing up. Josh had the digestive system of a goat. He had decided that night that next time he saw Roger he would tell him to piss off. Only Roger must have known – he must have received the beam of hate pulsating in his direction – because he had disappeared a week later of his own accord. That had given Josh such a rushing sense of his own power – if he could get rid of Roger just by thinking about it, he could do anything. Maybe he'd try for a new bike in a week or so. He put the empty bowl into the sink and shouted, 'Where are my sandwiches, Mum?'

Jenny awoke with a headache. Oh God, it's Friday morning, she thought. Henry clearly was not going to come now, his flight was at two, from Heathrow. He might even have gone down the night before, although he hadn't mentioned any intention to do so. She could not believe he would leave without a proper goodbye, but clearly this was exactly what he had done. Jenny tried to phone one more time, but there was still no answer. He must have gone. Perhaps he could not bear to have a last time together. She should not have said that about last farewells, he always shied away from strong emotion. She should have been more casual. More relaxed. She should have shown no more reaction than if he was going to London for a week, instead of Greenland and America for nine months. She blamed herself. She had frightened him off with all that arguing and self-doubt in the weeks before. She should have been more happy for him, celebrated this wonderful opportunity with him, instead of selfishly thinking about how much she was going to miss him. It was her fault he had not come to say goodbye. Or perhaps some last minute crisis had occurred. Perhaps he was even saying goodbye to some other girlfriend. She dismissed this thought, as she needed to cheer herself up, not make herself feel worse. Either way, he was gone now. She had better, in a Henry-like, sensible, understated way, get used to life without him. She got cold waiting for Janice to finish in the bathroom.

Men always looked at you – it was just that the age group who noticed you got older. At least, they always looked at you until you married one of them, then from that time on all you saw of him was the back of his head. That was how it had been with Mark, anyway. She wondered if they were all the same. Perhaps even Henry would turn out like that. She stared at her face in the mirror. She was getting to that age, she reflected, when she could look either terrible or not bad, depending on the lighting, the amount of sleep she'd had the night before, and the skilled powers of delusion of the Boots make-up counter. It was amazing how quickly that age seemed to have arrived. This morning she looked terrible, and she wasn't being hard on herself: she really did. Bloodshot eyes, crêpey skin beneath them, distinct grooves either side of her mouth (that still, mercifully, disappeared with a good moisturiser), and a little comma-shaped mark where she habitually scowled in the sun. Oh dear. She was quite safe, nobody would look at her today. Especially not beautiful young men like the one she had met yesterday. She really should give up red wine. She peered at her nose, which was suspiciously bulbous-looking and red. Oh God – it would have purple veins on it next. No wonder most men wanted a girlie. Fancy eyeing someone up who was at least ten years younger than you, she thought, remembering Sanjay. It happened quite often these days, and if she wasn't careful to keep her mind occupied, that renegade organ would dive into a writhing quagmire of fantasy that would make a tart blush. Perhaps it was the prospect of the long months of celibacy. But since Henry had not even been in touch the entire week before leaving, she did not know how things stood. Perhaps he had wanted to end it, finish it off neatly before going away. That would be just like him, with his tidy, well-ordered mind. It would be just like him, too, not to be able to say it, just to assume she could read his mind, which she often could. That must be it. She could think of no other reason for his behaviour. Her sadness began to assume a bright streak of anger. The coward, she told herself. He could at least have had the decency to say goodbye.

She and Janice could do with some company, she decided, once Henry was well dug into the snows in Greenland. They had made no agreement, he had not promised to be faithful, or asked her to be. In fact, come to think of it, whenever she had raised the subject he had skirted round it awkwardly. So there was nothing stopping her and Janice seeking out some harmless, platonic male company. That would be plenty to start with. They could make it a project – a project to boost self-esteem and widen social horizons – just like the ones she devised for the patients, only a little more adventurous than going to the shops on your own without running screaming into the nearest doorway whenever you saw a dog, a man with a beard, or whatever your own personal bogey might be. She just hoped that Janice's bogey wouldn't turn out to be men, as it very well might after the moribund yet strangely devious Roger. Suddenly she could smell toast burning. Listen to your mother, Jenny Burdge, she does occasionally talk some sense. You've got to do something. Dragging both her face and her mind into some sort of shape, she shouted to Josh and began the day.

Janice lived the life of an outraged hygienist. She could never get her hands clean. She felt guilty saying that about Roger – telling Jenny about the wet wipes – for it was she, Janice, who had insisted on it. Roger had agreed with her mind you, yes, he agreed, it was much nicer. More hygienic. Why should she feel guilty, it was he who had dumped her, run off with another woman. Initially she'd felt as betrayed as if they had been married. But already in the light of day she didn't feel so bad. He was a bore, always putting her right when she ventured an opinion different from his. Telling her about accounting, auditing and how you must not be caught netting off, whatever that was – she'd switched off for a second there. Anyway, you must not do it. Like eating a meal without washing your hands. Come to think of it, her teeth didn't feel quite clean; that new toothpaste wasn't as good as the other. She would have to do them again. After that she would just have time to clean the toilet after the others left before she had to go to work. She never felt right leaving the house without doing it. If she had to give it a miss because Josh was dawdling and she had to leave before him, it preyed on her mind all day. But Jenny called up 'Bye, see you later,' and she heard the door slam. Good. She dashed downstairs and greeted the bleach like an old friend.

On Friday evening the phone rang. It was a call box, a poor line.

'It's Maggie here. Jen? That you?'

'Where are you? Mum said –'

'Forget what Mum said, I think she got the wrong end of the stick. I'm fine. Honest. Look, can you put me up for a few days? I've had a problem with a room I was promised, and I need to disappear for a bit. That OK?'

She took Jenny's sigh for assent. 'Great. Actually, I'm only round the corner in a call box, so I'll be there in two minutes. Looking forward to seeing you. Love to Josh –' the phone died.

Where can she sleep? Hope she hasn't got some stray man with her. Before her mind could invent numerous other trivialities to worry about, there was a knock on the door. Automatically Jenny darted over to glance in the mirror, as she always did, before opening the front door.

It was a warm, rainy June night with some grey light still in the clouds. The drizzle was small and drifted gently across the street light outside, some floating in as she opened the door. There was a smell of wet tarmac and green leaves. She expected the pointed, cat-like face of her sister, her elegant form gracing the grey street. Instead, a fragrant shred of warmth reached her as she adjusted her mind to a different figure. A taller, more familiar one, with big shoulders from which all the rest of him seemed to fall away. One she had thought was somewhere high above the Atlantic being fed champagne and a plastic dinner. In the street light she could see the glisten of stubble, the broken outline of his nose cracked in a rugby injury years ago. Her mind gave a terrific jolt, trying to adjust itself.

'My God, Henry, I thought you'd gone.'

He laughed. 'That's a nice greeting. I'll go away again if you like.'

'No – no, please – it's just – oh never mind. Don't go.'

'Well I'm getting pretty damp out here.'

She gave his wet coat a hug. It was not very satisfying; he did not hug her back. All of a sudden her arms were awkward appendages dangling at her sides, her legs threatened to trip her up if she moved them. He must have come to finish it. But why was he here at all? She held the door open and he brushed past her. That same warm familiar smell again, like bracken, or very ripe apples. Everything about him seemed more dear to her, because she had thought him gone.

'They offered me a hundred-pound cash voucher to fly tomorrow instead of today. Over-booked the flight or something; peak season I guess. Tomorrow I'll go club class, too, so I took it. Not a bad offer.'

Already he was speaking in his old, confident tone, the one she hadn't heard since she had first met him, the tone of the seasoned traveller that he had almost forgotten he was. So he had not come because he could not bear to leave without saying goodbye. He had come because they had paid him to travel a day later. She tried not to make this into anything. She slammed the door, then had to open it again to release his coat which she had stuck in it. As she bundled him in he said, 'That's what I like – a really warm welcome.'

'I'll get you a cup of tea.'

She stood stunned in the hall, her mind racing. She had not expected to see him again for nine months, her mind was occupied with adapting itself to that, shutting down some pretty important stations, then all of a sudden here he was again and she had to change back to being warm and welcoming, as if there was nothing unusual in this visit. She took him through and almost pushed him onto the sofa, more annoyed with him than anything. He had disrupted her grieving for him. He had been right first time, the finishing did not need saying, it was too painful. She wished he had not come.

The doorbell rang. Maggie. He must not see Maggie. Not after last time. The doorbell rang again. Maggie was just paying the taxi driver and giving him one of her sweet, confiding smiles, touching his sleeve for a moment before saying goodbye. She's got some money, then, Jenny noted. Her sister stood on the street in a long, flowing dress that clung to her body in the dampness. Her long hair was loose; she gave an impression of wildness. She is like a gazelle in the rain, thought Jenny. Henry will love her.

'This really is a bad time. Can't you go for a drink or something and come back in half an hour?'

Maggie looked affronted. 'Sorry,' she said in the tone of someone who knows perfectly well they have nothing to apologise for and that really it is you who should be apologising to them. 'I've just spent six hours on the train,' she went on, 'subjected to tasteless sandwiches and some Irish bloke who couldn't stop talking. I'm longing for a cup of tea and a chat with my sister, but if it's really too much for you to –'

'All right,' Jenny caved in. After all, what did it matter? Henry had come to ditch her. What added humiliation was there in his obviously fancying her sister at the same time? Either way, it was Goodbye Henry. She suppressed something. There was no need to let the past poison the present. If you let that happen you ended up like half of Jenny's cases at the hospital.

'Great place,' said Maggie, looking around. 'Where's Josh?'

'Out. Staying with a school friend. Can I get you something to eat?' Jenny was frostily polite.

It was all so sudden; she had not had time to adjust her mental furniture and some pretty hefty pieces of it were grinding around in her head. But Maggie did not answer. She had seen Henry and set about greeting him effusively like a long lost friend. Her slender arms slid around his neck as she hugged him and pecked him on the cheek – quite unnecessarily, Jenny thought, considering she had only met him once before. The thin body pressed itself sinuously against him. I don't have to watch this, Jenny decided, so she dived into the kitchen, blasted on the hot tap and began washing up furiously. She wished Janice was here as an ally. 'Sandwich?' she shouted through, and received a 'Yes please,' and an 'Ooh, lovely,' in return. Maggie was sitting next to Henry, lips parted in ecstasy at the migration patterns of Arctic Char. She doesn't even like fish – but at least she can tell him how to gut them, she thought savagely.

Shaking with impatience, she made tea and sandwiches, slapping on cheap margarine and some wet ham. She plonked it down in front of them. Maggie was laughing at some minor joke of Henry's. He looked big and outdoorsy next to her fragility. Feeling like a fishwife, Jenny planted herself in front of them with her hands on her hips and said in her firmest voice – the voice that had brought Eric back from the window ledge on the top floor of the hospital when he had been about to jump: 'Maggie, piss off. Henry is going away tomorrow for nine months and he has come to say goodbye. Go for a drink, walk around the block, do what you like, but go. Now. Please.'

Maggie put on her look of injured innocence, a handy one to have in her repertoire when outraged wives came round, as they had on two occasions. Henry tried a 'No, really, I don't mind –' but was snapped down with a 'Yes you do, Henry. Maggie is just going.'

He saw Matron's starchy bosom in front of his eyes and subsided meekly.

'So insecure, you do surprise me,' murmured Maggie on her way out. Jenny ignored her and pushed the front door decisively shut. Then she went back into the sitting room, flopped down beside Henry, buried her face in his neck and burst into tears.

He had had some idea of staying the night, making love to her once more, then saying what he wanted to say, transforming her sorrow into joy and leaving her eagerly awaiting his return, confident that everything would be all right. But Maggie would be back soon and somehow he could not stay and be intimate with Jenny with her distracting presence in the house. She was attractive, any man would think so, but he found her unnerving and intrusive, not his type at all, she would invade his privacy and start wanting to change things. He did not have the heart to make love to a sobbing woman and Jenny was inconsolable. So he just comforted her gently, murmuring into her hair, while she cried solidly for half an hour. Then, prompt to the minute for once, Maggie returned, and he left. So, what with one thing and another, the moment had not presented itself and he had not got around to the purpose of his visit, which had been to ask Jenny to marry him.

CHAPTER 2

Dear Jenny & Co
Am sending this out with the supply plane.
Flew into Thule Air Base safely. Nothing here
except a lot of rock and fish. Pleasantly
warm for the time of year! Hope
you are all well.
Henry xxx

This card (with a picture of a Boeing 747 on it, for some reason) arrived on the mat one morning and incensed Jenny. How could he fill a card with so frustratingly little information? The big H of Henry took up half of it, with the large curly loop of the y, and how unnecessary to put his name – how many other people sent her cards from Greenland, for goodness sake? And the '& Co' must mean Maggie. Really, she could spit. No address to write to, either, but perhaps that was his intention. So certain was she that he had intended to finish it before he went, and that only Maggie's presence and her own distress had meant that he hadn't had the heart, she was surprised to hear from him at all. He had been gone three weeks. She should be pleased that he had written, however briefly. Instead, just when she thought she might be beginning to get over his departure, it made the pain last longer.

The worst thing about old age is how boring it makes you, thought Jenny, as she was cleaning out her mother's cupboards. The young don't want to know you any more, with your sensible advice that seems well past its sell-by date to those who think they are discovering everything for the first time. They can't believe it was ever like that for you; what could you possibly know about their lives and feelings? You're old. Your ailments dominate your conversation (why is it after sixty when people ask you how you are, you suddenly feel a compulsion to tell them?) and the same old worn phrases trundle out again and again, down the same familiar grooves in your mouth. You can't be too careful, plenty more fish in the sea, never trust a man who wears grey shoes – Jenny had heard all these for the hundredth time, repeated and repeated, worn like a pebble that has been sucked on for years, rolled around in the mouth until all shape and meaning is lost.

Alcohol makes you boring too, she reflected as her mother ground on with some interminable tale about Sylvia's nephew that she tuned into from time to time, just enough to realise she had heard the story several times before. It doesn't have to be like this, she thought mutinously, as she handed her mother a duster. 'Go through and do the telly and Dad's ashes,' she told her, just to get her out of the kitchen. It's all in the mind. Astrid isn't like this and she must be about Mum's age. Lots of old people are just as nice – interesting, fun-loving, considerate – and as clean as they have always been. It is just a quirk of life for these people that they now happen to be old. Mum's not even old, really, thought Jenny. But her mind is. She opened a cupboard and a dozen or so bottles rolled out onto the floor. A smell of old dregs came off them. Jenny stood up.

'Mum.'

'What's that, dear?' Her mother stopped singing a song from *Oklahoma* and came through. When she saw the bottles she feigned surprise. 'Good gracious, what a lot of bottles. They must be left from last Christmas. Or even before that. Perhaps your father left them there.'

Jenny opened the next cupboard. This one was so jammed with bottles that only the necks stuck out. They were all green and the faint, bitter scent of gin floated up.

'Dear, dear,' cooed her mother, completely mystified. 'How ever did they get there?'

Jenny didn't even bother to say anything. This happened about twice a year, which was as often as she got around to cleaning out her mother's cupboards. It was always the same. 'Take these down the bottle bank, Mother. Better take them in batches. We don't want to flood the recycled glass market, do we?' Her mother was still rubbing her chin and frowning exaggeratedly as if completely stumped by this mystery. She seemed to be enjoying this little charade, as she always did. Jenny sighed, bent down and started piling the bottles into used carrier bags. 'Mother,' she said wearily, and for the thousandth time, 'Stop drinking.'

The time when you can do exactly what you want to is always a little bit ahead. When you are a child, you long to be an adult because then you can do what you like. When you reach that longed-for status you promise yourself that when you are rich, when the children leave home, when you get a job, when you ditch your partner, then you really will be able to do what you like. Some, or all of these things come to pass and still doing what you like is an illusion on the horizon, like a rainbow, always moving ahead of you just as you reach the place you think it is. Then you say, when I'm old, before I get decrepit and lose my marbles, which of course I won't do until I'm about eighty-five, *then* I won't care what people think. I'll flout convention, dress in gaudy colours, drink in the day, surround myself with animals and fill the house with plants and interesting people who will delight in me for being an eccentric old lady with wild hair in a bun. Then, when you get there, you realise gradually, without really knowing when, that you have missed it. It dawns on you that the magic time, the time for pleasing yourself, when you would be free to be the person you really wanted to be, passed you some way back – some fleeting moment when you had your mind on something else, and it will never come now. That was it, that was your go. Perhaps this was the problem with Mother. Well, thought Jenny, Henry is certainly doing what he wants to do, Maggie has always done exactly what she wanted to do, so I will too, I'll make this my turn. Watch out, world.

Maggie did not say how long she intended to stay, she was evasive about anything serious, appeared to have no plans, and just said that she deserved to have some fun for a bit. She really is doing now what she wants to do, Jenny thought on that first evening, I must just make sure that it is not at my expense. But gradually over the next few days, she began to doubt whether Maggie was really enjoying life as much as she liked to make out. That was certainly the impression Maggie liked to create, that she was living, while everyone else was merely existing. Since a child she had always been a consummate actress. But as shreds of information emerged, this image grew a little tarnished and cracked.

She looked as gorgeous as ever. Her long hair was still dark and silky (a shade too dark, perhaps?) and at the moment she dressed in long robes of rich materials, curtain fabrics that she had ingeniously made into medieval-type garments. She smoked dark cigarettes which made Josh cough ostentatiously – they'd just had a horrible video in school telling you about the evils of smoking and showing the tarry, gelatinous squelch of black that was the lungs of someone who had died of smoking.

'Smoking is slow death,' Josh told his aunt (though she wasn't very auntie-like, but then his mother wasn't always very like a mother).

Maggie put her head back and blew out a sensuous wreath. 'So who's in a hurry?'

Josh couldn't quite work this out, but he thought it was very clever. Even so, perhaps she didn't know how bad they were for you. He thought he'd better tell her about the video anyway. Especially that terrible bit where that man is lying in bed and can't get his breath, his poor old purple neck all skinny and straining to get the air in. It said at the end he died the next day. It had reminded Josh of a turkey's neck, like you pulled out in a plastic packet. 'You wouldn't like a neck like a turkey, would you?' he admonished her.

'Jenny, where's the volume button on this child?'

He went off her a bit then. She was a bit of a skinny old bird herself. He did not know what twenty-six looked like, all grown-ups looked fairly much the same to him, except the really old ones, but she was too old to be a friend to him. She wasn't fun. He decided to go up to his room and carry on practising drawing fish. Perhaps he would think up a curse to get rid of Maggie – she wouldn't let him call her auntie, said it made her feel old. A girl in his class had an auntie who was only in the first form of secondary school, so Maggie needn't think she was too young to be an auntie.

43

He'd have to give the curse some thought. It had worked all right on Roger, and James had been very impressed. James had put one on fat Pauline who lived over the back, but it hadn't worked. She still sat on the wall eating crisps and shouting rude names after them when they threw stones. Josh was pleased that James's curses were evidently not as powerful as his own. He pictured fat Pauline with the cluster of warts on her knee. Some people, he thought, were just *so* ugly that you wanted to shoot them.

But Jenny saw a new hardness in her sister. Even before, when Maggie had behaved outrageously without a thought for anyone else's feelings, she had an enchanting softness about her when she chose to show it, and all those who fell under her charm could put her monstrous ego down to youthful self-absorption and lack of thought. But qualities just about excusable in a girl of seventeen, with the dew still on her and with the time to grow, are less acceptable and less easily dismissed as a passing phase in a woman of twenty-six. And although she still had a body to fill men's fantasies, there were downward lines of discontent around the perfect mouth. When she ate there was a slackness in her lips as they encircled the food and a devouring quality about her that made Jenny uneasy. She couldn't believe that all she had really come for was a few nights' hospitality. A few nights looked like turning into a few weeks, or even months. And she didn't really want to be friendly; Jenny caught the barbed glances when Maggie thought she wasn't looking. There was a hidden purpose behind the brief smiles flashed across a coffee mug and the firing of inconsequential questions.

Maggie had the habit of all egoists – of asking a question then not listening to the answer. 'So where does Josh go to school?'

'Same as before, Meads Road Juniors.'

'How's work? Still enjoying looking after lunatics?'

'Well, you know, it gets a bit routine sometimes. Only three rapes and two murders last week, and that was just the staff.'

'Good, mm. Have you read this article on pelvic inflammatory disease? Scary. One of the girls on the typing course had it. Left a tampon in for two whole days, can you believe it? How could anyone be so disgusting?'

Jenny grabbed the magazine from her. 'You're getting as bad as Mum, wallowing in all this muck. You'll be gossiping about the royal family next. You don't bother with us for ages, then you waltz in and act as if nothing ever happened. What do you want, Maggie? Do you want to be friends, or is this just a convenient place to sponge? Be straight with me, if you know how, or get out. I can't do with all this clutter.'

Maggie looked mildly affronted. 'All right, keep your hair on, I'll have a really good tidy up while you're at work tomorrow. OK?'

'I didn't mean that sort of clutter.'

It was impossible to get beneath the surface.

At least she went out most evenings, as the days turned into weeks. She must have some friends locally – after all, she had grown up in the city – for she dressed up smart and always came back in a taxi in the early hours. But none of them seemed to be the friends she had known before. Sometimes she said, 'Don't cook for me, I'm eating out tonight.' Jenny felt like a bossy older sister asking, 'Who with?' and she only ever got the oblique reply, 'Oh, just some friends,' or 'Someone I know.' Perhaps she was seeing another married man. Beautifully detached, she never felt any guilt by association. 'Well I'm not the married one,' Jenny could imagine her saying. But perhaps she was misjudging the girl. After all, that other thing was long ago. And it might have happened anyway. The pull of the currents in a family can be strong. Strong enough to drown you.

It was lovely and sunny those weeks in late June and July while Maggie was staying, the bright sunlight intensifying the quiet English colours of the countryside, the smell of tarmac acrid and sickly in the hot streets. The air was warm and soft until quite late in the evening, when Jenny and Maggie would pull out two faded deck chairs and sit in the scrubby back yard. On these occasions they did not talk. Jenny read a book while Maggie filed her nails, smoked, or read a magazine. At least they were not actively hostile on these evenings, and managed to share the yard like a pair of street cats who have decided to tolerate each other in a shared patch of territory. These were days when the afternoons were long and slow, when the grass was blue in the shade. At the mental hospital the heat made the patients drowsy and the staff bad-tempered. People sunbathed in the Museum gardens and the Minster grounds, hitching up office skirts and rolling up shirt sleeves in the lunch hour. Women sat with pushchairs while energetic toddlers chased the pigeons, and old men basked on benches, warming their bones in the sun.

Jenny, in between the sweat and struggle of work and home, gradually got used to the gap left by Henry and wondered what the weather was like in Greenland. She could picture a short, golden summer of bare rocks, snow still hiding in the cracks, light nights and tiny, unobtrusive mosses and flowers in the foreground, gigantic billowing white mountains and cliffs of ice rearing up in the background. For some reason a group of lively penguins kept intruding into this mental picture, like a crowd of eager film extras huddling and jostling in front of the camera so that their mothers can see them on the silver screen. She knew this was inaccurate, yet still she saw them, small comic figures dressed in spotless black and white, playing on the ice. Her mind must be playing strange tricks, she thought. Of course there were no penguins in Greenland, how ridiculous. On days spent sitting in hot traffic jams surrounded by other irritable drivers and poisonous fumes just to get home during the rush hour, she played with the idea of leaving everything and flying out to join him in that quiet land, remote and wild, and living with him in a rocky, romantic little hut with nothing to do but be together and study fish. It sounded idyllic. For a brief time she would feel that elusive thrill of freedom that he must feel all the time. Usually at this point she felt angry yet again with him for going, unstuck herself from the hot plastic seat of the car and longed for the traffic lights to change. Maggie meanwhile donned a minuscule bikini, coated herself in oil and spent her days decoratively basting herself in the yard. Once he realised she was there, Gavin found excuses to potter about in his mother's yard, and while doing nothing here and there, he carefully removed a loose brick from the wall and spent hours peeping through the hole he had made.

Jenny was still curious about Maggie's life, so she tried to probe a bit. The air had cooled outside one evening and the midges were biting, so they had come in. They had seen Astrid strolling down the back alley towards her house with a man who looked like a librarian.

'See anything of Cath these days?' Maggie and Cath had been inseparable since the age of eight.

'She's moved to Liverpool with her boyfriend.' Maggie did not lift her head from the magazine she was reading.

'Oh, she's living with Paul now, then?'

'Not Paul, another one.'

'What about Sarah and all that crowd?'

'What about them?'

'Well – what are they doing now? Are any of them still around?'

Maggie sighed and looked up at last. 'I really don't know, Jenny, and quite honestly I really don't care. What's so interesting about my old school friends all of a sudden? I haven't seen any of them for years. Grow up, for God's sake. Everyone else has. Stop doing the big sister bit, you're years out of date. You don't know any of the people I know, and quite honestly I don't think you'd want to. You might find yourself shaken out of your comfy little rut.'

Her irritation with Maggie had been building up for weeks and suddenly something snapped inside her head. You don't know me at all, you just don't know me at all, she thought. Jenny could only just trust herself to speak. 'My comfy little rut, as you call it, which you have been enjoying for over a month now, needs some money to keep it going. How about a contribution? Rent, for instance, or something towards the groceries?'

Maggie stared up at her from the only armchair, the pages of the glossy magazine still open on her knee. Her naturally pointy features adjusted themselves into soft, appealing mode. I expect it works every time, Jenny thought wryly. 'Oh well, if I had any, you know I'd give it to you. I really appreciate you putting me up, Jen, I really do. It's *so* kind of you, especially as we haven't been in touch for a while. I'm just not particularly flush at the moment – you know how it is.'

'So, no rent then.'

Maggie just shrugged apologetically.

'You can still wash up, presumably? Or don't you do that any more, either?'

'Janice likes that job, doesn't she? Bit of a cleaning fanatic, isn't she? I wouldn't like to deprive her of her hobby. Anyway, I have to keep my hands nice for work.'

'What work?' A thread to pick up at last.

Maggie reddened. 'Oh, nothing, only – you know, if I did get any work, I wouldn't like to have my hands all cracked and chapped at the interview.'

'What are you, for God's sake, that makes your hands too good for washing up? Do you do telly adverts or something? That must be quite well paid. No, they don't do that in the evenings, do they? Let me think – an evening job that you have to look gorgeous for, especially your hands. A private masseuse?' A fleeting, intense glance lasting less than a second told Jenny that she was on the right track. She grabbed Maggie's expensive carpet bag off the table and opened her purse. Three hundred pounds or more was rolled up in an elastic band.

'What's this – last night's takings? No wonder all you're fit for in the day is lying around. Poor you – you're shagged out – literally.'

'Don't be so quick to judge, Jenny,' Maggie began, 'it's not what it looks –'

'Why so secretive, then? What have you got to hide? Come on, now's your chance to put me in the picture and tell me why you're so rich all of a sudden and why none of this money can go towards housekeeping.'

Maggie flushed even redder. 'I just – don't think you'd understand.'

'Bloody right I don't.

So angry she could watch herself doing it, she grabbed Maggie roughly and flung her out of the front door. 'I don't want any of your dirty money!' she shouted out through the letter box. She didn't want one polluting scrap of her left inside, so she ran around frantically grabbing anything she could see that belonged to her, stuffing it all into a bin liner, then she opened the door again and threw the whole lot out onto the street. She glimpsed Maggie bending to pick up the bag, bundling her dresses and shoes into it, for they had spilled out a little in the fall. She was looking round to see if anyone had noticed. Only Astrid's curtains twitched.

'I'll burn the rest,' shrieked Jenny and slammed the door.

Leaning against it, panting slightly, she actually felt quite good, elated and strong. At last that horrible anger was out. Really it had nothing to do with rent, or Maggie's mysterious occupation. It did not matter in the least to Jenny how her sister chose to occupy herself these days. This outburst was a legacy from long ago. It was so sudden she hadn't seen it coming, she thought she had it all under control, safely mothballed and put away in the cupboard marked 'Things to Forget' – rather a crammed cupboard, that – and then out it had thrust, a fierce, hot, self-righteous force like a cleansing flame. She could breathe again freely, in a way that she had not been able to do since it had happened, the thing she had tried to forget. She had never shown any reaction to the unspeakable thing Maggie had done all those years ago, until now. Only now, in the act of throwing Maggie bodily out through the door, was Jenny free of that terrible rage she had kept inside. She had been paying the price for someone else's action a long time.

'What's the matter?' asked Josh, coming down the stairs.

'I thought you were asleep,' said Jenny. 'It's after nine o'clock.'

'I was too hot. Anyway, you woke me up. Were you arguing with Maggie?' His face was pink with sleep and he looked worried. 'Why were you shouting? Are you cross?'

Jenny hugged him very tightly. 'Not with you, sweetheart. Maggie can be a bit annoying sometimes, but it's nothing to worry about. Grown-ups do shout at each other now and again,' she said gently. 'It doesn't mean they don't care about each other. Maggie has gone for a while – she was only ever staying for a holiday.'

'You can't be cross with her – she's your sister.'

Jenny sighed. 'Sisters can be very annoying. I'm sure you'd find yours annoying if you had one.'

He grimaced. 'Yes, I would,' he said. 'Going in my bedroom and wanting to borrow my things. James's sister Sarah is a right pain in the butt. She always wants to play with us.'

'Of course she does. She thinks an older brother and his friend are very exciting. She wants to be like you.'

Josh looked gratified. 'She can't ever be like us, though,' he said with satisfaction. 'She's a *girl*.'

'Girls can do exactly the same things as boys,' said Jenny.

'No they can't. They haven't got willies.' He laughed nervously, feeling daring and wondering whether she would let him get away with saying this. She let it pass.

'Anyway, even if they could, I wouldn't want to play with them. They always want to play stupid kissing games, and keep falling out and making up again. Pathetic. Nothing's the matter, is it?' he asked again, peering into her face. 'You're a bit red.'

Jenny laughed. 'Nothing. You like James's family, don't you?'

Josh nodded. 'They're cool. His Dad does things with him. His Dad's *really* cool. He lets James play on the computer, and gives him rides on the back of his motorbike. They go to rugby matches. Real ones, not just school.' Josh looked awkwardly up at her. She thought he was going to cry. 'Mum, *why* haven't I got a Dad?'

Jenny's heart was wrenched and she wanted to weep for him. 'You know what happened. He was killed in an accident. He didn't choose to go.' God forgive me for that lie, she prayed.

'Yes but –' Josh's face was twisted with the effort of what he was about to ask. 'Couldn't we – get another one? Other people do. I mean, I know it's not the same as the real one, but I don't even remember him. Couldn't Henry have been my Dad? He was nearly as cool as James's Dad. He did fun things with us.' He let out a sudden huge gusty breath, as he used to do as a much younger child when he was trying to be brave. 'He could at least have said goodbye. I miss him.'

'So do I,' Jenny whispered, unable to get a normal speaking voice out. 'But he had to go away, for work. He didn't want to leave us behind, he just had to. He was a nice friend, though, wasn't he? They haven't got schools and all that kind of thing in Greenland.'

'Is he coming back, then?'

My God, she thought, how children put you through it. 'I don't know, sweetheart. I don't know. He'll always be our friend. We just may not – see him much.' I'm blundering here, she thought, feeling angry with Henry, and with herself for not being stronger.

She realised that Henry had no idea of the hole he had left in their lives. Perhaps it was her fault, she thought, for not making it clearer to him.

'Well if he's not,' said Josh pragmatically, 'maybe you could go and find another nice one?'

'You can't just go into a shop and buy one,' Jenny said, laughing. 'And not all of them are nice. By a long chalk.' She patted him briskly. 'Anyway you and me are fine by ourselves, aren't we? We're buddies.' She kissed him. Now it was getting soppy, Josh lost interest. Reassured, he broke away from her and went into the bathroom. 'She's left a lipstick here,' he shouted. 'A bright red one. And some dirty pants behind the door.' That's Maggie, thought Jenny. Bright red lipstick and dirty knickers. Trust Josh to point it out.

Janice had accepted Maggie's sudden departure with the same unquestioning resignation that she accepted the weather. She must have heard the goings on, for she had been upstairs, but she did not mention it. Nor did she demur when Jenny proposed a night on the town. So on Friday night they got their glad rags on and went out.

Janice was only twenty-three, but Jenny felt decidedly old for this sort of thing. They went to a wine bar that Janice said some of the nurses frequented.

'It's not all youngsters, though,' Janice said tactlessly. But it was. Most of them looked about fourteen to Jenny's paranoid eye. I must be getting old, she thought, a lot of them look as if they have forgotten to get dressed. And jeans as tight as that will keep the birth rate down. Most of these young animals in the cattle market were out for the evening, but near the bar stood a group of men in suits, clearly left over from the drinks-after-work brigade. Jenny nudged past them to get to the bar. The music was deafening – another sign of old age when you notice it's too loud, thought Jenny. One of the dark suits called her name above the din. She looked. It was Sanjay. How embarrassing to be seen trying to pass herself off as a young thing out on the town. She felt lumpy and frumpy and divorced. He looked pleased to see her. That smile again, she really must get a grip, he would notice her positively drooling.

'Let me take you for a corned beef sandwich,' he said. 'They're my favourite.'

'What, now?'

'What?'

She felt a fool repeating it.

'What?' he said again.

'It's not worth repeating,' she bellowed.

'What's not what?'

'Never mind.'

'So can I take you out to lunch? Tuesday? I work near the hospital, I'll call in about one o'clock.'

She nodded enthusiastically, not daring to risk another reply that he would not hear. So they nodded at each other for a few minutes like a couple of toy dogs.

'Fine. See you Tuesday.'

She edged up to the bar and saw her reflection in the long mirror behind it. She was bright red. But she could put that down to a touch of sunburn and apart from that she didn't look too bad. That's soft lighting for you, she thought. I must let the dust build up on the mirrors at home, it makes them so much kinder. She must put her hair up more often, it showed off her cheekbones, and you couldn't see the silver bit like a sixpence on the top. Not bad at all.

They had to leave shortly afterwards, as Janice was being pursued by a pimply youth who kept saying things like, 'Do you fuck?' and 'You're like a spanner – you tighten my nuts.'

'Whatever happened to chatting up?' asked Jenny as they breathed the fresh air gratefully. Perhaps the circumcised Roger had had his attractions after all.

'I don't think I fancy this any more,' Janice said. 'Let's get some chips and go home.'

'We might even catch the nine o'clock news.'

Astrid had the television on loud and was knitting a sweater for Gavin. 'Purple's his favourite,' she said. 'He likes everything purple. He's decorating the front room for me when he's finished his rest. He's gone in for a bit of a rest.' She used this term to describe his periodic stays in hospital. She was surprised to see them so early, and shared their chips. Each time she bit one there was a waxy ring of lipstick left around it before she popped the last bit in her mouth. The lipstick reminded Jenny of Maggie. They told her about their evening. Jenny kept quiet about Sanjay, though, partly out of embarrassment and because she didn't think she would go, and partly not to hurt Janice's feelings.

'What's happened to men, Astrid?' asked Janice. 'Were they always like this, and did we just not notice?'

'Were we blinded by the rush of hormones towards the sack, you mean, before the cold light of maturity peeped between the curtains and showed us their grubby underwear and dirty socks?' Astrid laughed. 'Well, there is a lot of frogs, in my opinion, who'll tell you they'll turn into princes, but you has to kiss a lot of 'em before you find one prince, and I'm still looking! Mind, I quite enjoys the kissing,' she added with a naughty twinkle.

'Hmm,' said Jenny. 'At the moment I think I'd rather have a talking frog.'

As the saying goes, 'Never agree to anything on a Friday night, because Tuesday lunchtime always comes.' Or if there wasn't a saying before, there is now, because Jenny said it to herself five thousand times between Friday night and Tuesday morning. She even considered ringing in sick, except it was her stress management workshop, and she wouldn't let them down. She might even benefit from it herself today. He was there on the dot. Kate gave her a knowing look as Sanjay escorted her out.

'You *are* a dark horse, Jenny Burdge,' and she winked heavily, and in Jenny's view, tastelessly. 'Who is he?'

Jenny didn't answer. She preferred to keep her private life private, and it might not look too good, going for lunch with Dr Baljekar's son. Sucking up to the boss. Especially after all the abuse they gave the older man behind his back. But really, this was nothing. After all, what was a corned beef sandwich? Even creative Kate couldn't make anything out of that.

In fact, Kate was fed up. She lived on her own, and although all this independence and self-sufficiency business was fine, she sometimes wished she didn't have to pretend to be quite so independent and self-sufficient. She enjoyed her own company, but you could have too much of a good thing. She hadn't had so much as a sniff of romance in her life for far too long. She sighed heavily after Jenny had skipped out of the door and decided to start her sandwiches early. Just then Damien put his head round the door.

'She's out to lunch,' said Kate. Like most of the people round here, she thought as Damien made a silent retreat. The only thing Kate had to look forward to was an evening at the Women's Refuge, a grim, decaying pile of Victorian masonry where she worked three nights a week. Not many laughs in that, she thought glumly and bit fiercely into a hard, sour Granny Smith apple as green as her spirits when she pictured Jenny out to lunch.

Kate had spent her childhood in Newcastle in a large Victorian house very like the women's hostel. Except that instead of housing women and children in need and being in dire need itself of extensive repairs, her home had been equipped with two academic parents and every modern convenience that money could buy. Her mother and father both taught at Newcastle University. Her mother taught French and Spanish, her father Economics. Kate was their only, much-cherished offspring. So cherished in fact that she had been assigned to the military regime of a superbly trained and very expensive Swiss nanny from the age of three months. When Kate was two the Swiss nanny had left in a cloud of stolid Swiss indignation after accusing Kate's father of rubbing himself up against her in the bathroom. 'Delusional, clearly, poor girl,' Kate's mother had commented drily while giving her husband a steely glare. Another one, just as authoritarian but gloomier, had followed, from Finland. Kate had been distraught at the loss of the Swiss nanny, so had been bought a teddy in compensation. The teddy was handmade, ludicrously expensive and over-stuffed – the sort designed for wealthy, maladjusted adults – so that it was too hard to cuddle. It sat on top of her chest of drawers and stared down in mute disapproval.

Her education had been a matter for extensive debate and the disposal of vast sums of money. Teatime conversation concerned the latest (in her father's opinion) insanities of the government, so that for many years as a child Kate was genuinely under the impression that most of the Cabinet was suffering from senile dementia, and that the few who were not yet afflicted were obsessed by a compulsion to 'climb over the backs' of the poor, demented ones. This childhood picture had been so vivid that when the House of Commons was televised Kate had been surprised to see that they all looked relatively normal – well, most of them – and that no one was clambering about over anyone else. Her father's other pet subject for teatime chat was the desirability of the Japanese economic model, despite its obvious drawbacks as perceived by Western individualist thinking.

Kate's mother had written a critique on Molière that had been well received in academic circles. 'Home-making' was a word she used only when she intended to be patronising, and she had never mastered the complexities of cooking. A very quiet woman called Gina saw to all the housework. Gina had peroxide hair and wore skin-tight jeans. At about the age of fourteen, Kate had once seen her father squeezing Gina's bottom in the kitchen. Gina had been asked to leave shortly afterwards and a stout lady called Mrs O'Leary had replaced her. She wore a flowery wrap-over pinafore, she stood no nonsense and her ample bottom was eminently unsqueezable. Kate had been expected to excel at school. She had endured half an hour's French conversation with her mother every evening after supper since the age of twelve. Her French was impeccable. She had found out about periods only when she had soaked the back of her skirt at the age of twelve in school, and had thought she was about to die.

As a result, Kate had rebelled against the sort of career her parents thought desirable – a well-established degree at a red-brick university, followed by something steady and lucrative, probably in London. Instead, she had spent a year from eighteen to nineteen living in a caravan and travelling around Britain with a crowd of similar vagrants, many of whom were also the children of high-achieving parents, some of them quite well-known public figures. After this she had qualified as an occupational therapist and, to her parents' horror, spent two years working in a refugee centre in Zaire. As she pointed out to her mother, all those years of French had come in useful after all. At the age of twenty-five she had returned to the north of England, although comfortably far from the leafy part of Newcastle where her parents still lived. She had become semi-reconciled to them on her return to Britain. That is, she had spent a few only mildly uncomfortable weekends with them, enjoying good sherry and biting her tongue. The things she had seen and experienced on the compound in Zaire had made her want to repair the rift. The differences that divided them now seemed trivial. But paradoxically, the gap between her and her parents was now wider than ever because of her experiences in Zaire. She was even less likely ever to conform to their ideas of what was acceptable for their daughter. She had also realised that she was gay. With this revelation, less than two years after her return to Britain, relations had been terminated permanently. Since then, Kate had lived quietly in York, establishing her own life, enjoying her work and establishing a few loosely connected and undemanding friends. Her one or two forays into relationships had been brief and unsatisfying, so she had decided to leave such matters to fate. Fate, she believed, had a way of sorting these things out. She just wished it would hurry up.

Sanjay took Jenny to a little dark café off a side street. The stress management workshop hadn't helped a bit.

'I usually have lunch here, it's a good contrast to the office. They do really good pitta breads too, if you prefer.'

He probably wanted her to sit and listen to his problems, that was her usual role.

The man behind the counter greeted Sanjay by name. Jenny wondered how many other women he brought in here. He was a partner in a firm of accountants round the corner – not the same one that celery-stick Roger had worked for – but his caste, he told her, was the caste of the barber. 'So whatever profession we go into, and my father was very ambitious for us all, we learn to cut hair. Only the men, though. My sister's a chiropodist.'

'Even your father?' Jenny couldn't see Dr Baljekar with a pair of scissors, asking if you'd had your holiday yet, and saying, 'All ready for Christmas, then?'

'Oh yes, he's an expert. He cut my sister's hair for her wedding, and dressed it. He's done very well to go into medicine, though.'

Jenny thought it best not to go into how well or otherwise Dr Baljekar had done. I daresay his mother is proud of him, she thought.

'Cutting hair is very therapeutic. It makes a good bond between two people.' He touched the ends of Jenny's critically. 'I could do yours for you some time.' Her stomach lurched. 'You need to look after it, it's very lovely. And natural. It's the same colour as the woodwork in here, look, you match that door. Antique pine. Your eyes are the same.'

'Same as each other, or same as the door?' she burbled, thinking this is unreal, this is not happening.

'Will you let me cut your hair one day?' he asked. She said she would. They had coffee, and she eyed the sticky banana toffee cake, but felt too embarrassed to pig out on it in front of him. She must come back here again. He asked her about herself, not merely to be polite, but as if he really wanted to know. He listened when she talked about Josh, Janice, and he asked about Josh's father. She told him he had died in a car accident.

'You must have been devastated,' he said, which people usually said, and she usually agreed with them.

'No,' she said with an honesty that surprised her. 'He had what you might call – a problem with fidelity. I had already lost him. We had lost each other. I don't think I ever really knew him. We'd been divorced for two years, he had some student with him in the car when it happened, in France. She walked away without a scratch, thank God. He was a terrible driver – fast, always showing off.'

She had not talked like this to anyone for years, not even to Janice. Pouring your heart out to a virtual stranger was a bit pathetic, the sort of thing some of her patients did when they came out of hospital – sit on a park bench and do the 'Ancient Mariner' bit to anyone who would listen. She had seen them at it when she walked across the park in her lunch breaks, and she usually went over for a chat to the ones she knew. It was not something Jenny indulged in herself, confiding in strangers. She suddenly wished that she had not. He was so young and privileged, she thought, he could not possibly understand. She felt a bit shaky, as if they had trodden on forbidden ground. Perhaps he didn't care at all, perhaps this was all a ploy of some sort.

'I don't want to talk about it, it was so long ago, I've forgotten it really. All part of life,' she shrugged. Then she stood up briskly. 'Look, you're very nice, I've enjoyed lunch very much, thank you. But I don't talk like this to people, especially to complete strangers. This is how patients talk to me – all this pouring out your life story stuff. Perhaps this is some new idea for undercover staff assessment by your father? Find out what the staff are really like?' She was doing this all wrong, being too aggressive. But what did it matter, she thought, she was old enough to be his mother. Well, nearly. 'How old are you, Sanjay?'

'Twenty-six. And you, since you have had the impudence to ask me?' He was smiling.

'Thirty-five.'

'So, *not* old enough to be my mother.' He leaned forward and kissed her, a warm, dry brush across her lips. 'You see, your eyes show your thoughts. Be careful what you think.' His dark eyes were unfathomable, teasing her. 'When can I cut your hair? Those ends really need it.'

Jenny laughed. 'Now you sound like a hairdresser.'

'Shall I see you a week today? Where do you live? I can cut your hair at your house in the lunch hour, if it is not too far.'

She told him. It was only a few minutes away.

'So, one o'clock at your house?'

For the second time she agreed to his request, and for the second time, she wished she had not. She thanked him for lunch and offered to pay for hers, but he wouldn't let her. She sensed that he was not just gentlemanly in an old-fashioned way, but proud. She did not mind, she was at the stage where everything about someone is interesting, even down to what they wear in bed and what they like for breakfast. Perhaps especially that.

Outside, the hot August street was gold with the slanting sunlight of late summer. He didn't kiss her again. 'Goodbye, Antique Pine.' It was all so corny and innocent, somehow. She hadn't even realised people still talked like that. It had all the freshness and play-acting of a schoolgirl romance. In perfect keeping with his part, as if he knew just what was expected, he smiled, turned and was gone.

Well, what was lunch? Nothing. Almost nothing. Henry would be having lunch, tea and who knows what else, with people she knew nothing about. It was weeks since he had gone, she had heard nothing from him except that one hopelessly uninformative postcard, and this was the first time she had even spent more than half an hour alone in the company of a man, on anything that might even remotely be described as a date. She need not feel the slightest pang of guilt. In fact, she told herself, she had been rather slow to console herself with other company. She still missed Henry every day. But being faithful to his memory was being pointlessly faithful to a lost cause, she reflected sadly. And she had to admit, she had really enjoyed Sanjay's company. He had an openness, a lack of reserve that exhilarated her. It was the openness of the young, the unbruised. It was refreshing.

Yet when she came to think about what she had learned of him, it amounted to very little. He had done to her what she usually did to others – asked them open questions and then listened while they talked. Thus, he had left her with a feeling that he was clever and sensitive, that he really cared, and that *she* had had a lovely time. He had given the impression that, for the time they had spent together, she was the most important person to him. That is a skill indeed, she thought cynically. It probably gets them into bed every time. Maybe she had been rash, letting him know where she lived – after all, she still knew practically nothing about him, and you read such terrible things in the papers, you couldn't be too careful. That was her mother talking, she told herself. Be careful, Jenny Burdge, that you don't turn into your mother.

She had no illusions about her own motivation – she was colliding with Sanjay on the rebound. She was looking for a bit of fun and harmless consolation for the aching gap left by Henry. But he was firmly out of the picture now and she was simply trying to help herself adjust to that idea, by getting out and about and meeting new friends. That was what they advised in magazines, wasn't it, for this sort of situation? She must just ensure that harmless fun was all it remained with Sanjay. It was too soon for any more painful involvement. In the meantime, normal duties had to be maintained and she must forget about it until next Tuesday – or until she went to bed at night, at least. She might allow herself a little *frisson* of anticipation then.

On the Friday she considered suggesting another outing with Janice, only the last one had been so depressing (apart from Sanjay) that she didn't have the heart. But as it turned out, they had a visitor. Jenny got home from work to find Janice sweating over the internal organs of some animal in the kitchen, and a stranger sitting on the sofa. Oh God, thought Jenny, she's not done something like put an advert in the paper, has she? He looked like the product of a lonely hearts advertisement. 'Sincere forty-something would like to meet understanding lady, any age, good sense of humour, for nights out or in (know what I mean?) Beard-lover preferred.' He had the mournful, begging look of a spaniel that hopes to be given a scrap from the table. He stood up to greet Jenny, and there was a whiff of something not very fresh about him. He was tall and gangly, with a gaunt but not unfriendly face and rather savage teeth that lurked in the straggly beard. Oh no, Janice, she said silently, this can't be Roger's replacement. No, no, no. When he sat down again his legs fell apart, almost disjointed, like a pile of wood.

'I don't think we've met.' Jenny made her voice sound as unwelcoming as possible.

'This is Frank,' said Janice, appearing in the kitchen doorway with a tomato impaled on a knife. Jenny followed her back into the kitchen.

'I'm sorry to be rude, but who the hell is Frank? And what is he doing in my sitting room? And why has he got such a horrible, scabby beard? And why does it make me so angry to see him sitting there like bloody Pinocchio?'

'Because it's Friday night and you want your glass of wine,' said Janice automatically, in her nursey voice. 'Josh has gone to James's for tea. I said to be back by seven, I hope that's all right.'

'Yes, fine. I'll go up and get him. I'd like to meet this wonderful family who have captured my son's heart. But who is *he*?' she asked, gesturing towards the sitting room.

'Oh, *him*. Says he's a friend of Maggie's. I thought you must have heard of him.'

'What's he doing *here*?'

'Ask him.'

Frank fumbled apologetically when Jenny asked him. God, I have enough of life's inadequates all week, she thought harshly.

'She owes me some money. I knew she was coming to stay here for a while. I hoped to catch her.'

'Well, you're too late, she's gone. So if that's all you came for,' she moved to show him out. He was clearly not a man open to hints.

'The thing is, I need the money. I lent it to her for the furniture that the boyfriend broke when he – er – called round. The chairs and the pictures and that. And the plates. I live in the bedsit below, you see. In Brighton.'

'You came all the way up here to get some money back? It must have cost you more than she owed you.'

He shook his head. She could almost see flakes of stuff from the beard floating down onto the carpet. Janice would have the hoover out as soon as he was out of the door. He had hitched up, he said. 'And she owes me two hundred pounds.'

'I'm very sorry, but really it's nothing to do with me. So I really think you'd better go. I'm afraid I can't help you.'

But this did not make him move.

'I've got to have my money,' he said more stubbornly. 'I'll lose the room if I don't pay the rent.'

Suddenly Jenny felt uneasy, the same sort of uneasy feeling she had had when she had been in the training kitchen at the hospital and had turned to find a patient poised with a knife behind her. (It turned out that he had mistaken her for his mother, on whom he blamed all his present problems. What a lot mothers have to answer for, Jenny had reflected.) It was nothing more than an intuitive feeling that made her cautious. She spoke to Frank more carefully.

'I'm sorry, Frank, we can't help you. Perhaps the police will be able to trace my sister. I'll just give them a ring.'

'No.' His voice had changed from rather weak and frail, to

hoarse and low. His teeth were suddenly more visible. 'Give me my money. It's mine, she took it.'

Jenny put a hand on his shoulder, kind but firm. He was shaking.

'Your sister lied to me. I need the money.'

'I'm very sorry, Frank,' Jenny repeated, easing him up out of the chair and steering him towards the door. Calmness on her part was everything. 'I know nothing of my sister's affairs, and I don't wish to know. If you leave me your address, I promise I will get in touch if I hear from her.'

He looked at her doubtfully. His eyes were yellow and rheumy; there was a glint of desperation there. However, he let Jenny lead him to the door and out onto the pavement. 'You will tell her I need it, won't you? Because otherwise I'll have to come back,' he said just before she closed the door. She assured him she would.

Just then the phone rang. It was Josh. 'Mum, they've invited me to stay the night. Can I? Please? I can just nip home to get my stuff.'

Jenny agreed. It must be much more fun for him up there, she thought guiltily. All we have here is two lonely women, and the occasional nutter asking for money.

'Oh, great,' he said enthusiastically. 'Thanks, Mum. See you in a minute.'

One upshot of the incident with Frank was that Janice spent the whole evening cleaning, hoovering and dusting, and still claimed to be able to smell him in her nostrils. Another was that a man came on Tuesday (at Janice's insistence) to put locks on all the windows and put a spy hole in the front door. Janice was at home that morning and stayed in to supervise. The man finished early, so she took the opportunity of some privacy to henna her hair. One of the girls at work had said it would really suit her. So when Sanjay called, scissors in pocket and flowers in hand (he had an eye for detail), it was Janice with a shower cap on and thick, greenish liquid running down her ear, who opened the door. It was hard to tell who was more nonplussed.

'Is Jenny here?'

Janice looked at him doubtfully. 'You're not here about the windows? Because the man's just been and gone. You're not him, are you? He was the man, wasn't he, not some conman?'

He shook his head. Perhaps she was on medication. Never one to appear ill at ease or lacking in grace, he handed Janice the flowers.

'Thank you, that's very nice. How very kind.' She peered at him. 'I'm sorry, I haven't got my lenses in. Do I know you?'

Sanjay told her he was Jenny's hairdresser. 'Your henna's running, by the way.'

'She never mentioned it,' said Janice. 'But then, she might have forgotten. We've been quite busy.'

When Jenny arrived, hoping to intercept him, Sanjay was sitting at the table having a cosy cup of tea with her friend. Janice was in full flow, describing Frank and why she had thought Sanjay might be the lock man, and Sanjay was listening with his usual undivided attention.

'Let me take you out to dinner,' he said to Jenny when Janice had finally stopped talking.

'Oh, thank you,' said Janice. 'Jenny, isn't that nice? Dinner as well as flowers. Where would you like to take us?'

She is definitely mad, thought Sanjay, as well as exceptionally plain. He was acutely aware of appearance, his own and other people's. Jenny must have her here out of the kindness of her heart. He adjusted his tie and coughed. 'I have to go now, but I will look forward to seeing you – er – both.'

'What about Friday?' persisted Janice excitedly. 'We're both free Friday, aren't we, Jen?' Jenny was trying not to cringe too obviously.

'OK, Friday,' Sanjay agreed, rallying gallantly. 'I will book a table and pick you up at eight. You like Italian? Good.' At least I will see Jenny, he thought, and perhaps we can get rid of the strange one.

Jenny tried to catch his eye as he left, but failed. He thinks I set this up, she realised, to make fun of him. He thinks I did it deliberately. His large dark car pulled smoothly away. Handled with my usual knack for winning over the opposite sex, she mused. It wasn't Janice's fault, I should have warned her. She would never have guessed that someone so young and gorgeous would be here to see me. She had a sudden pang about Henry. But he had chosen to take himself so far away, she told herself. He wouldn't have made that choice if he had wanted her. She was confident she could keep Sanjay as an interesting friend, with just that little extra sparkle of attraction.

'How many times must I tell you – don't let strangers in,' she told Janice. 'Even goodlooking ones who say they are my hairdresser.'

'Isn't he?'

'Well, yes. Sort of. Prospective hairdresser. I'm going to try him out, anyway. And I might even let him cut my hair,' she added, and they laughed the predatory laugh of two unattached women assessing potential prey.

CHAPTER 3

Dear Jenny
It's getting colder and darker here –
fantastic skies. Have had several trips
upstream to see the fish before it freezes.
This is another world. Hope you are well.
Henry xxx

On the front was a picture of a small jet plane with red wings. The one he flew in on, perhaps? Or the supply plane? Jenny could see no other possible relevance in the picture, and she always looked for a message in the picture as well as the words, on a card. One thing he was right about, though – he certainly was in another world. I can no more imagine it, she thought glumly, than a flea can imagine a trip on the *Queen Mary*.

Sanjay was angry. He felt he had been wrong-footed, out-manoeuvred. The two women had made a fool of him. Fancy giving the flowers to that girl, that terrible skinny one like a bird with half its feathers off, a plucked chicken with a sharp nose like a beak. She had those freckles that melded together into blots, as if her skin were blotting paper. He hated those kind of freckles. He liked the small, precise ones his wife had, tiny clear ink dots on her dark shoulders. He had kissed them on the wedding night, discovering them with joy, but she had shrugged him off, stopped him. He hadn't seen the freckles since, but it made him ache sometimes, knowing they were there under the thin stuff of her shirt.

He'd always been at the top of his world – the crown of creation, a position he kept hold of mainly because of his mother's unshakeable faith in him, which had developed into an unshakeable faith in himself. He always wanted things that were worth wanting, things that other people wanted and he nearly always got them. But his wife, his clever, talented, prestigious wife, whom any man would have wanted to own, thwarted him. Because she, so delicate and elusive, refused to be owned and thwarted *him* – Sanjay the handsome, Sanjay the strong – she shook his whole judgement of himself.

His wife was very beautiful, like a bird, but not a chicken like that Janice. A dark, shy bird that flitted in the undergrowth and wouldn't let you see it. A blackbird with rainbows in its wings. He had agreed to marry her only because she was so beautiful. He had also done it to please his father, but it was her appearance that clinched it. He had been so struck by her dark, glossy hair, her velvet skin, her hard little hips, achingly slender. He would never have agreed to it otherwise, he told himself. He often wondered why *she* had agreed to an arranged marriage. She didn't have to, after all. With a good degree in social sciences, trained as a social worker, she must have met plenty of men. She didn't even seem to like him very much. When he asked her if she liked him yet, she would say, 'Of course', in an abstracted way, without looking up from her book. Perhaps it was his timing that was wrong. When he said, 'Why did you marry me?' she would look up, annoyed, and say, 'What sort of question is that?' If pressed, she would say because he was a good man, a kind man, and if she had not married him she would have risked hurting her parents. It was as if she owed something to them, he felt, not to him. Perhaps she felt she had to repay them for all that money they had invested in her education – the very education that had made it unfitting for her to have married him, he thought. He had not been to university himself, a choice which had pained his father, until Sanjay had explained that he wanted to start earning money straight away. His father could understand the pull of money. It was that and the prestige of psychiatry that had guided his own career, more than any feeling for the sufferings of his fellow men and women, or a strong curiosity to understand what tortuous stories went on inside their heads. She worked in child care, the worst area. She saw it all.

The toughness and compassion that this work required was one of the things he liked about her. It was the sort of work people admired. As a hobby, just for fun, she helped out in a home for battered wives two nights a week. She stayed over on a Friday night, to give the mums a rest from night feeds, she said. What about my night feeds, he thought, then realised he was being a baby. She wouldn't respect him for thoughts like that. She was big on respect. It seemed to be a substitute for a lot of other, stronger feelings.

He wasn't sure if it was sex she didn't like, or just him. She just let him do things to her. She never, ever gave him what he thought of as a 'proper' kiss – the kiss of a lover rather than the peck on the cheek of a member of the family or a very close friend. He didn't seem to do it right for her, but without any other experience he went on instinct. Once or twice he had tried to exercise some imagination, but she hadn't liked that. He tried to be gentle, but it seemed to hurt her. She would wince and turn away, but he carried on, not knowing what else to do, dreading the silent impasse that he knew they would reach if he gave up trying. 'Hurry up,' she would say from time to time. She was tight and he always came quickly. Especially as she only allowed it once or twice a month. He did nothing else in between, although the lack of intimacy between them worried and depressed him. He wondered if she had some sort of mysterious women's medical problem, or whether there was something wrong with him. He was fastidious as a cat.

She wore baggy, loose-fitting clothes that hid her neat, hard body. She had had her hair cut short and shaggy, which accentuated the small bones of her face. She wore a red jewel in the side of her nose, her small delicate nose, with its arching nostrils he would have liked to lick. Her hands were small and chalky, the nails short and very clean. She wished she would touch him in his warm places with those small, cool hands, but she never would. If he tried to place them there she took them straight away.

He didn't really know why he was drawn to Jenny. She wasn't beautiful like his wife and he was very much governed by appearance. But she had a sort of animal charm, a primitive, earthy quality, of sensuality only just damped down. She had large breasts and a rounded stomach. He could bury himself in those breasts – big, squashy, doughy breasts, warm and fragrant, smelling of bread in his imagination – he wanted to mash them gently round and round and bury himself in the scent. She wasn't even pretty really. She was quite wrinkly, as if she had seen a bit of life which she obviously had, but that closeness to the grubbiness of experience, that touching of the real energies, attracted him. He didn't really know what he wanted from her. Some sort of learning, perhaps, a bit of truth to nourish his own life. Some sort of key to it all. He had a dim sense that there should be more, that there *was* more, and that if anyone knew what it was and could teach it to him, Jenny could.

He turned the big quiet car into the smart, modern cul-de-sac, then into the driveway of his smart, modern house. He had been very pleased to be able to buy detached first time. There was a path down the side of each house, just about wide enough to walk down if you turned sideways. It pleased him to know that the house was as immaculate inside as it was outside. Just like his own mind, he liked to think. The busy lizzies and marigolds in their regimented rows were fading a little, he'd have to remind his wife to pull them up. Her shiny red car was in the drive, she was home first. He felt the usual pleasure tinged with anxiousness that accompanied his homecoming. He didn't know whether he would honour his offer of dinner on Friday. Perhaps he would not turn up, give them a taste of their own medicine. But perhaps they would just laugh at him, as they must have done today. Good at keeping his mental compartments tidy, he put away Janice and Jenny and thought about his wife. He hoped she was friendly today, not contemptuous, as she often was. He was not in the mood for barbed, clever word-play. He'd had enough teasing for one day. Like most men he didn't like it and with women, he usually didn't understand it. He didn't think they had a sense of humour, really. They just thought they did. He was a man limited by words.

'One of the things I liked about him was the way he comes straight out with it. You know, says something not realising how frank he's being. Very unreserved.'

'Perhaps it's because English isn't his first language. It makes him say more than he means, I think.'

'Isn't it?' said Janice. 'You wouldn't know. Except for the odd phrase here and there. I think just the hint of an accent's very attractive, don't you?'

'He certainly knows how to say what you want to hear,' Jenny said. 'Wonder if he'll turn up on Friday. I've never been on a date in a threesome.'

'It's not a date. It's just a meal. He just wants to be friendly.'

'Does he?' said Jenny. 'I've never met a man who takes you out for dinner just to be friendly. Not worth the investment.'

'Not all the world is as twisted as you think it is,' said Janice.

'Isn't it?'

Despite the major cleaning, tidying and general exorcism last Saturday after Frank, the house was untidy again, ordinary and profane. Janice's instinct to put things away was overcome by the tendencies of Jenny and Josh to get things out, so a litter of newspapers, clothes (clean and dirty) and a half-eaten yoghurt cluttered the small sitting room. Jenny had found a piece of starry muslin at lunchtime in the market and was hemming it in front of the television. Janice was wiping up. Josh was up in his room drawing cartoons of sharks eating people. Normality was restored.

Sanjay encircled his wife in bed, curling in behind her like two spoons in a drawer. Usually she allowed this. His erect member nuzzled her back like a small friendly animal. He kissed the back of her neck with warm, dry lips. She smelled of something herby. Sighing heavily, she edged away. He expected this and usually took it in good part, turning his mind to financial matters until he went to sleep. But tonight the picture of Jenny filled him, her white doughiness surrounding and enveloping his own hard darkness. He could imagine himself licking her, like a female lion licking its cub which they'd seen on television this evening – the pink liquid tongue that you knew was so rough, pouring out love and cleanliness onto the hard, tussocky head of the cub. He stroked his wife persuasively. She nudged him off. He'd had enough of this. For Christ's sake, he was a normal man, wasn't he? Was he supposed to go without sex for the rest of his life? He hadn't realised that was part of the deal. If he had, he would never have let himself be talked into it. He'd never even had a chance to get bored with it, yet. Cursing suddenly, he threw off the duvet and strode out, slamming the bedroom door. Those hollow wooden doors they put in new houses do not slam very effectively, so it didn't give him the satisfaction he required. It was cold downstairs. He wondered what to do now he had made his gesture. He lay on the sofa in the dark, wishing he had got the duvet from the spare room. He was cold, he'd have to go back up in a minute. But not yet. He got a blanket from the airing cupboard. Then he closed his eyes and, picturing Jenny (and a lot of other large, white-breasted women), he gave himself relief, and fell asleep.

Nita went straight from work to the hostel on Friday night as usual. It was a massive, rambling Victorian pile on the London Road, two houses knocked together with a crumbling, fusty air of decayed grandeur. But inside the atmosphere was anything but fusty. She knocked on the door and was let in by Sharon clad in black leggings, a tight top that emphasised her meagre breasts and scarlet lipstick that made her mouth look like a gash across her face. It was strange, Nita reflected, how as soon as these women had escaped from a brutal, brutish man, they gave out all the signals that would attract another, similar one. The real gash had healed to a fine line down the side of her face and Sharon was going soon, she had got a flat above a bakery in town. The stairs were littered with children and a radio competed with the television. She greeted everyone, and one or two of the children replied. Two of them were fighting, rolling over and over in the hallway.

'Come on Jade and Jack, tea's ready,' Cathy called from the little kitchen on the first landing. Marion, a vicar's wife, was reading to a child on a sofa. Someone had made a paper mobile of colourful fish that caught the light in the small back room where the television was.

'Do you like it?' asked Sam.

'It's lovely, Sam. Did you make it?' Nita asked. He nodded, pleased. She stroked his shoulder, smiling. 'You are talented, well done.' He grew about two inches in height.

Nita went down into the basement, where her friend Kate had a tiny office made out of the old scullery. They kissed each other on the cheek. Kate told her what hd been happening while she made coffee. 'Sorry there's only powdered milk, I didn't get out at lunchtime. We can go out to eat later.'

They exchanged news. Kate was the real reason Nita came here. She did like to chat to the women and help bath the children, and she also used the time to catch up on any of her case load who had moved on. But she got at least as much as she gave, in the sustenance of Kate's company.

The hostel was a fluid community. Most of the women moved on, either back to their homes – some to sink without trace, some to reappear in a few months' time – or the more determined, those with more self-esteem and a clear vision of a better life, into a flat or a caravan. For only those with truly nowhere to go ever came here in the first place. Anyone with a family would go there first. Even so, the hostel was always full to bursting. Marion was the only one who was a permanent fixture – she had no other home as she had no children and was too old to get a job. 'After all,' she said, 'who wants to employ a woman in her fifties whose main achievements have been flower arranging, making jams and running a demon jumble sale?' The last time her husband (the vicar, doted darling of the parish ladies) had hit her, it was for leaving a sardine tin on the floor for the cat to lick out. She and the cat had arrived together. So Kate had given her a part-time job and a room on the top floor. Now she ran a crèche for the working mums. For Kate, the hostel was the closest she could come in Britain to having the sense of usefulness and purpose she had had in Zaire.

Even though most of the women were passing through, there was a strong sense of community. If there was anything approaching sisterhood between women, and Nita didn't really think there was, there was a transient semblance of it here. If she had to describe it in a sentence, she would have said that there was an atmosphere of acceptance. Everyone was accepting of each other; they had to be in this sort of proximity. People fell out, of course, and got on each other's nerves, but on the whole it was a very accepting, accommodating place. A haven. All the experience that each woman brought into the house was valued, none of it dismissed as worthless. This was part of the healing. That was what Kate said, and the best help Nita could give was to listen and talk to people, which she did. It was hard not to get angry sometimes and frustrated, and very hard not to judge, but Nita was used to stepping back. She had practised detachment and compromise to perfection. She thought of Sanjay for a moment, secure in his picture of the world – a happy, tidy world with himself at the top, his badges of success clearly defined and worn with pride. She sometimes wondered what he would make of this, one of the refuges in the hinterland of existence. She did love him in a way. Who could not? He was so simple, so transparent, and he tried so hard to please. He thought he was the stronger one, so she let him. But she had made her compromise, her deal with fate, a long time ago.

'What do you fancy? Italian? There's a good one opened in Maurice Street, my treat,' said Kate. She was big in every way, her energy filled the room. She loved the sensuous pleasures and approached them all with equal gusto. Nita agreed. Being with Kate was like basking in the warmth, vitality and light of a large log fire. She enveloped Nita in a big, warm hug.

'You're like a little shivering sparrow. It's jumper weather now, you know. Here, borrow this.' She turfed a cat off a fluffy brown thing, shook it and threw it to Nita. It was an old sweater. 'Don't worry, it's clean. Baggy's only been sleeping on it a couple of days.'

Nita put it on and pulled up the huge sleeves. It smelled of Kate, warm and appley.

The meal was delicious, strongly savoury and stodgy. They shared a bottle of wine. It was dark on the way back and they walked together arm in arm.

'Thanks, that was a real treat.'

Kate smiled. 'You could do with a few more dinners like that. Put some meat on that skinny little bottom.' She patted it affectionately. This was as far as Nita would let her go. Theirs was a playful friendship, made sparky by the tautness of Kate's devotion and pursuit of Nita, and the certain knowledge in them both that Nita would never succumb. Nita was not, as she put it, 'that way inclined'. But she loved to be pursued, doted on and showered with affection, and Kate made her laugh more than anyone else she knew. It was a classic erotic friendship of the sort often seen between men and women, sustained because the eroticism was never allowed to blossom. Kate was the eternal pursuer, long having given up any hope of her feelings being reciprocated, but enjoying the pursuit. Nita was the eternal, unattainable pursued one, so attractive precisely because she would never be won. If Nita had suddenly discovered she was gay, she sometimes reflected, the whole finely balanced friendship would be upset. They would have a brief, intense affair that would fizzle out leaving them both disappointed and deprived of a close friend. Nita saw all this, and liked to keep the game finely poised.

'I've been giving Sanjay a bit of a hard time lately, poor thing.'

Kate had never met Sanjay. For some reason she imagined him to be little, fat and grumpy like his father. She made no connection between Nita's apparently pathetic husband and Jenny's mysterious, elegant friend.

'Is he expecting you back tonight?'

'No, he's not expecting me.' Nita was doubtful. It would be nice to surprise him for once.

Kate was silent for a moment. She put her hand on the back of Nita's neck. 'It's up to you.' She gripped harder, playfully. 'Your choice.'

Nita hesitated. A small drizzle started, blurring the street lights. She was warm from the dinner and the wine. 'I'll stay. I brought my sleeping bag.'

She always did. And Kate always said, as she did now, 'I could keep you warm.'

Nita always declined, as they both knew she would, and they were both contented when they went to bed. Although Nita was perhaps a little more contented than Kate. Kate was getting just a little tired of the game.

Sanjay was in two minds whether to keep his arrangement with the two women. His time was his own on Friday nights and it wasn't his fault if his wife neglected him, it was up to him what he did. He often went out with friends, there were quite a few young men his age at the office, single, without commitments, who went out to eat or drink. That was how he had seen Jenny that time, when he had impulsively asked her for lunch. He wished he hadn't, it was nothing but trouble. She was old, for God's sake and the other one was ugly. If there was one thing he couldn't stand, it was ugly women. They were an offence to society. Even if they didn't mind themselves, they owed it to everybody else at least to try to look half decent – after all, it was everybody else who had to look at them all day, they didn't have to see themselves. Just as well, or there'd be a lot more women jumping off bridges. But women in their thirties are in their sexual prime, everyone knew that. Paul from the office had a girlfriend who was thirty-four and he said she was insatiable. Said he hardly managed to come up for air all weekend last time he'd been down to Bournemouth to see her. He had certainly looked pretty rough on the Monday, but perhaps that had been the drive. Sanjay wouldn't go all the way to Bournemouth just for sex. He was sure you could get it much closer to home. You couldn't believe everything Paul said. He told some stories himself. He never let them think he was a virgin when he got married, they'd think he was a right prat.

He'd phone and cancel the table. That would show them. Then they couldn't eat, there would be no room, they would have to leave. For there was never a table on a Friday night. He'd chosen one of the most popular restaurants, of course, that new Italian one in Maurice Street. He picked up the phone. But what about Jenny? She was very nice, she was someone you could talk to, she actually listened, seemed to find him interesting. He would like to see her again. If he stood them up, he wouldn't be able to call in to the hospital and ask her for lunch. He couldn't say, 'Well, I wanted you but not your friend.' That would be very rude and he was never rude, he knew how to behave. She would be bound to take it the wrong way in any case and think he was after something that he was not. He would have to go. Perhaps they could ditch the friend. But he shouldn't even be thinking like this; he was a married man.

He believed in fidelity, in the promises he had made. The whole thing was a mistake. He would cancel. Jenny could think what she liked; he would probably never see her again anyway. He phoned the restaurant.

Jenny and Janice enjoyed their meal. (Janice always polished the cutlery surreptitiously on a napkin before she ate – you could never be too sure). The Italian restaurant was too crowded, there was no reservation for them and no sign whatsoever of Sanjay, so they went for a curry instead, washed down with plenty of lager.

'Funny he didn't turn up,' said Janice.

'Not really. Funny he ever asked us, really. I can't make him out.'

'Well, our success with men isn't anything to write home about, is it?' said Janice. 'One lunatic occupying the sitting room for two hours wanting money, and one film star look-alike who doesn't turn up.' They laughed.

'Give me a good tikka masala any time,' said Jenny.

A week or so later, Jenny remembered the sticky banana toffee pie and went back to the café to try some. It's the only pleasure of the flesh I've got at the moment and I'm going to make the most of it, she thought, as she plunged her spoon in. It was, unusually, as good as it looked. She ordered a second coffee and opened her newspaper. She had, of course, given the dark, low-beamed room a predatory scan to see whether Sanjay just happened to be in today. He wasn't. She was acting like a ridiculous, infatuated teenager. Worse, she was a ridiculous, infatuated mature woman. The barman had recognised her, though, and greeted her. He was worth his wage, she thought, with a memory for faces like that, and friendly with it. He probably doubled the takings just by smiling at the customers. How rare that is these days, she reflected, and then realised that she must be getting old. She was just about to leave after some banter with the barman about the weather (he didn't score highly on originality of topics) when Sanjay entered. Foolishly her heart, or stomach – she was not sure which bit of you it was that gives that funny lurch when the object of desire appears – lurched. He was with another dark-suited man, shorter and more thickset than Sanjay was. The friend had the stance and manner of a small, fighting bantam cock. He stuck out his chest and appeared to strut even when he was standing still. Small man syndrome, she thought dismissively. She let her eyes rest on Sanjay. Those shoulders in that oversized jacket – he looked almost as tasty as the banana toffee pie. So she said so. Shit, said her brain, but her mouth just went right on talking. The object of desire was maintaining a stunned silence.

'Given up on my split ends then, have you? A lost cause, are they?'

The friend was looking bemused. 'Are you the cabaret?' he asked. 'Do you know this person, Sanjay? She seems to be speaking to you.'

God this was terrible, she thought, telling herself, 'Shut up, shut up, shut up.'

But Sanjay was smiling. Ever impeccable in good manners, he gave a flourish. 'Jenny, this is Paul. Paul, meet Jenny. She's from the psychiatric hospital,' he explained kindly.

Paul nodded sagely. 'Nice to meet you,' he said, slowly and rather too loudly. 'Are you – erm – out for the afternoon?'

'Oh yes,' said Jenny. 'They do give us poor things time off for good behaviour.' Paul shrank back a little with a nervous grin.

'Must dash, I've got subjects to see and a country to run.' She leaned towards Paul and said in a confidential whisper, 'It's hard work being the Queen of Siam, you know. The tiara never will stay on.' She winked and patted his arm, then whisked out of the café, just catching sight of the barman's startled stare. 'She seemed so quiet,' he was saying. 'I had no idea.'

Out on the street she laughed to herself. It didn't matter that Sanjay had broken their date. She had caught his eye and seen the blench of embarrassment to be associated with this strange woman. She looked at her own reflection in a shop window, foreshortened so that she looked like a stunted dwarf. She'd seen him. The sun was suddenly shining, the trees were clad in their autumn colours, the street was dog-shit free thanks to the new bins the council had provided, and Jenny was happy.

Back in the occupational therapists' office after lunch, Kate was slumped at her desk looking decidedly disgruntled. Jenny was magnanimous with joy. 'What's the matter? You look less than your usual cheery self.'

'Domestics,' said Kate glumly, her chin resting on her hand.

'I thought you lived on your own.'

'Precisely.' She looked balefully at Jenny. 'Anyway, what's up with you? You look like you've been smacked all over with a copy of *Woman's Weekly*, you're all pink and pleased. Had a naughty lunch? That's what I could do with.'

'Not as naughty as I'd like,' said Jenny as Margaret came in. 'Only a piece of banana toffee pie.'

'If it has that effect on you, I must try some. What did you do? Get someone obliging to lick it off?'

Margaret pulled her thin lips in disapprovingly. 'Sometimes it's hard to tell the staff from the patients around here.'

Just then there was a knock on the door. It was Damien. He wanted Jenny. 'I had this dream,' he began, 'this amazing dream. There was this woman – '

'No, Damien, I'll talk to you about anything you like, but not sex. That's the rule, as you know. Now, what shall we talk about? Come on, let's go into the garden.'

'I rest my case,' gloated Margaret.

Kate just groaned and put the kettle on.

CHAPTER 4

Dear Jenny
Weather closing in here.
Getting fed up with a Nissen hut
and not much else, but people great.
(5 Great Danes – joke). Char looking
good. Here's a picture of the Nissen hut.
Henry.

The Nissen hut must be a joke too, for the card was a plain one, completely white. Nissen hut in the snow, ha ha, thought Jenny guiltily when she saw it lying on the mat that night, its chaste, snowy whiteness reproaching her. She remembered with a pang Henry's careful, gentle, ponderous humour. He reminded her sometimes of a Saint Bernard looking pleased with itself because it has just made a joke. Sanjay was more of an Afghan hound, really. She had a feeling Sanjay didn't joke. If he was ever funny, it would be quite unintentional. Suddenly she missed Henry with an almost physical intensity, a lonely, dull, dragging pain of longing. Oh Henry, she cried inside, where are you?

Kate started phoning Nita once a week, then two or three times, sometimes very late. When she came back to bed, shivery and wide awake, Sanjay would murmur and turn over. She didn't think the sound of the phone woke him and if he noticed her absence it was only in his sleep. First it was for chats, joking and exchanging news as they did on a Friday night, enjoying each other's company. Nita was never quite sure each time with Kate whether they were still where they had been last time, or whether things had slipped back. Kate could be moody and silent sometimes. Kate set the pace. Intimacy and friendship interwove and swirled like the currents in a stream, sometimes dark and still when nothing much could be seen, then fast and furious, shooting down rapids when they argued vociferously about everything from politics to the best way to give a tablet to Kate's cat without him craftily sicking it back up (Kate favoured the biro method and brute force, whereas Nita preferred the deception method with a bit of tinned tuna) and they would end up laughing. But gradually, over the next few weeks as late summer drifted lazily into autumn, Nita became aware of a conflicting pull between them. Kate would try to talk seriously but Nita would stop her, afraid of what she might say. So Nita would skate deliberately on the surface like a pond skater, flitting away whenever Kate threatened to step over the lines they had established – or rather, that Nita had established. Then one night, when they had been chatting on the phone for almost half an hour, and laughing a lot over this and that, enjoying each other's enjoyment, Kate said suddenly, 'I miss you, Nita.'

'I miss you,' she replied lightly.

'I don't mean just "miss you". I mean, come over. Now. The bed's warm, there's a bottle of wine in the fridge, I'll light the candles and – '

'You know I can't. You know that's not how it is with us. I'm not – ' she could not find a word that would not sound insulting to Kate.

Kate sighed. 'I know. See you, Nita. 'Bye.'

Nita was left holding the lifeless receiver. The abrupt end to the conversation left her suddenly cold and alone in the hall. She realised that beneath the light, bright surface of their friendship, something dark and hidden was shifting.

This became rather a pattern. Mostly it was playful banter, a sign that Kate wanted her, which flattered Nita and gave her a chance to call the shots a little, saying yes, or, I'm sorry, I can't today, or maybe, I'll have to see, to Kate's pleas to see her. She knew that she was behaving ambiguously. She also knew that she was not gay, but simply needy, and weakened by the loneliness of her marriage. She did not really know why she could not respond to Sanjay. It was not, she felt, for want of trying. But ultimately, she just could not love or desire him in the way he deserved to be loved and desired. Partly, she thought sometimes, it was because he loved himself so much already.

There was an unpredictability developing in this friendship with Kate that had been totally missing from the socially choreographed courtship of Sanjay. That had revolved around a set pattern, like a dance where everyone knew the steps and each participant signified the outcome to the other long before the dance reached its conclusion. For although Nita could have refused him at any point, right up to the last minute, in practice it would have been far from easy. It would have upset a lot of people, questions would have been asked, explanations expected. Brought up knowing that it was important for her to please others, Nita did not have it in her to shock and disgrace her parents. They would, she believed, never have got over it. And if the choice was between Sanjay and all that he offered her – their extended family and all their friends, material success and social acceptability – or Kate – and Kate alone, for whom she could never be a full partner any more than she could for Sanjay, although for different reasons, to sustain her through loss of her home and family and the experience of becoming an outcast to those she had loved all her life – Nita could not choose. She knew that Kate would always want more than she was able to give her. So, in her peaceful way, elusive of conflict, she chose the middle path.

But gradually Kate grew more insistent, more demanding, and her natural bossiness had less humour in it, more aggrieved irritability. They talked endlessly about how Nita could leave Sanjay, when would be the best time, how she could come to stay for as long as she liked at Kate's sunny attic flat near the station while she considered her next step. They had it all worked out, curled up side by side on Kate's squashy sofa. They would drink Earl Grey tea, eat buttery teacakes, look out through the skylight into the chill mist of the November dusk, and make plans. It was like playing houses when she was a little girl for Nita, it had that same element of 'Let's pretend'. Still, though, the tone was light, possibilities were tossed lightly around and discarded. They each appeared to be deliberately choosing not to take the other seriously.

One night in the last week of November Kate rang her up. Christmassy things were beginning to happen around the town, especially in the open market and Coppergate shopping centre, but they were the tawdry commercial Christmas activities that begin in November and Nita could not feel the least bit festive. It was a filthy night, with black, stinging rain sheeting from torn clouds and bouncing up off the greasy streets. Nita would not have put a cat out in it. She was glad to be cosily ensconced in her tidy, well-insulated home, the thick, expensive curtains shutting out the cold, devouring darkness. She picked up the phone with pleasant, warm anticipation. She knew it would be Kate, for it was around her usual time for calling, just after midnight. She kept strange hours because she lived by herself, she said. She sounded husky and slightly drunk.

'Where are you?' asked Nita. The line was crackly and she could hear the swish of cars passing in the background.

'In the phone box by the museum gardens. I've been out with some friends.'

It occurred to Nita suddenly that she had hardly ever met one of Kate's friends. They were an amorphous crowd who went on raucous bouts of drinking now and again, and who occupied the shadowy background of her friendship with Kate. It was as if she and Kate occupied a small, private corner of each other's lives. She knew that they would never inhabit the open, central area. How little she actually knew about Kate. It was all just play, she realised. Pointless, even perhaps dangerous, play. Suddenly she did not want to talk to her. Kate's breath was agitated. Nita said, 'Are you all right?'

'I want to kiss you. I've known you all this time and I've never kissed you, you know that? Do you know how hard that's been?'

My God, thought Nita, horrified. She's like a man. A drunken, predatory, lascivious man. She felt revulsion creep like a cold slime over her whole body. This was her friend, her kind, sensible, strong, funny friend. Her *confidante*. How, she asked herself, had she let it get this far? Verbal play was what she enjoyed, and she had thought Kate did too. After that other, awkward conversation, the open invitation that she had so definitely declined, she had thought

81

it was all clear. This was sickeningly not play.

'Kate – you know how it is – just friends, OK? You've had a lot to drink, you don't know what you're saying. Just go home to bed and you'll be fine. You're my best friend, you know that. I thought we had it straight.'

The line was silent. Nita could just hear the rain through the double glazing in her own blue-carpeted, uncluttered hall. It must be heavy. 'Kate? Are you still there? Talk to me.'

'You mean, *you're* straight.'

'Well, yes. You knew that. I thought – I thought we both knew how it was. I love our friendship, but that's what it is. Friends. I'm married, for heaven's sake.' Suddenly this conversation seemed ludicrous. She could not believe they were having it. She realised that Kate must be very drunk. 'What did you think was going to happen?'

'You're always going on about how you don't love him, you were forced into marrying him, how one day you're going to leave him – why did you keep saying all those things? We spend all this time together – as friends. You know – the way I am – but you still kept on coming round, to my flat and to the hostel. You still wanted to see me as a friend, just giving me enough to be going on with – *only just* enough to keep me hoping, without you having to change your happy, comfortable, straight little ways. Do you think a man would have put up with being kept dangling like this? You talk about how you're going to leave and come and stay with me. What was I supposed to think?'

'I didn't mean for you to take it – like that,' Nita faltered.

'How did you expect me to take it?'

Nita's heart began to pound with dread, and her voice clutched at Kate over the phone. 'You're my best friend. If I thought you didn't care for me I would just shrivel up inside.'

Kate was silent again. 'You led me on,' she said eventually, her voice hard and cold, enunciating every word. She must have had a lot to drink. 'You fucking led me on. You're unhappily married – so you *say* – but you don't go fooling around with another man –'

'Of *course* not!' said Nita, outraged. 'I would never do that to Sanjay.'

82

'But instead you fool around with *me*. All the endless joking and flirting – yes, flirting, that's what you were doing. Didn't you even realise? Come on, I can't believe that. What was it for? Curiosity? See what it would be like with another woman? An experiment? Except you haven't even got the guts to try? Why – in case you might like it?'

'No!'

'But when it gets serious, and you are asked to give for once instead of take, oh no, little miss tight-arse gets all prim and proper and jumps back onto the right side of the fence. "I was only playing." Is that it?'

Nita was shaking with shock. 'You're mad,' she sobbed, 'you're totally out of your head. Can't you have straight friends without – without – you're crazy, you're spoiling it all. You scare me. We were never – like that. I thought we understood each other.' She could still hear the rhythmic swish of traffic in the background. It was a dreadful night. She could imagine the tyres slicing the dirty water in the gutters into fans that caught the beam of the headlights. Kate must be cold and miserable. She could imagine her so clearly, shivering in the phone box in her old waxed jacket that smelt like a tent in the rain. Her hair must be plastered down and she would be able to see her own breath. Her own warm, living breath. If only, Nita cried to herself, if only I could give you what you want. But I can't, Kate, I can't. I don't want to.

In desperation Kate said, 'I love you.'

'*No!*'

There was a pause then, afraid of what else might be said, wanting to push away everything that Kate wanted and represented, Nita crammed the receiver back into its place. There was only the comforting, meaningless burr of the dead line. Nita was shaking and crying in the dark hall. Slowly she climbed the stairs and slipped gratefully into bed and curled up close to Sanjay's warm, sleeping back.

Kate pushed open the door of the telephone box and the rain immediately, remorselessly slashed across her body, whipping the skin on her face. She hunched herself against it, pulled up her collar and began to walk slowly down towards the station and her flat.

She was very drunk, drunk enough to be outside herself, looking down on the lonely figure in the rain, and to think with perfect clarity, you shouldn't do this to yourself, woman, you're better than this. You know it doesn't do you any good, after that first flush of *bonhomie* in the pub. At best it makes you gloomy and miserable when you go home alone; at worst you become an irrational, outspoken fool. A taxi rushed by close to the kerb and soaked her. She took several deep breaths, saying aloud to herself, 'I'll be all right. I'm *not* going to throw up. I'm all right.'

An elderly man, pausing by a lamp post in the rain while his dog had his evening constitutional, stared at her strangely. She was an outcast, she felt, as much as the sad piles of rags sheltering in the entrance of the station were outcasts, doomed to walk the streets scavenging for scraps of whatever they could find. People might be kind, but they could never really help. Most would prefer not to see and not to know. Kate felt that she would never find what she was searching for. Her face was covered with a sheet of water as hot tears mingled with the icy rain. Never in her life had she felt so completely, so bleakly, alone.

All the next day, while she was writing up case reports, Nita was in a state of tremor. That had been it, last night, the moment she had known must come, when she realised it was all too good to be true, that the gods would not agree to her bargain. They wouldn't let her have her cake and eat it. Kate had been very patient, they had been friends for nearly three years now, almost as long as she had been married. If only she had met Kate three months earlier, she thought, and had the benefit of her down-to-earth advice, she would have had the strength not to agree to the farcical social arrangement with Sanjay – poor Sanjay, as she had come to think of him. She was poised, like the year, nearing its dark end, slowing down at the top before the pendulum swung again. Time would move forward, the old year would tip over into the new but she, Nita, was frozen. She had rejected Kate and sooner or later she knew she would finally, irrevocably, reject Sanjay. She could sense the time crawling relentlessly nearer. The crisis with Kate was just a small rehearsal, a forerunner of what was to come. Beyond that, the only thing she could see was a gaping void. This knowledge kept her locked in a state of paralysis from which she could not yet see any means of escape.

Janice decided she needed to take herself in hand. Christmas was coming, work was fine – well, as fine as it ever was in geriatrics – she had settled into the new house and got over the well wet-wiped Roger long ago; but she was depressed. Not just the normal, curl-up-in-front-of-the-fire winter low, which she knew was more to do with lack of sunlight than anything else. She was really fed up. She couldn't say she was lonely, after all Jenny and Josh were around all the time, but she felt very alone. Her chief activity outside work was cleaning, and she was having to do more and more of it to get the same feeling of satisfaction. Even that wasn't filling the sense of emptiness inside her. She didn't want to burden Jenny with it, she had to listen to people's problems all day and anyway, Janice could see she wouldn't be receptive. She wasn't sleeping that well, either. She'd been to the doctor and he'd recommended iron tonic tablets and a keep fit class, which his wife just happened to be running in the community centre off Gasworks Street. But the thought of gyrating with a bunch of Lycra-clad dimply bottoms and willow-like teenagers depressed her even more. It would take more than a keep fit class to put her right, however much it trimmed her tum and tightened her bottom, as the poster promised. She was ready for a change.

She thought of booking a holiday and even went down to the travel agent to pick up a few brochures. Astrid lent her one on holidays in Majorca, two weeks of sun, sea and Spanish waiters and as much free lager as you can drink, but this was not quite what Janice had in mind. She toyed with the idea of a week in Jersey, but she had never been abroad on her own and none of her colleagues were free or keen to go, so that was as far as she got. She applied for two jobs and got an interview for one of them in Doncaster, but it looked so dreary, just more of what she was already doing. And more of the same was definitely what she did not want.

She'd given up cooking, more or less, and gone off eating, too. Her greatest indulgence of the flesh was cleaning her teeth, which she did six times a day it felt so nice, and rinsed her mouth out with diluted TCP in case she had bad breath. Gradually, little by little, more and more, cleanliness became all that mattered. Jenny bought bleach pretty often for the bathroom as Janice used it up, but Janice was buying extra in between, the same brand, so Jenny wouldn't notice. Once or twice Jenny said, 'Poo, it's a bit strong in here, isn't it?' with reference to the bleach, and in mid-November she remarked that Janice was looking a bit thin. But she had always been slight (Jenny was good-naturedly envious of her neat form) and she kept herself well wrapped in woolly clothing as they were trying to economise on the central heating, so it didn't really show. She felt dead and empty inside. Something was wrong, but she was not sure what, nor what to do about it.

She tried to analyse how she felt, but her mind was not naturally analytical and anyway, she felt that trying to understand yourself was like trying to see inside your own eye – you just couldn't do it. Only someone else could look in and tell you what was the matter. She just felt as though there was a big hole inside her, a vacuum, and that she just could not feel clean, really clean inside. She had bad dreams – nothing specific that she could remember, but she had a sense that they concerned nasty, dirty jagged things that she could not see and that hurt her. She would wake up sweating, her heart thumping, feeling petrified for no reason at all. The only way to get the fear out of her head was a frantic bout of housework.

Perhaps she needed God in her life. One of the girls at work had joined a new church in the town, so Janice went along with her. But the ecstatic hand waving, eyes closed while communing in some sort of spiritual orgasm, embarrassed her, and the man who played the guitar, again with eyes closed (that must be very important to help you concentrate, because Janice kept hers open and couldn't concentrate at all) came and chatted to Janice afterwards. He stood too close, smirking, had really awful breath and gave her the creeps. She tried the Church of England round the corner, but it was so long since she'd been, she had forgotten it all and kept standing and kneeling in the wrong places. And nobody spoke to her afterwards, which was worse. She even let the Jehovah's Witnesses in once and tried to talk about the vacuum inside her, but the woman didn't seem to listen, and Janice couldn't get her to go. In the end Jenny came home from work and threw her out, saying, 'We're all heathens here.' The woman had been there three hours.

So it was in this frame of mind that Janice approached the winter. The closing in of damp mists, cars nose to tail in the dusky streets puffing out poisons, depressed her and made her anxious about the levels of heavy metals and other toxins in her blood. She hardly dared breathe outside without a scarf across her mouth and she developed a persistent cough. The medieval city walls were floodlit at night and their creamy brightness shone beneath the black, skeletal branches of the bare trees. Steamy café windows where lovers met after work, snug in the warm, bright atmosphere inside drinking fragrant coffee and eating cakes, contrasted with the dark, smoky streets outside, where slimy leaves clogged the streaming gutters and the occasional stinking tramp picked over the rubbish bins outside the cafés, hoping for the droppings of seasonal goodwill. The Christmas lights were up before the end of November and everyone said, as they did every year, that it was much too soon.

One Friday, the second one in December, she was in a bookshop in town. She had just finished a long shift, but she had changed into jeans before leaving, as it was cold and she was walking home. The bookshop window had attracted her; a good read was often a distraction. She went to the novel section as always and started reading the backs of some of the shinier ones. Then two things happened, both of them small. One was that she caught sight of a tall pile of children's books, hardbacked and glossy, stacked up as part of a Christmas promotion. On the top was *Cinderella*. It was the version Janice had had as a child, a traditional one. The pictures were instantly familiar; they took her straight back to sitting up in bed in her nightie, on a winter's evening such as this, reading. She used to love this book; it had been her favourite. Then suddenly she had stopped reading it and never wanted to see it again. She couldn't remember why. She turned to her favourite picture, Cinderella all dressed up ready to go to the ball and the fairy godmother there, floating rather than standing in the dingy kitchen, all light, airy magic next to the big, old-fashioned kitchen range that poor Cinderella had polished, of course. The row of copper pans across the stone chimney breast shone just as brightly as they had when she had read the book as a child. The fairy godmother's dress was just as iridescent, Cinderella just as pure and graceful. She had loved that picture of them in the kitchen. It seemed now to symbolise all that had been missing from her own childhood home. Looking at it now in the calm, impersonal surroundings of the bookshop with its dark red carpet and fluorescent lighting that reduced everything to a uniform coolness, she got a sudden really sickly feeling inside. She could not, she just could not, remember why. The other small thing was that she became gradually aware that someone was watching her.

Kate was transfixed. This was love. Or at least the fiercest, most gut-wrenching infatuation she had ever experienced. For it is only with hindsight that we know for sure if we can call it love. The small young woman reading in the corner, slightly stooping, so unobtrusive that no one else would have even noticed her, had drawn Kate as if they were connected by a cord. The thin neck stuck out of the faded jacket, it was white, fragile, stained with blotches of tawny freckles. Something about the angle of it suggested deep thought. The short hair was reddish and stuck up in tufts as though its owner had ruffled her hand through it just now. There was a piece of something stuck to the sole of one shoe, sticking out at the side. Kate didn't think the bookshop would want it deposited on the carpet. She stood staring at this figure for a few minutes, willing the worn, shabby appearance to yield up something significant about its owner, something to explain the magnetism that was pulling her in.

Feeling eyes upon her, Janice turned. Someone was staring at her. She reddened slightly, so intent was the stare. She wondered if she knew her. She didn't think so, but she smiled vaguely just in case. In nursing, grateful patients whom you don't recognise in their ordinary clothes, transformed again into human beings, accost you in the street from time to time, to thank you for what you did for them. It didn't happen much in geriatrics. The woman smiled. She must know her. She had a very nice smile, warm and friendly. The corners of her mouth turned right up. Janice's own smile widened in return. The woman was quite tall, broad, athletic looking, the set of her head implied a certain strength of will. Her features were determined, strong and attractive, although 'pretty' was a word that would never describe her. She had something more than that. She looked quite weather-beaten, for York in December. Janice liked the look of her, but she was sure she did not know her.

So here we are, thought Kate, at this momentous point, this moment we will remember perhaps always, just smiling. 'Excuse me,' she said at last, 'you have some dog shit on your shoe.'

After the inevitable shrieking and running outside, frantically searching for a tuft of grass to rub it off onto (not all that easy to find in the middle of a crowded street in the dark) Kate suggested going for a coffee. Not one to take the initiative much herself, Janice was never surprised when other people did, in fact she took it for granted as the normal state of affairs.

They chatted easily about all sorts of things. Janice looked out onto the dark street and remembered being on the outside, looking in, how nice and warm and light it had looked in the cafés with their wafting smells of bread and savouries. And now here she was, on the inside. She told Kate her thoughts.

'You've been on the outside for too long,' Kate said.

'I have. I do have that feeling. How do you know? We've only just met.'

'Because I've been there too. But like you just said, I feel as if I'm back on the inside now.'

She wondered if she had gone too far. She wasn't sure if Janice had understood her. Janice wasn't sure if she had either. 'What do you mean?'

She studied Kate's hands on the table as she waited for an answer. They were large, smooth and brown, the nails short and tidy, not chewed like her own, and very clean.

It was like being an early Christian, Kate thought, when they were persecuted, always on the outside and in order to recognise each other they had to draw the shape of a fish in the sand. You drew the shape of a fish cautiously, for to show it to the wrong person could mean betrayal and death. Most people would not know what you were doing, would not even recognise it as a fish. They would think you were just doodling idly with your foot. But someone, every now and again, someone would recognise the fish, would understand. And that person would look you straight in the eyes and with their toe they would dot in the eye of the fish. 'Well, you,' she said carefully. 'Meeting you.'

Janice was looking her straight in the eyes. Kate was thinking, she has wonderful eyes, almond-shaped, blue, the lids are translucent, I can almost see through them, into her mind. She has a very direct gaze. The blotted freckles had a muddy appearance in winter, giving her the look of a grubby, neglected boy. She appeared to be waiting for Kate to say more. But Kate had been down this path before. Say too much too soon and you blow it, she told herself. After Nita, she could not take another rejection too soon. If Janice rejected her, she knew with a bleak certainty that that would be it for her. She would not try again. She would prefer to be on her own for the rest of her life. Nothing would ever match the intensity of this moment. How sudden and inexplicable, she thought. It is as if a spell has been cast on us. The colours of the world have changed.

They stared intently at each other, completely absorbed, waiting. With a rush Janice understood. She was shocked and excited. This was certainly a change, perhaps it was the change she had been waiting for. She was a strong believer in Fate. 'Yes,' she said.

Then a few minutes later, after a long silence, Kate said, 'Your coffee's cold. Let's have some mulled wine.'

As they sipped it and the warmth ran through her blood, Janice looked out of the steamed-up window and said, 'We're in a bubble, just us, in here, in the warm.'

'Yes,' said Kate. 'We are.'

They walked home arm in arm to Kate's flat. It felt strange to Janice, yet she was elated, holding tight this incredible person, in whose personality she could sense no limits. It was drizzling and she lifted her face to the orange clouds with a huge smile. She couldn't say anything. Squeezing Kate's damp arm, she sniffed her, breathing in deeply, breathing her in. 'You smell of apples,' she said.

Kate turned to face her. They were in a wide street with large trees which were almost bare now and dripping. She was thinking, Nita was a humming-bird, beautiful and exotic, never coming to rest. This one is a sparrow. A small, brown, unobtrusive, nesting sparrow. A necessary bird. Vitally necessary to my life. Dare she move in, or was it too soon? She dived in. 'If I were a man I would be kissing you now,' she said.

For a second they paused under the dripping trees. This was the moment when Janice could no longer possibly misunderstand. If she is going to leave, Kate thought, it will be now. This might be it, the end before the beginning. Perhaps I have blown it again. A heavy drop of water fell on Janice's nose. Kate brushed it off as if she were a child. Janice turned her face up towards Kate, put her hand on the side of her cheek. Just before they touched she felt the sweetness of Kate's breath. For a split second it felt strange. She thought, my God, I'm about to kiss a woman, I don't think I can do it. Then curiosity tinged with excitement took over – would it be the same or better, or just different? Roger had had a big fat tongue like a toad, which he had thrust too far into her mouth. Then she thought, how lovely, no bristles. Then she was lost.

It was six weeks since Jenny had flitted past Sanjay and out into the sunny street, but he thought of her often. She had been like a butterfly that day, a flash of glowing colour across his otherwise grey day. Paul had called her 'a tonic' and 'a laugh' and wondered who she was. Sanjay had been deliberately vague. He didn't want Paul getting in there before him, not with his track record with older women.

'I tell you,' he said to Sanjay, 'no inhibitions, loads of experience – they're brilliant. They know just what to do,' he added, with the look of a boy who has seen his first girlie magazine. Sanjay wanted to get in touch with her, but the hospital seemed too public, now that his purpose was more private and clearly defined, and he didn't want to call at her house in case that terrible girl with the bath cap was there. Goodness knows what colour her hair had turned out, she must have had that henna on an hour or more. In the end he wrote to Jenny, a short, formal note asking her out to lunch again, leaving his work number. It felt a bit tacky, but the slight feeling of seediness excited him. It had the same air of almost inviting chaos to take over as Jenny's messy sitting room had and to his well-ordered soul it seemed a daring thrill. Tightening his impeccable tie whenever he thought about her, he waited for her call.

Jenny opened the expensive envelope with the unfamilar writing. It was flowing and ornamental, a feminine style. She was surprised to discover it was from Sanjay. She had not exactly forgotten him, but he had been assigned an insignificant place in her busy life, crammed with planning ideas for work, being endlessly open-minded and non-judgemental about the problems of her patients however mundane or bizarre, violin practice and clean sports kit for Josh, worrying about her cellulite, trying to fit in some thigh-trimming exercises and deciding what to get for tea. Frivolities such as young men who ought to be on the cover of a magazine came sadly low on her list of priorities. Janice had been a bit peaky lately. Nothing she could put her finger on, but she wasn't the bright, benevolent presence Jenny was used to. She'd lost her sparkle, somehow. But Jenny had too many other things to think about to worry about Janice. Every day was a dash, from the moment the alarm went off, to setting it again at night. If Janice wanted to talk, presumably she would.

She actually felt pretty crusty and disinclined to bother with Sanjay. Weeks had gone by; it had all gone a bit cold. Sanjay's letter lay on the table in front of her while a blob of marmalade soaked through it and Josh toyed with his cornflakes. He was having one of his phases when he insisted on Super Space Snax or some other new breakfast gimmick, which Jenny always refused to buy, so in return, for a week or so, he would turn his nose up at anything else. Still, thought Jenny, it wasn't every day she was asked out to lunch by the sexiest animal on hind legs. She might as well go. She could do with a bit of cosseting, even if it was only the verbal kind, and Sanjay would certainly give her that. There was little enough to look forward to on the horizon. Christmas dinner with her mother promised to be the usual joyless occasion. Yes, she decided, she deserved to give herself a treat.

By the time Friday lunchtime came, this treat had taken on rather alarmingly graphic proportions in her head. She pictured herself (with the perfect body of course – her sister's body) making Sanjay lie down on the bed and watch her as she stripped for him, slowly, slowly, peeling every item of clothing off until she was completely naked, except for black stockings and suspenders. then she would smooth herself all over, smooth her hands over her buttocks with her back towards him, showing off, inviting him. Then she would move slowly, sinuously towards him and undress him gently while his hands explored her breasts. His bronze body would be hard and fit, as she could see it was beneath the expensive suits. He would be stretched out on her bed, ready for her like a wild beast, quiet and tamed. She would sit on him and start to move rhythmically, then faster, fully in control. Reality stuck its grubby finger on the stop button of her imagination at this point, as she remembered that her thighs didn't look that good from behind, and even in the dark he could not fail to notice the crimped skin of her stretch marks. Woman, she said to herself firmly, what you need is a bloody good time.

But not with a beautiful boy ten years younger than you are. But then again, why not? People have done worse.

The effect of all this was to make her rather pink and awkward by the time Sanjay called for her. When she had rung to accept his invitation he had suggested that she should wait for him on an obscure street-corner near the hospital and he would pick her up in his car. This did not strike her as shifty or strange. As she climbed into the car she wondered if she had overdone the perfume; it wafted off her and seemed to fill the car. He must have noticed it, she was nearly gagged by the scent herself. He smiled his big smile. She realised she had forgotten how attractive he was. There was a real warmth about him. He suggested somewhere to eat.

'Why don't we go to my house?' she said. 'You can cut my hair if you like, if you've got your scissors, and it's more private – ' Then, thinking that sounded like innuendo she added, 'I mean – I don't mean – that is, if you'd rather – ' Oh no, I'm doing it again.

He patted her hand. 'Your house will be fine,' he said. 'Have you got any corned beef?'

Jenny put the key in the door. The net curtain in Astrid's

window twitched. In the kitchen, as a reflex action, she put the kettle on. He turned the pages of last Sunday's colour supplement, removing an open jar of fish paste from it first.

'Oh, that's from Josh's packed lunch,' she said, whipping it away and sniffing it before she put it in the fridge. 'Did you bring your scissors?' She said this more out of embarrassment than anything else, to provide a distraction, but he laughed and produced them with a flourish.

'And where would you like to sit, madam?'

'You're really going to cut my hair?' she asked, taken aback.

'Of course. You said – '

'Yes, but I didn't think you thought I meant it.'

'What?'

'Nothing. I was joking, that's all. I think I may have misunderstood.' He was looking very put out. 'A haircut would be lovely, thank you very much. Just a trim, mind,' she warned. 'Nothing drastic. I don't want to look as if I've had chewing gum stuck in my hair and had to cut it out.'

'Certainly not,' he said proudly. 'I can cut hair well.'

It felt strange sitting on a kitchen chair in the middle of the sitting room with this velvet-skinned man trimming her hair. He was very deft and quick.

'There,' he said, standing back professionally, eyeing his work. 'Just a bit of a reshape at the back, and I've made it look thicker.'

Jenny went to the mirror. The effect was subtle, but definite. 'Yes, you have. That's very nice, thank you. Now I can get you lunch in return,' she smiled. He smiled back happily. He really did look as if lunch was all he had come for. What a disappointment.

She went into the kitchen and he followed her. Just as she reached for the bread she felt his hands on her waist. Then his lips were nuzzling the back of her neck, just on the spot that sent a shiver down her spine and gave her a funny feeling somewhere around the kidneys. His hands slid up to cup her heavy breasts and he brushed his thumbs across the hardened nipples. She twisted round so that she could kiss him full on the mouth. His hand slid up and found her. His fingers came out wet and slippery straight away. He was kissing her hungrily, with an urgency she had forgotten existed. This was not a hunger that would be satisfied by a tuna fish sandwich. She could sense he was not experienced at this kind of thing. But then, neither was she. Fumblingly he produced a crumpled, well-travelled condom, whose packet looked close to its sell-by date. Jenny thrust any suggestion of tackiness out of her mind and told herself it had been specially reserved for her. With her back against the fridge she put him inside her and he gasped. The kitchen was narrow, so she put one foot up behind him on the sink for a bit of extra leverage. He was shoving so hungrily that it was over quickly. It was far clumsier and more full of feeling than her fantasy. This was not about control. This was an act of giving.

They laughed, exhilarated, as they tidied themselves. He carried on kissing her as he tucked himself in, saying, 'You are so *warm*. So generous. You have lovely big bosoms.'

He gave them a gentle mashing. She laughed again.

'And you are a hungry boy,' she teased. Then more thoughtfully, 'I've never done it up against a fridge before.'

Her frankness amazed and delighted him. He had never heard a woman talking openly about sex. It excited him. Boldly, wanting praise, he asked, 'And did you like it?'

She answered him with a kiss. 'You know I did.'

He felt fantastic, like a new man. No one had ever wanted him like this, a woman had never taken him in her hand and put him inside her, showing that she really wanted him. He wanted to leap and shout. Instead, he squeezed her very tightly so that she had to say, 'Hey, I can't breathe.' He sank his teeth ferociously into the doorstep sandwich she put in front of him. They ate standing where they were. Afterwards, she produced some fresh apricots from a brown paper bag (the appearance of everything pleased him) took the stone from one and put the fruit straight into his mouth. The intimacy of this gesture touched him. Then she ate a banana in a silly way as a joke, slowly playing with her tongue on it, teasing him, exciting him so that he wanted to do it again. He had never known sex as a jokey thing, except in the crude jokes of his friends. He hadn't realised women enjoyed it and claimed it as their experience too. She had blossomed in the last hour, he could see it. He cuddled her so that she could feel him ready again. But she brushed him off kindly, saying there would be other times. He treasured this like a rare bird in his hand. They would be able to do this again, she had said so. She was like an actress playing just for him. Delighting him with foolishness like a puppet in a bright, mysterious show, in a language he had only just discovered and couldn't yet fully understand. But it was she, not he, who held the strings and played them in and out.

It was that night that Janice went to the bookshop and did not come home. She rang Jenny about nine o'clock. She and Kate had just finished something from the takeaway and were halfway through a bottle of wine. Jenny sounded very chirpy, Janice noticed.

'Where are you?' Jenny asked.

'I'm – with a friend,' Janice said cautiously.

Jenny picked up her tone. 'Anybody nice? Do I know him?'

Janice glanced across at Kate, still not quite believing that this was herself, Janice, on this adventure. 'Yes to the first,' she said, 'No to the second.'

'Well, have fun.'

Janice assured her, smiling across at Kate, that she would. 'I'm on a journey, Jen,' she told her, becoming profound because she was slightly drunk. 'I don't know where I'm going.'

'Are you phoning from a train? The line's very clear.'

'A journey of self-discovery.'

Jenny laughed. 'Oh, *that* sort,' she said. 'Well, make sure you only discover what you want to find out. And make sure you discover where the spare key is; you left yours here. If you're coming back, that is. Take care. Bye.'

'Jenny who?' Kate asked when Janice came off the phone.

'Jenny Burdge.'

'Not Jenny who works as an OT?'

'Yes, that Jenny.'

'Well,' said Kate. 'She's often suggested going out, doing something. I've just never bothered, I always seem to have too much to do as it is. To think, if I had, I might have met you ages ago. Think of all that wasted time.' And all that wasted emotion, with Nita.

Janice snuggled up to her on the sofa. 'I'm glad I've met you my way,' she said, 'not through Jenny. This way it's just us.'

Kate could not believe how quickly things had burst into bloom. She wondered if Janice would be very possessive. She suspected so, and wondered if she would mind that. Probably not, she thought, and realised she must be settling down.

Sanjay did the unthinkable that afternoon after his lunch with Jenny: he made a mistake in his calculations. He had to go right back to the beginning of a set of accounts and start again. The filing cabinet in his head had never failed him; everything was kept neatly in compartments: a drawer for home with numerous individual files in it, several with 'Nita' written on them, which were the most disorganised; a drawer for work, extremely well organised, and one drawer marked 'Social' which contained everything else, including his extensive and chattering family. They assumed right of access to all the other files and commented freely and critically on every aspect of Sanjay's life they could get their hands on. But he didn't know where to file Jenny in his head. She just didn't fit into any category he had ever devised. Perhaps he should start a file labelled 'Sin', except that it didn't feel like sin. It felt like waking up. It felt like living. He wandered across to the coffee machine thinking it was as if he had been short-sighted all his life and suddenly, someone had placed a pair of spectacles on his nose. He looked around at the world in wonder. Things that had been vague and muzzy before – like his notions of love, his understanding of sexuality – were suddenly clear and three-dimensional. Things he hadn't even imagined were there, were standing out in glorious colour. Even Moira, the stout, grey-haired secretary, took on a new aura in the light of his new-found knowledge. He pictured her being taken from behind at the kitchen sink by George, her husband, who wore one of those cardigans with imitation leather buttons. It had never occurred to him that Moira had a sex life. That she, and everyone, had access to this amazing life force, this jet of energy that he had just discovered. He beamed at Moira benevolently. She could have been quite pretty in her youth. Perhaps George had found her 'good in the sack', as Paul would say. She stopped keying-in on her computer for a moment and looked at him strangely. 'Are you feeling all right, Sanjay?' she asked with concern.

She had small teeth, very white, one top front one crossing slightly over the other. He'd never noticed them before. That could be very sexy, he was thinking, to the right man. 'Me? Oh yes, perfectly fine. Tea, Moira?'

Anyway, even if he could think of a way to categorise Jenny in his head, Jenny would refuse to stay in any drawer he put her in. There was an abundance about her, a generosity, as he had said to her. She spilled over into her surroundings, into him. She filled up his whole being. He, Sanjay, was neat and tidy in his own skin, but who could tell where Jenny began and ended? Even the way she dressed, which was terrible really, he thought, expressed this freedom. The messy chaos in her house breathed life into him, its sense of being lived in, rather than a show-piece of achievement like his own. There was an earthy directness about her, she was straightforward and open in her pleasures and her thoughts. In her presence he felt that things were permitted that up to now he had not even dreamed of. All of a sudden his marriage appeared to him like a well-oiled machine – no friction, but no warmth or spirit either. No life. Nita would be at the hostel tonight doing her bit for society. He no longer needed to ask himself, what about her bit for me? He would see Jenny again, he would phone her, call on her when her boy had gone to bed. Nita would be gone all night – she camped there, she said. He couldn't see why she wanted to; it had always seemed a dreary idea to him. He could lie down with Jenny, make love to her again, do the things that kept cramming into his imagination. They would do it in different ways, she would show him, teach him, he would please her more than any man. She had wanted him, she had really wanted him. She had taken him eagerly and put him inside her. This individual gesture filled him with joy. But what about that other girl, Freckles? He'd forgotten about her. Jenny would be able to get rid of her somehow. He took it for granted that Jenny felt the same as him. He was beautiful and successful, who could not? He would phone her as soon as he got home.

As he turned the dark, quiet car into the driveway, his heart plummeted. The red car was there, lined up neatly against the beech hedge, whose leaves were all brown and dead, shrivelled in the cold. He felt shrivelled too. He shut the car door with a depressing clunk and went into the kitchen. Everything was bleached by the bleak strip–light and his disappointment. Nita had her back to him. She must be agitated, he thought, because she was picking all the nuts and pieces of dried pineapple out of the muesli. He did not kiss her. Irrationally, he was angry and irritated with *her*, not himself.

'No helping the needy tonight, then?'

She turned and smiled tightly. 'No, not tonight. Actually, not ever. They've told me they don't want me any more,' she said and burst into tears. He hugged her.

'Why? No women being beaten any more?'

She smiled through her tears, more bravely. 'If only. No, they've got enough volunteers now. They don't need me.' She cried afresh.

'Hey,' he said, patting her gently. 'It's not that bad. Who wants to spend Friday nights in some pokey old women's refuge, when you've got a nice home you could be in instead?'

She pulled away from him angrily. 'I do!' she screamed and ran upstairs. He didn't know what he had said.

Janice didn't go home all weekend. She loved wandering around the flat, high up under the eaves of the large Georgian house, almost touching the horse chestnut trees outside – tall and bare now, like the charred, delicate bones of some extinct creature stretching its limbs to the sky. On Saturday she borrowed Kate's clothes, which hung off her. She tied a huge floppy jumper with a belt and felt about sixteen. She wandered around the sunny flat, touching things and admiring them, asking Kate about them. Each of Kate's small treasures, picked up here and there, had a story behind it, for she had travelled quite extensively. Janice was interested in everything.

There had been a touch of awkwardness on the Friday night. They had both had quite a lot to drink. Then, at bedtime, they had each been overcome by a (for Kate, unusual) fit of modesty. She had stripped off in a matter-of-fact way down to her T-shirt and pants. Janice had perched on the edge of the bed, fully clothed.

'I'm not – you know,' she had tried to say to Kate.

'Not what? A lesbian, you mean? You can say it, there are worse words.'

'It's not the word, that doesn't matter – although it does sound strange, I can't associate it with me. It's just – '

Kate waited as she searched for expression. Her eyes were bright and intense with what she was trying to say. She wasn't looking at Kate, but sat staring at a Matisse print on the wall. 'I feel just the same as I always have done. I mean, I'm not suddenly someone different – look, I know this all sounds pathetic – '

Kate stroked her cheek. 'It's OK,' she said. 'If it matters to you to say it, I want to hear it. Right?' Janice nodded.

'I mean – I just feel, it's just you, not the fact that you're a woman. I want to be – I feel it's very important to be – close to you. You make me want that, and I do want that. It's just all so – sudden and – extraordinary. I can't believe this is me – yet it *is* me, and I feel very happy about it, really – just a bit shocked, too. It's the person that counts, not what sex they are. Although the sex *is* the person – ' Kate nodded. 'It's no good, I can't think of the words. Words hold me up, I always use the same ones, I can't make it come out the way I think it in my head. I get frustrated.' Kate just carried on stroking her neck and tracing the outline of her ear while Janice struggled with unaccustomed self-expression. This was important, she had to get it out. She wanted Kate to know her, to see into her mind. In the end she said, 'I just feel as if I've come home, that's all. And I'm clean now.'

'You are,' murmured Kate, kissing her neck with dry, small nips. 'Squeaky clean. And we'll just cuddle up. OK?' Janice nodded. We can take it slowly, thought Kate, and get it right. After all, we have plenty of time. All the time in the world.

On Sunday morning they read the papers. Then they went for a walk in the Minster grounds, chasing each other in the leaves, holding hands when no one was around. It was a golden day. The pale yellow stone of the Minster, recently cleaned, shone mellow in the sunshine. They had lunch in a pub and strolled by the canal in the afternoon, watching the squirrels dart down to collect acorns, then sprinting back up into the safety of the branches. Everything was new, invested with the oblique amber sunlight of a fine December, and the magic of this amazing force that had drawn them together. They talked all the time and when they didn't talk, they smiled. For Kate it was delightful simply to have Janice there with her. All the things she enjoyed doing on her own were now doubled in enjoyment because there was someone with whom to share them. It had all the glowing misty magic of a first relationship, which for Janice, Kate reflected, in a sense it was.

When they got back they had crumpets for tea, and Janice had a bath. She was on earlies in the morning and would have to go home. Kate came in and sat on the lid of the lavatory to watch her. They chatted, continuing the conversation that had been ebbing and flowing all weekend between them, the conversation without an end that is the sign of an enduring relationship. As Janice's thoughts meandered on aloud, deepening the knowledge between them – for to Janice intimacy meant filling in the other person on every bit of your life that they have missed, however trivial or significant, right up to the moment when you met – Kate began to wash her back. The soapy hands felt so wonderful to Janice as they stroked up and down her spine and around her neck, that she stopped talking. They slid round and washed her breasts, slipping under them. Kate laid her back gently and poured water over Janice with her cupped hand to rinse her. The bath water started to slosh back and forth until it leapt right over the back of the bath and soaked the floor. They laughed and Kate threw a towel onto it. They laughed a lot, Janice noticed. Everything was fun.

'Come on.' Kate pulled her out, put a towel round her and led her back to the bedroom. Janice felt warm, fragrant, relaxed and squeaky clean. She *was* clean now, Kate had said so. Kate had made her so. Her soft nakedness rubbed against Kate's jeans and hairy jumper. Her trepidation had washed away with the bath water. She let the towel drop and they fell backwards, laughing, onto the bed.

Neither of them heard the key in the door. They were too engrossed to notice the footsteps on the wooden floor, approaching the bedroom. The door was flung back and crashed against the foot of the bed. They both heard the shriek of outrage and stared up together, horrified, at Nita.

In the screaming, shouting and general disarray that followed, Janice took no part. Like the squirrels they had seen this afternoon (was that really just today? She couldn't believe it) she darted around, grabbing her few things, then made for the door. She couldn't find the top she had come in so she flung on the jumper and belt she had been wearing earlier. Superstitiously, she felt that if she left with something of Kate's on she might see her again. The clothes obscurely made her feel safer. She raced for the door as they emerged from the bedroom – the bedroom where she and Kate had just been. Kate was restraining the girl, pinning her arms to her sides, steering her out towards the door. Her heart thumping as fast as a rabbit's, Janice got there first and dashed out. Kate was calling her name, saying, 'Wait, wait,' but she ran, almost falling headlong down the stairs, and was regurgitated like an owl pellet onto the dusky street.

She ran to the end of the block, then round the corner, then further. On and on, past the station, past small streets of terraces, some with the curtains open so that she caught glimpses of plastic flowers on a windowsill, a child playing the piano, a man watching the purple flicker of a television, someone holding a baby on their shoulder. She stopped at last, far enough away to be sure she couldn't be followed. Panting, she leaned against a wall. She hadn't realised she was this fit. The air was clear and frosty; it scraped at her lungs. Just ahead were the black, spiky railings of the Minster. Were they there to keep the unbelievers out, or the faithful in? Janice approached them slowly, still breathing hard. The Minster soared, glorious, pale and ghostly now in the floodlights, cold and beautiful, a petrified symbol of man's divine inspiration and his earthly aspirations. The tons of stone looked weightless as it streamed upwards into the dark orange sky. Evensong was on; she could hear faint, high singing and the deeper sounds of the organ. The gate in the railings was open. It squeaked when she pushed it. The side door to the Minster was heavier; it didn't seem to want to let her in, its studs were black and cold. Inside was pitch black, much blacker than the night outside. Then she realised she was underneath one of those horrible, heavy tapestry curtains that go up for miles and smell of something very old – the stuff of nightmares. Shrinking at the touch of it, she pushed it aside and entered the church.

The nave was empty. The ornamented ceiling, famed in books on church architecture, was barely visible, far and high above her. As she got to the centre, she could see the service going on far away in a blob of light further up the church, a glowing, indistinct activity, remote and distant, because in the mêlée she had forgotten to put her lenses in. The small figure of the priest in heavy robes moved slowly in some ancient pageant in a bubble of light, while the rest of the church lay in darkness. She seemed to be the only observer of this ancient ritual. Here, in the scented darkness of dead flowers and dusty robes, the city and traffic outside did not exist. Here, the events of two thousands years ago in a far-off, dusty country, were more real than the events of this afternoon. She walked slowly to about halfway up the nave, wondered whether she should genuflect, decided eventually on a sort of nervous, jerky nod of the head, and sat down. The organ was pouring music like dark treacle out into the nave. Then the singing started, the aching sweetneess of it soaring up into the dim rafters. The fluted pillars rose up on either side of her like the bones of the dead. With tears pouring hot down her cold face, she knelt on one of the tapestry kneelers, and without knowing who she was speaking to, or what to say, she began to pray.

CHAPTER 5

Dear Jenny
Hope all is fine with you and continuing
much as usual. Dark here all the time
now. Freezing cold. Ice formations
outstanding. Merry Xmas
Henry xxx

Jenny had this on the mantlepiece and was looking at the picture. Concorde – the pattern was dawning on her at last. He must have bought all these at the airport before he set off. Typical of Henry – forward planning down to the finest detail. She was ironing. Oh Henry, you and your ice formations, your life is so simple. I do miss you. What am I doing? How could you ever understand my weakness, my neediness, the chaos of my life? I wish I could be detached like you, never touching the sides. I wish I was there.

There was a knock on the door about nine o'clock. Jenny put the iron up on end and went to look through the spyhole. The head of Janice, grossly enlarged by the fish-eye lens, looked back.

'Where have you been?' asked Jenny, shocked at her friend's appearance. The weekend had clearly not been the voyage of pleasant discovery Janice had hoped. Jenny could have told her that on Friday night, she thought, but what would have been the point? Sadly, some learning only comes first hand.

'Are you all right?'

She obviously wasn't. Her teeth were chattering, she looked frozen, she had on some terrible garment that looked as though it had begun life as a potato sack. Her eyelids had the look of an albino rabbit's and she was breathing in the gusty sobs of someone who has been crying for hours. Jenny pulled her into the warm, dark hallway and hugged her. 'Whatever's the matter?' Something horrible dawned on her. 'You haven't been attacked, have you?'

Janice shook her head. 'I've been walking. In the Minster grounds and down by the river.'

'At night? You must be crazy! Why the hell did you do that? What's been happening, Janice?' Janice's thin shoulders were still shaking.

'Oh, nothing. Well, not nothing, but – ' She bit her lip and her eyes fixed on the middle distance, which was somewhere around the kitchen door. She couldn't tell Jenny. She just couldn't. In the cold light of reality and Jenny's wry cynicism, her experience would shrivel into something small, grubby and pathetic. A shrunken acorn not destined to grow. Her bubble, that had made all the world iridescent from inside it, had floated for forty-eight hours before it had burst, leaving her dumped, shivering on the wet Minster grass. Forty-eight hours was not long to last you the rest of your life. But there was one bit she could tell her. She needed to tell someone and she couldn't tell the one she most needed to tell, so she would tell Jenny instead. Jenny was used to being a surrogate for people's loved ones. That was part of what she did, part of how she helped them. Well, now she could help her friend.

'I went to evensong,' Janice began 'at the Minster.'

'That's nice. But I didn't know you were religious,' Jenny interrupted.

'I'm not – well, not like that, you know, churchy, but I – shut up, I'm trying to tell you something.'

This spurt of urgent irritation silenced Jenny. She had never heard Janice speak like that before, she was always so quiet and good-tempered. Something had changed.

'Well, no, it was before that, there was this book in the bookshop on Friday – *Cinderella* – well, I remembered.' She looked triumphantly at Jenny.

'Remembered what?' I must be losing my grip, thought Jenny, I think I missed something there.

'What it was. I remembered what it was about the book, why I stopped reading it.'

'Did you? Is that good?' Jenny was mystified. 'Look, come in, have a drink, and let's start again.'

Janice wished suddenly that someone else was saying those words to her, and started to cry. Jenny shepherded her into the sitting room and dispatched Josh off upstairs to fetch a hot water bottle for Janice and afterwards to put himself to bed.

'I'll be up in a few minutes,' Jenny told him. 'Give me a shout when you're ready.'

He huffed a bit, and stamped on the stairs, but he did as she had asked. When he came back with the bottle he peered at Janice. 'You look a bit rough, where have you been? Not with that horrible Roger.'

'Don't be so rude, Josh. Get up to bed.'

'Oh, did you think he was horrible?' asked Janice with interest. 'Why was that?'

Josh shrugged. He wasn't going to say about the grunting. 'He wasn't the sort of person you could – make into a friend.'

'You're right,' agreed Janice. 'I'd never thought of him like that before, but you're quite right. I don't think he had many friends. Only people he worked with.'

'You've got to be – *interested* in things to be a friend.'

'Come on, Josh, you're stalling,' said Jenny. 'Bedtime, it's after nine.'

'He's right, though, Jen. You don't miss much, do you, Josh?'

Josh threw his mother a look of satisfaction. 'No,' he said. 'I don't. So you two people, watch it.'

'That's enough,' said Jenny firmly. 'You're being cheeky. Bed. See you upstairs in a minute.'

He shut the door behind him emphatically. When they were sitting comfortably, Janice began.

'When I was eight, my Auntie Cath got married. She was my favourite auntie, always smiling and that, she always brought us sweets when she came to stay. My Dad's sister, she was. Well, I say my Dad, but – anyway, I'll get to that. I was a bridesmaid and I had this gorgeous dress. It was pale yellow taffeta, lemon, my Mum said, but it was a much softer colour than lemon. More of a primrose. Anyway, I felt like a primrose in it, it was lovely. I pretended I was Cinderella. My Mum called it my Cinderella dress. I had this book of Cinderella – '

'The same one you saw in the bookshop?' asked Jenny, hoping that by prompting her they could get to the point. She still had a pile of ironing. 'Look can I iron while you talk?'

'Of course,' said Janice. 'Well, the wedding was beautiful, the first I'd ever been to. Me and my cousins played on some bikes they had in the hotel, riding round and round in the entrance hall – it was big enough for that – anyway, I was Cinderella, this bike was my horse, I pretended I was a real princess, you know, like you do. I felt just like in the picture. When we got home I couldn't wait, I went straight upstairs to read my book in my Cinderella dress.'

'That's nice,' said Jenny absently.

'No, I haven't got there yet. Me Dad was really drunk.' She was slipping into the Lancashire accent she had had as a child, but which had faded over the years. Her voice had gone flatter, like a child's, halting but matter-of-fact.

'Anyway, they started rowing, they did that quite a bit, mostly when they thought I were asleep. Well, this was a bad one. And there's me, sitting on me bed reading *Cinderella*, in me Cinderella dress. I really thought I was it. I got to the picture where she's just about to go off to the ball, you know, all dressed up, then me Dad bursts into the room. He smells funny and he's breathing really loudly. But I'm not scared; he's me Dad. But he shoves me back on the bed, pushes me like, he doesn't hit me, he never did, and he's saying something about me not being his, me being 'no blood of his', how he can't love me because I'm not his. I don't know what he's talking about, I can hear me Mum screaming up the stairs, she comes in after him, she says to him, 'Don't you lay a finger on 'er, she's mine,' and I realise they mean me. And me Dad calls her a bleeding whore and a lot of other stuff I've not heard before, says she's conned him into loving me, that I'm not his child. Says he washes his hands of me, those were his words, because they seemed funny to me, I'd never heard anyone say that before, about washing your hands. Says he wants nothing more to do with me. She grabs me and hugs me to her, then he punches her while she's holding me, in me own room. I'm feeling sick as a pig at this stage, what with all that rich food and staying up late and that, then this. Punches her right in the face. He gives her a bleeding nose. I don't realise first off, then I look down, and me dress, me beautiful primrose dress, and the picture of the fairy godmother and Cinderella, they're all bright red. Soaking. Even the white sheet on the bed has got spots on it – big, red spots. I remember thinking, how could so much blood come from one nose? I never knew there was that much in there. Everything's soaked. Drenched with blood. Me Mum's blood.'

She looked towards Jenny with glazed eyes. Jenny was frozen at the ironing board. The only sound was the hum of the fridge and the subdued murmur of Astrid's television through the wall.

'And that was the last I saw of me Dad. So you see why it was important that I remembered.'

Jenny looked at her friend for a long time.

'Are you coming?' shouted Josh from the top of the stiars.

'I'll be there in a minute.' Jenny was still looking at Janice. 'I think you've been washing the blood off ever since.'

Janice stood small and still in the middle of the room. 'I think I have.'

After saying goodnight to Josh, Jenny went to the fridge, her first instinct whenever solace was needed.

'Get that down you,' she said, handing Janice a plate and a glass of red wine. 'There's nothing like food and drink to nourish a starved soul.' She took a deep gulp from her own glass. 'So when did you remember? In the Minster?'

Janice nodded, her mouth full. 'It sounds corny, but it was really weird. Something – ' or someone, she thought – 'unlocked it. And it's all right now. It's gone. I'm clean.' Kate had cleansed her, she had bathed her, baptised her, washed her clean, and she had told her she was 'squeaky clean'. She loved that phrase.

'And what about your father?'

'My real one? He was some plumber my mother had a fling with while my Dad was away. He was a lorry driver. He really loved her. He was right, though, she was a whore.'

'Or just lonely and weak, maybe?' Jenny suggested.

Janice shook her head. Perhaps she still had to protect herself by having someone to blame. 'My Dad – you know, the one I thought was my Dad, well, he was. He was the one that looked after me, he loved me. He did love me, I know it. Least, he did till she told him.' Her eyes filled again. 'He should have been me Dad. She robbed me of him. She had *no right* to do that. Why did she have to tell him? Why?'

'Guilt, perhaps? Maybe she felt too terrible about it? Couldn't bear it on her own?'

'Well, she got herself into it, she should have lived with it. It was her guilt, not his or mine. She should have carried it inside herself instead of smashing us all up.'

Jenny could see that her friend had gone straight back fifteen years in her reactions, back to the point where she had cut them off. Time plays strange tricks on the mind, leaping back and forth. In the deeper parts of the ocean there is no current, no night and day, and so it is in the dark passages of the mind.

'He never even knew, the plumber. Never even knew he'd done it. I used to see him around, here and there, chatting up the housewives. She was one of loads.' She gave a dry laugh. 'So was I, probably.'

'Have you ever tried to find him – your Dad?'

Janice shrugged. 'What for? He didn't want me, did he? I don't even know where he is. Could be dead for all I know. He wouldn't want to see me.'

'He might,' said Jenny gently. But she left it at that.

With the cold weather, Jenny's mother got bronchitis. She had it every year, regular as clockwork. Jenny sometimes thought she caught it deliberately, just because of all the fuss and attention it demanded. Jenny collected her medicine from the chemist's.

'Avoid alcohol,' she read aloud from the label on the bottle. 'Hear that, you old trout? No more whisky for your chest, or tots of rum to get you off to sleep at all hours of the day. No drinks except tea, squash, and lemon and honey.'

Her mother was grumbling between deep, hacking fits of coughing. Jenny felt guilty at her own callousness, for it did sound pretty bad. The usual odours of the house were masked by the overpowering smell of vapour rub.

'I'll pop in at teatime,' she said. 'I'll get meals on wheels to bring you lunches.'

'Meals on wheels? I'm not a geriatric yet, you know.'

'You're poorly, though, and you don't look after yourself. I'll go to the supermarket for you tomorrow, stock you up with fruit and things.'

'Fruit's no good – goes to me bowels. You're a bully, you are, you know that? A proper bossy little madam.'

'Yes Mother,' said Jenny as she tucked her into bed, 'I love you too, you old bag. See you tomorrow. Now be sensible and look after yourself.'

As soon as she heard the front door shut, Jenny's mother climbed out of bed like a mischievous child, crept down the stairs, stopping halfway to have a coughing fit, and went into the kitchen. She pulled a chair across to the tall cupboard, clambered precariously up onto it and grinned with wicked satisfaction as her hand closed around the cold, smooth neck of an unopened bottle. 'I'll give her meals on bloody wheels,' she said.

Kate tried to phone Janice several times, always during the day, when Jenny would be at the hospital, but there was never any reply. Once, about four o'clock, a boy answered. It must have been Josh, but Kate left no message and didn't give her name. Nita had been round, every day she had come home from work to find her sitting on the doorstep, it was terrible. Thank God she had got the spare key from her that Sunday. She had forgotten even that she had lent it to her. Kate wouldn't let her in the flat, it was her space now, not to be shared. To let anyone in might destroy the aura of Janice that Kate told herself was still there. She had only been there two days, but Kate felt a cold space in the bed and fancied she could still feel her in the bathroom. She hadn't had the heart to have a bath since Janice had occupied it and always used the shower instead. There were a few leaves Janice had picked up in the Minster grounds because of their colours, yellow and red. Kate had called her a kleptomaniac, and Janice had said innocently, 'What's a clectomaniac? Someone who collects things?' They were still on the windowsill where she had left them, but they had brown spots on them now and were beginning to curl up at the edges.

Eventually, she agreed to meet Nita, just to talk. She did not see what there was to talk about. As far as she could see, Nita had strung her along, flattered by her attention, then dropped her as soon as the inevitable became too obvious and Kate had wanted something deeper. But Nita insisted that they needed a chance to talk. Kate agreed reluctantly to her request, but she made it clear it was just to tidy up the ends. She agreed to meet her in town, then spent days worrying in case Janice saw them out together.

They met in the stagnant middle of a grey afternoon three days before Christmas. They had each come out of work on the pretext of a dental appointment. Kate had suggested somewhere out towards the ring road, slightly out of town, a sleazy café full of sad people with bored eyes and dominated by the smell of chip fat. It was in a row of dingy shops, all of them run down, many of them closed, with just a launderette, a betting shop, and a late shop with some dreary vegetables outside. A tawdry Christmas tree hung with a few red light bulbs made a token gesture towards Christmas. Crisp packets and dead leaves scuffled around on the dusty pavement. It had no previous association for either of them and it befitted an ending. It was also well away from anywhere Janice might frequent.

The stout woman behind the counter looked askance at them over a tray of aged doughnuts. Nita looked out of place with her glossy, elfin looks, but her clothes were dull and ill-fitting enough. All the others in the café were regulars and looked up when the two women came in. For a moment the low hubbub of talking stopped, then continued. These people were indifferent to most things, they were not going to be roused to interest by two women having a cup of tea. The tea was as grey as the afternoon and the faces of the people. They sat in the corner by the window, next to a remarkably grubby net curtain. Nita tried not to brush against it. She was beginning to think she had made a mistake, insisting on this meeting. Perhaps she should have left it alone, while the good memories still dominated. The ceiling was stained brown by years of nicotine. She could see Kate was itching with irritation already.

She didn't make eye contact, but kept glancing out of the window as if she was expecting someone to go past. Nita didn't know what to say. 'It's nice to see you,' she tried.

'Is it?'

'I had to come and see you. I couldn't just let it go like that.'

'Why not? You hadn't been in touch for weeks. And last time we spoke, I made an idiot of myself and you put the phone down on me. That seemed clear enough to me. Did I get the message correctly?'

Nita started to cry, and a man looked round. Kate's irritation spurted out in an acid jet. 'Shut up, for God's sake,' she whispered savagely. 'We're in public.'

'I don't know any of these people,' said Nita out loud, abandoning herself to crying. 'What do I care what they think?'

'Well I care. You're making an exhibition of yourself. Come on, we're leaving.'

She grabbed Nita roughly by the sleeve, paid the woman, and they went outside. 'Walk,' she ordered. Then more kindly, she added, 'It's more private out here.'

They walked round a bleak housing estate. The wind chased grey clouds and bit into them, tearing them into tattered shreds across the darkening sky. They walked arm in arm for warmth.

'Who is she?' Nita asked. 'The one you were with?'

'She's no one you know. And mind your own business. You're not interested in that kind of thing, remember?'

'If you had really cared about me, you'd have given me time to think. Not sprung it on me like that.'

'I'm sorry. I was very drunk. But I have waited longer,' Kate said furiously. 'I've been waiting for three years.' She sighed with exasperation. 'Look. I've been straight with you all along. You must have seen the way things were going, you knew I cared for you. You knew I was attracted to you, for God's sake – I made it plain enough. And you liked it – you *enjoyed* it – what was I meant to think? I thought maybe you were – changing your mind. You knew from the start, I wanted a home, a companion, a best friend, a lover, for *every day*. Someone to be there when you come home from work. Someone to share things with. To have a laugh with, to get angry at sometimes, and make it up. To go out with, to stay in with, someone to *talk* to every day. Like you've got. I don't just want to be part of some heterosexual fantasy, something to dip into every now and again, just to see what it's like, then put away in a box marked "My Lesbian Experience".' She looked at Nita for the first time. 'That's what everyone wants, isn't it? Is that so bad? Can you understand?'

Through her pain, she could understand. 'I just wanted it to be me,' she whispered.

'Then why did you put the phone down on me – just when – God, your timing was incredibly cruel, do you know that? Just when I'd finally said I loved you? Have you any idea how long ago I loved you, and I never said anything in case you ran away?'

Nita shook her head, the tears streaming down her face. 'Is it – because of this other girl – is it too late?'

Kate looked at her. Nita saw a new hardness in her features. Her eyes were dry and defensive. Nita sensed that Kate was experiencing something in her life that she herself had yet to discover.

'Yes,' Kate said quietly. 'It is too late. Not because of anyone else, but because of us. Be honest, when it actually came to it, and you might have had to commit yourself – or, God forbid, finally gone to bed with me – you were shocked. I could hear it, even on the phone. You were shocked and disgusted. If you'd really wanted what I wanted, you'd have known it there and then. You wouldn't have been taken by surprise. You'd have known it long ago.'

'But I do want it now – I made a mistake – I want to be with you.'

Kate hugged her and put her face to the top of her hair. 'Not quite enough to give up everything else, though,' she said quietly. 'Because that's how it would have been. Lots of people you care about would never have spoken to you again. You wouldn't be the pride of your family any more, you'd be their disgrace. Their daughter who ran off with another woman. Stuck on the outside of everything you know now. I don't think you could take it. Some people' – she thought painfully of Janice – 'have less to give up than you do. You have a lot of good things in your life, Nita.'

Nita was quiet. 'You underestimate me.'

Kate smiled. 'You may be right. If so, and if your feelings about yourself are lasting ones, not just because you're unhappy now, then I really hope you find what you're looking for, Nita. And when you do, next time go for it. There is the right life for you out there. You *can* find it. For all you know, you may yet find it with Sanjay. But opportunities are not there for ever. You've got to grab them when they come.'

Privately, Kate thought, I wonder how much her change of heart is because she found out about Janice. Perhaps this is just one more attempt to flatter herself, to reassure herself that she really could have had me. And she could have done. But not any more. It would have been a mistake.

Nita could hardly speak for crying. As they walked back the way they had come, she said, 'There's one more thing.'

'Yes? What's that?'

Nita stood still. Spots of rain were just beginning to mottle the pavement a darker grey. Her lips were purplish with cold, but she didn't feel it. She turned to Kate. 'Promise to answer me truthfully.' Kate promised. After a long, cold minute Nita said, 'Did you love me?'

What sort of question's that, thought Kate, there's only one answer I can give. 'Yes,' she said, 'I did.' And to her surprise she found that it was at least partly true.

Sanjay got quite used to his double life. He went to see Jenny three or four times in December, and every time he was due to go he woke up that morning with the same feeling of excitement and pleasure he used to get as a child when he had a new pair of shoes. For a second after he woke up, he just felt full of anticipation, the day held a promise of something wonderful, he couldn't recall what it was. Then he would remember the shoes, shiny, untouched, neatly lined up beneath his chest of drawers, smelling of that special smell of new leather and shoe shop, waiting just for him. Now it took more than new shoes to give him that pleasurable feeling, but the feeling was just the same. When he recalled the source of it a few moments after waking, while he was still in the hazy dreaminess of sleep, he would surface slowly and lie gazing at the ceiling, hands behind his head, remembering what he and Jenny had done the last time and anticipating what they would do today. Every time was different, he reflected, oblivious of the sleeping form beside him. He and Nita did not talk in the mornings. He always woke before her, about two minutes before the alarm went off. That way he could switch it off, she would sleep on, and he was free to be alone with his thoughts. Nita hated mornings, they were her worst time, whereas he rather liked them. He felt fresh and full of energy first thing, especially on mornings when he was going to see Jenny. He started work before his wife, so she was usually still in bed or in the shower when he left the house. He knew, of course, rationally, that he was betraying his wife and that if he ever had reason to suspect she was doing the same to him, he knew he would be absolutely devastated. But he felt no clash between Nita and Jenny in his heart. They were so different, they inhabited different universes, he thought; they didn't even touch. They even occupied different parts of him. They were safe, completely separate. And what's more, he was safe.

He usually went for lunch and they made love, often combined with eating. She seemed to be particularly keen on mixing sex with food. Once they had made love at the bottom of the stairs, another time she had licked yoghurt off him. He hadn't liked that much, it had felt cold and made a mess and he'd had to have a shower afterwards to get the stickiness off. He never declined anything she suggested. He was like a special guest at a top restaurant, going back again and again to try everything that was on the menu. He was developing a well-educated palate. Gradually, though, it wasn't a question of enjoyment; he was hooked. It became torture to him when she was busy and would not see him (for she rationed the lunches). The affair filled his mind; Jenny became a compulsion.

Nita started to notice he wasn't listening when she talked. She had been pretty down in the dumps lately, since she had stopped going to the refuge centre, but he hadn't felt the need or obligation to ask her why, or make any effort to cheer her up as he would have done before. He made mistakes at work. He wanted to ring Jenny up at ridiculous hours and occasionally he did so, then he would panic and put the phone down if it wasn't she who answered. Once he had even stepped out to cross the road without looking, right into the path of a double-decker bus. Paul, who was with him, had hauled him back by the collar just in time. 'Jesus, Jay, you fed up with living or what?' The clear vision she had given him at the start had turned into an addict's haze. His judgement was clouded by his growing obsession. He arranged his life around when he could see her next. Those times became points at the centre of his existence – Jenny was the huge, magnified image at the centre of his fish-eye lens; everything else fitted in small and insignificantly round the edge. His life was just a passing of time between sex and intimacy with her. For it wasn't just the sex, although that was amazing and energising to him; it was the chat, the laughs, the sense of fun and light-heartedness she brought to everything. She had a light touch on life. She was so casual with him, she inflamed his desire even more. She would never give a definite yes to seeing him until the day before. Nothing was a problem, she would belittle obstacles and whisk them away, whether it was that the only milk she had in the house was off, or that Josh was off school with a bout of tonsilitis. Everything was all right, not too serious. In Jenny, he believed, he had found the answer to the gap in the middle of his life, the gap he had only been dimly aware of until he had met her. She was both the problem and the solution. She was, it seemed to him, his path to fulfilment.

More and more he wanted to impress her. Christmas came and went without his noticing, his main concern was what he could buy Jenny that would be suitable. He got his wife a jumper from Marks and Spencer, and he didn't even notice when she took it back and swapped it for a barrow-load of sensible cotton under-wear. He was paralysed by indecision, so that for Christmas itself he got Jenny nothing. But that didn't really matter, he wasn't due to see her until after the New Year. By then he knew what would be just the thing.

He wanted to show her first, so he called in on his way home from work, even though Josh would be there. This time it didn't matter. He could even face the prospect of the miserable, freckled one. He was keyed up and shaking like a boy while he waited for her to answer the door. Josh answered. They hadn't met before. He looked rather an unprepossessing boy, Sanjay thought. He had a truculent expression (he practised it in the mirror every day) and he looked Sanjay up and down coldly. Sanjay felt a stab of jealousy that such an unworthy individual should claim so much of Jenny's love. 'Mum,' he shouted back into the house. Sanjay could see the glow of warm reddish light from the kitchen and a savoury, mouthwatering smell of chicken casserole wafted out onto the frosty air. He yearned to be inside, sitting down with them and eating in the warm, untidy sitting room. Jenny came to the door, wiping her hands. She looked solid and heavy-footed, she was wearing a horrible green apron with grubby embroidery on it, years of food had embedded itself in the stitching. He felt a split second's repulsion, then the zeal of his mission took him over again. She exclaimed in surprise.

'I thought it was someone collecting for charity,' she said. 'I was just about to give you a pound.'

He stood back with a flourish. She stared. Josh, who was just behind her, peered out and let out an impressed, 'Cor, smart.'

In the icy night, parked on the gritty road, stood a large black motorbike. Its sides gleamed like the skin of a snake and even standing still it looked fast. It was the symbol of his aspirations, his manhood, his new sense of self that Jenny had given him. It *was* him. It also symbolised his desire to whisk her away, clinging on to the back of him, trusting, dependent. Sanjay hovered expectantly next to it, waiting for her impressed reaction.

'Susuki 950,' breathed Josh. 'That's some power.'

All of a sudden Sanjay was glad Josh was there, because his mother was decidedly under-reacting. He even began to warm a little to the boy.

'Very nice,' she said. 'Don't get yourself killed on it.'

He shrank a little. But undeterred, he opened one of the panniers. 'And this,' he said proudly, 'is for you.'

He was holding a large package. Her heart sank. Really, not now. The chicken would be sticking to the bottom of the casserole. 'Come on in,' she said, and he followed her, holding his parcel.

It was embarrassing. She knew before she opened it that it would be something inappropriate and far too expensive. It was. Shaking out the folds, she held up a heavy, black leather jacket. 'Oh, Sanjay, it's lovely,' she said, holding it to her face to breathe in the leather smell. It was supple and shone with a subdued silky sheen. 'But I can't take it, you know.'

His face darkened. 'Why not?'

'It's too much. Too generous, too – lavish.' Too generous and serious a gift for this frivolous relationship, she thought. The implications made her uncomfortable.

'Why have you given my Mum a Christmas present?' asked Josh. 'We don't know you – do we?'

Jenny put her arms protectively around her son's shoulders. Suddenly to Sanjay they looked very close and united. They had the same eyes. He was the intruder.

'Sanjay is a friend of mine,' Jenny said. This was all wrong. Her relationship with Sanjay seemed squalid and dirty when scrutinised by Josh's young, perceptive eyes. A pathetic attempt to clutch at happiness by embracing a cheap imitation of it. 'His father works at the hospital. He's – a very generous and kind friend.'

'You don't like it,' said Sanjay, as a statement, not a question. She had wounded and offended him. In his eyes it was the epitome of excellent taste and style. It was a very sexy garment, it made a statement about the wearer. It did not occur to him that on Nita it would have been entirely appropriate and stunning.

'It's beautiful, Sanjay, really beautiful, it's just that – ' Her tone was wrong, she was saying the wrong thing, she had to make him feel better, this was cringingly awkward. 'I just don't deserve it, that's all.' I don't feel enough for you, she meant. What we do is playing. This is a serious gift.

This he could understand. She thought she wasn't good enough for the jacket. He took her firmly by the shoulders. 'Of course you do. Anyway,' he added, knowing that common sense would sway her, 'you will need it. For when you come on the bike.'

She laughed. She never would take him seriously. 'You're so sweet, Sanjay. And I'm really flattered that you can even *picture* me on the back of a 950cc motorbike.'

He couldn't understand her. Of course there was risk in it, of course there was danger. That was why the bike was such a mean, glamorous machine. But he would be master of it, she would be safe with him. She would hold on tight to him, rely on him. This was what he wanted to show her. He couldn't find the words and even if he could, he couldn't drag them out, but he could show her through objects, through possessions, which spoke more to him than words. His own achievements and identity were marked in possessions, in the things he owned. He could not grasp that it might not be the same for Jenny. She must understand that he was laying a trophy at her feet to show her that he loved her. Because suddenly, as she stood there amid the clutter in that filthy green apron, with her tall son draped around her elbow, her hair escaping from its loose ribbon in a gesture of abandon, pushing a stray strand of it behind her ear, then nipping through to stir their dinner, he knew with an overwhelming rush of pain and longing that for that moment he loved her. A lump of suppressed emotion was blocking his throat, as if he had just swallowed a boiled sweet. His face and throat ached with the effort of not bursting into tears. But Jenny was smiling at him, completely unaware of the cataclysm that was occuring in him. She smiled a lot of the time, he really couldn't tell when she was serious and when she was joking.

Josh said, 'Can I have a go, Mum?'

She laughed down at him, although he was taller than her shoulder. 'We'll see. Maybe up and down the road.'

'Brill, Mum, thanks. When can I go on it – tomorrow? Can he come back tomorrow, after school? Wait till James sees me – I'll be the same as him!'

It must be wonderful to have a mother who laughs a lot and lets you go on the back of motorbikes, thought Sanjay. He felt another wave of fleeting jealousy for Josh. He supposed he would have to give him a ride one day. He would try to put it off. Jenny was still holding the jacket, awkwardly scrunched under one arm.

'Try it on,' he told her. 'I want to see you in it.'

Laughing, embarrassed, she put the jacket on. It made her honey-coloured hair glow like golden syrup as it flopped down the black leather. She twirled for him coquettishly. They were back to the playful tone that he so enjoyed. Something that he had feared was about to slip away had been retrieved. She saw the appreciation – and the relief – in his eyes.

'You will keep it?' he pleaded. She saw he couldn't bear to have his present shoved back at him, it would be too humiliating.

'Yes, I will, Sanjay, it's really lovely. Thank you.'

Back in the beam of her warmth and approval, he was content. His mission had been a success.

'I'll never wear it, of course,' she said to Janice later.

'Can I have it, then?' asked Janice. 'I'll buy it off you. It's more suitable for my age.'

'What's that?' said Nita when he roared home and parked the motorbike in the garage. 'We've got a car each, why do we need another vehicle? Is this an image thing? You're a bit young for a mid-life crisis, aren't you? How much was it?'

He maintained a dignified silence. He'd never really been alive before, he was in torture, he wanted to leap for joy. But there was no point in saying anything. Except for one woman, women never did understand.

CHAPTER 6

Happy New Year
Love from Henry
Off to Illinois on 16/1.
xxx

Picture of a Boeing 737. For goodness' sake. Was this the equivalent of train spotting? Was Henry a closet plane spotter and she had never known? Couldn't he at least have found a picture of an Arctic Char? Or a scenic view of Number 4 Terminal at Heathrow? Why was he sending the cards at all? If he really wanted to keep in touch, she thought, he could have written letters and phoned. Actually said something meaningful. She stuck the card on the kitchen cupboard along with the others and felt unreasonably angry with Henry for making her miss him. She was trying to heal the wound he had left, and every time he sent a postcard he pulled the stitches out.

Janice was so confused she began to wonder if she had somehow disappeared altogether, if this ordinary person who went through her daily routine, getting on with things – making conversation, being nice to patients, tolerating Josh's violin practice and his habit of switching channels with the remote control just when it was something she liked – was a shade, an illusion, a kind of living ghost. It was as if the real Janice, the one she knew, the one everybody else assumed they knew, had gone off somewhere never to return. She was certain of nothing, everything she had taken for granted before was now open for negotiation. Even her sexuality, a mild, muted energy that she had taken for granted all this time, was now wide awake and in a torture of uncertainty. The whole world had been turned on its head. Only the incessant cleaning lay between her and the dreadful abyss of uncertainty that yawned in front of her. The only way she felt she could control her life and herself, was by destroying all germs. Since this was of course impossible, her daily life was a constant battle. She had really thought that she had been made clean and whole again by Kate, as if their brief, extraordinary time together had been some kind of essential healing, cleansing process. But since everything had turned into chaotic disaster on that Sunday night, when she had felt caught up in some surreal nightmare, all that healing had been undone and she was right back where she had started. Now that she had remembered, too, what she had tried so successfully to forget, she became even more obsessed with scrubbing away the past. But she knew she had to face up to certain things in order to heal herself, and that not all toxins can be scrubbed away with a scrubbing brush, especially toxins of the spirit. Even so, she could not escape from her obsession. She was not yet ready to leave it behind, it was her comfort and her stay. At least it made her feel better, if only temporarily, and it was safer than turning to drink or drugs as a way of blocking things out. At least in her case, she told herself, it was only Domestos. She knew she had to sort herself out in order to create a future in which she could grow healthy and strong, but she was not quite ready to begin the task yet. And before she could move forwards she had to revisit the past.

She told Jenny she was going to see her mother.

'I thought you weren't on speaking terms.'

'We're not. Well, not for five years. We fell out when I was eighteen. She lives in Swansea now, with some bloke called Reg.'

Jenny wondered why they had fallen out.

'Something pathetic, you know how it is. But I think really it was that I just couldn't forgive her – about me Dad.'

Jenny nodded. 'When are you going?'

'Saturday. I'll get the train.'

'Would you like us to come? We wouldn't mind a weekend by the sea. Even in January. Even in Swansea.'

Janice thanked her, but she had to do this on her own. 'It might be a total disaster. I may like her even less than I did then. Or she may just kick me out again. But I've got to try, then at least I'll know. Anyway, it's bound to be raining, isn't it, down there? It's worse than Manchester for rain. We camped down that way once. Rained every day for two weeks. Worst holiday I ever had. Spent the whole time sitting in cafés in wet anoraks, drinking Coke and listening to Mum and Dad falling out. Or was that Tenby? All the same sort of area, anyway.'

'I'm sure it will be better than you expect. Just don't expect anything, then you won't be disappointed.'

Swansea was bleak on a rainy Friday night in January. The train arrived at nine o'clock and Janice was loath to leave the snug security of the carriage, with its scarred seats and stale air. She stepped out onto the platform which was black with rain, and pock-marked with ubiquitous blobs of old chewing gum. She fingered the small card in her pocket, a Christmas card from four years ago which had said simply, 'From Mum and Reg', and no kisses. She presumed she had sent it just to show she had moved, because there was a small pre-printed sticker on the back of the envelope with a new address. Janice read the address out to a taxi driver and was whisked along on a nylon fur tiger-skin car seat cover, to number 2, Heol Derwen.

When the taxi had gone, Janice stood outside the house. It was the bottom one of a row of terraced houses, straggling up the side of a very steep hill like a row of jagged teeth. The mean houses staggered together, their roofs making steps up the hillside and the bottom one appeared to be propping all the others up. Her mother must have been desperate to follow a man named Reg to a place like this. But then, thought Janice, her mother's judgement had never been the best.

Reg, though, was just as she had expected. Fat and ginger-haired, he opened the door with a cigarette stuck to his lower lip. He looked her balefully up and down. 'No thanks, we're Mormons,' he said before she had opened her mouth, and slammed the door.

She stood there for a moment in the rain, at a loss. Then, to keep warm and regain her composure, she walked up to the top of the hill. This must keep people fit, she thought, as she panted up to the top. Imagine doing this with a push chair. The exercise elated her and got her circulation going again after the train journey. Swansea lay out across its hills and valleys below her, the rows of terraces bright with white and orange lights, and in the distance the cranes and derricks of the docks stood like ancient dinosaurs. Suddenly she felt better about her mission. She'd come all this way, the train fare hadn't been cheap, and she wasn't going to go home unsatisfied. She was still unclear about what she wanted, or what she hoped to gain, but she would make this meeting a success. She turned to let the steep hill take her speedily back down.

'I've come to see Irene,' she said firmly, before Reg could finish saying, 'What the hell did I just say to you?'

He curbed his irritation. The cigarette had a long pile of ash on it now. She looked at that rather than at his face, wondering curiously how it managed to stay there without falling off. There must be some sort of scum on his lip to hold it in place.

'Rene,' he shouted. 'Somebody to see you. Who shall I say it is?' he asked, turning back to Janice.

Irene had appeared behind him in the doorway. She looked small and frail next to her husband. Janice wondered for a second if he hit her. She patted her thin hair that was pumped into stiff curls and shone a dull, brassy yellow in the hall light. Then she saw the visitor. Janice looked straight into her mother's horrified eyes. 'Tell her it's her daughter,' she said.

'You've lost weight,' her mother said. She had kept her back to Janice almost the whole time since she had come in, fussing with the ornaments along the mantelpiece and on top of the giant colour television, then fiddling around in the kitchen, putting cups on a tray and making the tea. She was a tiny woman, smaller than Janice, and time and cigarettes had toughened her sinews so that she was shrunken, wiry and tight, with a face like a peach stone.

'You've gone – blonde,' said Janice, for want of a better word.

'This is Reg.'

'I know.'

'How do you know?'

'The Christmas card.' Janice produced it from her pocket. 'Remember?'

Her mother jerked her chin. 'Oh yes. Reg wanted me to tell you our new address. Said he didn't want to start our married life with "bad feeling"' – she isolated the words ironically. 'Didn't you, Reg? He's very kind, is Reg. Kinder than me.'

'I didn't know you were married.'

'What, wanted an invitation to the wedding, did you? Wanted to come and judge me, say your bit, like you did before?'

'Why? What did I say?'

Her mother looked at her for the first time. 'You mean you can't remember? We fell out for five years because of something you said and you can't even remember? Well, I hardly think I'm going to remind you, lady.'

'Come on love,' said Reg, giving his wife a soothing pat. 'Let bygones be bygones, eh? She's come to make it up. Let's have that tea, it must be mashed by now.'

They sat down, Reg and Irene on the sofa, Janice on a chair, in a parody of a polite little tea party. Irene passed some Battenburg cake around. Janice had not eaten since breakfast, but she couldn't manage any. The combined sweetness of the cake and the all-pervading acrid smell of stale cigarette smoke made her feel sick. Some ash from Reg's cigarette fell onto the pink part of the cake as he took a piece. Janice had to rush for the toilet. This was terrible, she thought, sitting on the lavatory and looking up at the over-blown roses on the wallpaper. There was a little plastic lady with a crochet skirt covering a spare toilet roll and some back copies of *Plumber's Monthly*. So Reg was another plumber. At least her mother was consistent. Perhaps it was all that free washing-machine maintenance and giving the boiler an overhaul that attracted her. Or overalls and oily hands. It took all sorts. I've come all this way, thought Janice, and it's awful, there's nothing to say. I shouldn't have come, it was a daft mistake. Pathetic to think she would have changed, that we might get on now. What did I say last time I saw her? She couldn't for the life of her remember. It must have been something pretty bad. But Janice was not in the habit of saying things that were pretty bad. If only she could remember. I've got to make a better go of it than this, she thought, peering at her reflection. Bracing herself, she joined them again.

Her mother seemed to have mellowed a little in the interval; Reg must have said something. 'Where's your glasses?' she asked, as she had every day before school when Janice was a child.

'I've got contact lenses now.'

Her mother sniffed. 'Nice,' she said. 'You look better.' This was the first positive remark. Reg got up and appeared to be sprucing himself up in preparation to leave the house.

'He always goes down the club on a Friday,' Irene explained. 'He likes a pint before bed, don't you, Reg?'

'Don't you want to go?' Janice was conscious of intruding.

'Oh no, it's men's night out. He likes to go on his own. We go on a Wednesday.'

Irene was definitely making more effort after the initial shock of seeing Janice. She asked about her job, and pulled a face when she said the word 'geriatrics'.

'But you wanted to be a theatre nurse, didn't you?'

Janice explained that it wasn't as easy as that, she had lost her job in theatre and mumbled something about cutbacks. If anything wasn't as easy as that, Janice generally tended not to bother. She liked the line of least resistance. 'Geriatrics is a growth area,' she said brightly.

After Reg had gone, her mother asked her, 'Why have you come?'

Janice said she didn't really know. No reason, really. 'I suppose I wanted to set the record straight. Sort things out. Understand things. So I can put them away and move on.'

'What things?' demanded her mother, immediately on guard.

'Well,' Janice hesitated. She hadn't meant to broach it quite this soon, in this way. 'Things about me. About you. And my Dad.'

Her mother's hard, wrinkled face set itself into a mask. Janice noticed that the skin on her neck was brown and had cracked into a mosaic of dry segments. It reminded her of the skin of a crocodile. With a bizarre flash she had the sensation that her mother was slowly turning into a reptile in front of her eyes. She must be more light-headed than she realised. 'What things?' she repeated. The stagnant air was thick with hostility, and Janice knew she had trodden on forbidden ground.

'Where is he?' she said, blunt with desperation. 'Where does he live? I want to know.'

'Are you going to see him?'

'Yes, I am,' said Janice, making the decision after she spoke, surprising herself, for it had floated up from nowhere, although she realised it must have been the true purpose of this trip all along. She was firmer now that the choice had been made. 'I am.'

Her mother bridled a little and lit a cigarette.

'Do you have to smoke so much, Mum?'

Her mother tossed her head in an old, familiar gesture. 'You're still a little nag bag, then,' she retorted, but Janice could see she was pleased. Nagging is perceived as a kind of concern to those who cannot show love, or whose love is warped and distorted into criticism – those who have lost all other ways to communicate. At least nagging shows an interest, albeit of a starved and unproductive nature. Irene blew a plume of smoke up towards the yellowing light shade, enjoying the effect. She looked at Janice through narrowed eyes. 'He won't want to see you, you know. He never bothered with you from the day he left.'

The day you made him leave, thought Janice, but she said nothing.

'He's got another family now. Remarried pretty quick after, I think. Several more kids, anyway. Probably never even told his new wife about you. After all, why should he? You weren't his.'

Janice felt as if a tight corset was holding her in and she wanted to burst and shriek and scream her pain at her mother – to give her some of it back. Hold on, she told herself, hold on till you've got his address. Her mother was waiting for a reaction, but Janice gave none. 'Where does he live?' she persisted, managing to keep the quiver out of her voice.

'Bridlington, I think. They run a guest house, of sorts. Or they did. Probably folded by now, knowing his head for figures. Never had a bloody clue about anything. I only know that because your Auntie Cathy and her Frank met him on the front there once, years ago. They may have gone now, for all I know. The "Shangri-La". I ask you. In bloody Bridlington.'

Janice stood up. The presence of so much bile in the atmosphere was giving her acid in the pit of her stomach.

'You off?' said Irene. 'Well, I won't ask you to stop over on the couch. Might have known you wouldn't have come to see *me*,' she said with her old habit of self-pity and wounded pride. Suddenly, she remembered something. She appeared to think for a moment, then swiftly she left the room, cigarette clamped in her thin lips, permanently puckered after years of habit. Janice pulled her coat on. The need to get out of this house was rising in her throat. Her mother returned holding a small bundle of letters. 'You may as well have these now. They can't do any harm any more, he won't want to see you.'

She handed Janice the bundle, tied with an elastic band. They were letters, opened, but still in the envelopes, all addressed to her in her father's careful hand. The date on the postmark of the top one was October of the year he had gone. She stared at her mother with pure hatred. Understanding was beginning to dawn.

'You kept them from me. How many are there – ' She flicked through them with her fingers ' – twelve – fifteen? He wrote to me, more than fifteen times, and you kept the letters from me. You stole *my* letters. You hid them from me.'

It was her mother's smile that did it. A slow, triumphant, hateful smile across those prematurely wizened features, just like the smile of the wicked stepmother when she would not let Cinderella go to the ball. Or a crocodile that has just gobbled someone up. Janice let out a scream that ripped from her body, taking years of pent up pain and rage with it. Grabbing her mother by the throat, she shook and shook her as if she was a guy ready for bonfire night. Screaming abuse, she wanted to mash that head, with its false, metallic hair, into the vinyl-covered wall. Her mother was a limp, scrawny thing in her hands. Then just as suddenly, she was filled with horror, her hands felt filthy where they had touched the dry roughness of the over-washed acrylic cardigan and felt the bony frame beneath. She had to get them clean, to get the feel of that woman and the stench of that house off her. She let her mother

128

crumple slowly to the floor, darted to grab the bundle of letters, then ran. Frantically she was thinking, I can't have hurt her, I didn't do enough to hurt her, I only shook her. How hard did I shake her? Not that hard, she's all right, she must be all right, but she was too shocked to wait around to see. She was vaguely aware of a door opening as she ran by, a neighbour coming out and shouting about all the fuss, but she kept on running and running, down a dark tunnel in her head. She felt as light as air, as empty as a dry leaf, nothing was stopping her. For the second time, Janice felt as if she was running for her life.

Nobody notices somebody running in Swansea city centre late on a Friday night. The pubs are disgorging students and drunks (often one and the same thing at this time of day). Gangs of youths are going noisily home or on somewhere else, taxis lie in wait, engines permanently running. A few dogs nose around the drifts of rubbish and the Friday night messes of sick, and plenty of people, either escaping or perpetrating harm, have reason to run. Janice ran all the way through the brightly lit shopping streets, past some more run-down shops and takeaways, where gangs of loud men thought it was a good end to their evening to menace the Chinese and Indian staff, shout noisy abuse and order a whole load of food they did not want. She ran down past the darker area near the Leisure Centre, where couples kissed in doorways and behind concrete buttresses, across a bit of park where the shapeless outlines of tramps adorned the benches and the grass squelched with an occasional used condom, until at last she came to where the cranes stood tall and silent, bowing their heads over the black water of the docks. The water had its own smell, one Janice would always recall, a mixture of oil, salt water, and the heavy stench of mud. She slowed to a walk. A couple of bright security lights were on and she could see a man sitting in the warm fug of a prefabricated hut. He was watching the purple flicker of a small television. She could just hear the babble of the programme he was watching, the bursts of canned laughter sounding senseless and far away. There were still tramlines in the tarmac, although the trams had vanished decades ago and the whole area had received the benefit of an EC grant to make it a place for young executives to come for lunch.

But at night it still held the mystery of a working docks and the old ghosts of obsolete machines hung around the scaffolding bases of the derricks.

Janice walked along the tramlines right to the end of the dock. It was darker here, where the industrial stone ended and plunged down into the black water below. The rain had stopped now and it was a clear night, still and calm. The wetness on the pavements had turned to ice and the stars flickered in the frost-laden air. The water shivered and reflected the lights like a piece of the sheerest fabric imaginable being lightly shaken. The faint, occasional breath of wind made tracks of feathered water in the shiny stillness. Glancing round to check no one was about, Janice sat down on the edge of the dockside and looked out to sea. The letters formed a lump in her pocket, but she wouldn't read them yet, and besides, it was too dark. Gradually, her breath settled back to normal after the long, frantic run. She was numb. Now she was further out in the cold than ever, drifting away. Exhausted, she couldn't think, she couldn't feel, she just gazed out to sea and let the cold creep up from the chill concrete and seep into her bones.

Janice was a nurse. She knew that if your inner body temperature dropped only two degrees Celsius, hypothermia would set in. Any lower than this and you are in grave danger. Her clothes – jeans, a jumper and a thin anorak – were inadequate for outdoor conditions on a clear January night. Her suede boots were drenched from running through icy puddles and the damp had soaked through to her socks and feet. The previous months, culminating in this disastrous evening, had flayed her to a pitch of starvation and exhaustion so that her body had no reserves to draw upon in need. She had not eaten all day. Sitting there, alone on the frozen dockside, there was need now. Her body got colder and colder while her spirit drifted away on the tide.

At four am the night security guard pulled on his boots, wrapped his scarf round his neck, buttoned his jacket, wedged his flat cap down on his head and reluctantly dragged himself away from the comfort of his gas heater. He locked the door of his hut and came out into the cold to do his round. Shining his torch around in a routine check, he could see what looked like a small heap of clothes at the end of the dock. The pile looked too flat to have a body inside it. Cautiously he approached it. It could be a tramp – though it would have to be a small one – who might kick and curse and spit at him if disturbed. But no one could sleep rough on such a night; he reckoned it was the coldest yet this year. It could be something worse. It was.

She was so cold and her breath was so slight, he thought she was dead. He started to curse quietly under his breath as he lifted the thin arm. The stuff of the anorak had frozen onto the tarmac. A corpse, he thought, just my bloody luck, a bloody corpse, and a young one at that. His old throat got choked up in spite of himself and hot tears bulged and spilled over his purple-veined cheeks. If only he had listened to Meryl, his wife, he could have been tucked up with her in his own bed now, with her ample backside in its long flannelette nightie slotted comfortably into the cushion of his belly, instead of picking up the corpses of young girls on the freezing dockside. He'd lived mostly out of doors himself, being brought up on a farm, and he'd taken this job only when they'd had to sell the farm because of the new milk quotas. He'd seen a few things, what with the way society was going these days, no values any more, but he'd never had to deal with a corpse before. He wished he'd sorted out his pension, paid his extra years and retired months ago like Meryl wanted him to. His mouth began to work frantically but silently. He put his head to her chest. There was a heartbeat. Thank God for that. Meryl would have made him ask for a rise if he'd had to start dealing with corpses. There was no mention of that in his contract. That would have constituted a change in terms and conditions. Meryl wouldn't let him stand for that. His own heart was pumping like a piston engine. He shook the girl's shoulder. 'Wake up, girl, wake up.'

Very young she was, tiny. White as a sheet. Perhaps she was a drug addict, taken an overdose. He'd better be careful how he handled her, she might be savage suddenly, or throw up over him. He didn't want to go catching anything, and Meryl wouldn't thank him for the washing. The Lady of Shalott, he thought, the only poem he had ever read, fifty years ago in school. The Lady of Shalott, that's who she reminded him of, she was blanched like an onion. Carefully he picked her up. She was so frail and light, it was like catching a turkey in the yard before you took it into the cow shed to wring its neck. They always surprised you, how light they were; you could feel the breast bone and the heart beating fit to burst. Only her heart was a flutter. As he lifted her, a bundle of letters fell out of her coat and into the black oily water of the dock. Quickly they became soiled with the grime in the water, and a thin rainbow slick of petrol floated over them as they drifted away. He hoped they were not important. He took her back to the hut to phone for an ambulance.

Janice surfaced as he was carrying her; she could feel the cold clamminess of his waxed jacket. But she couldn't make sense of anything, so she floated off to that warm place again. When she woke up she was in an ambulance, she thought it must be part of a dream, except that she was shivering violently. An ambulance woman was sitting next to her, taking her pulse and steadying her. Janice tried to sit up, but the woman restrained her.

'I shouldn't be here,' she said frantically, then she realised that her words were blurred, slurring into one another. Her voice felt and sounded as if it came from someone else. Why wouldn't her mouth work properly? What was wrong with her? 'I should be there, where you are,' she tried to say. 'I'm a nurse, I don't get ill, I'm a nurse.'

The ambulance woman spoke in a calming tone, the tone Janice used herself when talking to the patients, like Mr Tomlin, whose caved-in face floated up to her now, who had been in for eight months and would never get out. They were just looking after him until he had another stroke, which would probably kill him. Rehabilitation was out of the question. But Mr Tomlin told Janice every day that he had to get home to see to his garden. 'There's nobody to do the pruning,' he would say through his toothless mouth, half paralysed by a stroke. They even had to help him chew. 'I digs it over every winter, that's what's kept me fit as a fiddle till eighty-five. I've got to get home to get on with it.'

He would get very agitated and fall off his chair in his desperation to get home, then Janice would haul him back up, change his underclothes for him and tell him they would try to get him home soon. Nobody would ever again call Mr Tomlin by his Christian name. No one would ever tell him that they loved him. Quite possibly no one did. Janice thought of Mr Tomlin who had been a fine lad in his youth, as he told the nurses on his clearer days, showing them a crumpled photo of a dark, handsome man in uniform whom they could not recognise in the gaunt, broken frame sunk in the hospital chair. She started to cry as if she would never stop.

They kept Janice in for forty-eight hours, just for observation. She slept most of Saturday, waking just at teatime to eat some white bread sandwiches, a banana and a yoghurt. After tea she wandered into the TV room and watched some quiz show she usually detested. On Sunday she managed breakfast and a women's magazine, and she rang Jenny to let her know she would be home on Monday. As she had told the staff she had no relatives in Swansea, that she had been there on her own for the day, had got lost and so had missed the last train, they gave her a paper nightie to wear and washed her clothes. Janice had often dressed people in paper nighties, but she would never do so again without a silent prayer, saying, 'God preserve me from getting old and having to wear a paper nightie.' By Sunday afternoon the noise was getting to her, too, as she tried to sleep through rowdy visits by bored grandchildren, breezy conversation, over-loud, as relatives (prompted by guilt alone) came to visit the sick, trying to pretend that there was really nothing wrong with them at all. It was really quite an eye opener to Janice. The woman in the next bed was the sort who makes a doctor's heart sink, constantly calling the nurses for trivial matters such as opening her sweet tin, or needing the toilet then changing her mind. Her shoulders were permanently hunched in her brushed nylon nightie and she blinked about fifty times a minute. She regaled Janice proudly with all the juicy details of her condition.

'They've done every test under the sun, but they really don't know what's wrong with me, you know. They've named a syndrome after me – Murdstone's syndrome. Fancy having your very own syndrome – that's something, isn't it? Have I smudged my eyeliner? The mirrors in here are terrible, they make everybody look so ill, have you noticed?'

Janice pretended to be asleep.

They let her out first thing on Monday morning. With typical hospital timing (which makes six am feel like time for elevenses) she emerged into the fresh air at what she thought must be mid-morning, to find that only a few early birds were on their way to work. It was a beautiful morning, bright and crisp with pockets of frost in the hollows of the valleys and the promise of some weak winter warmth from the pale sunshine later on. The Bristol Channel was glittering with a brilliant dazzle beyond the town. She reached the station in time to catch the early train and arrived home about two in the afternoon. It was a golden afternoon in York, though the frost had not melted in places, and she could smell the warm, dark odour of chocolate on the still air from one of the two chocolate factories. The house was empty and quiet; even Geoffrey didn't raise his furry head from his pillow in greeting. Outside, Astrid was chopping with some rusty shears at her spindly climbing rose that straggled up the wall of the back yard, and pulling up a few intrepid weeds. Gavin was gingerly picking up the prickly clippings and putting them in a bin liner. He looked less doleful than usual. Astrid waved cheerily and cawed out a loud 'hello'. Janice waved back. Everything was beautifully, wonderfully normal. Then she ducked out of sight before Astrid could engage her in conversation, cleaned the toilet, made herself a good, big, satisfying lunch, as they had told her she should eat better at the hospital, phoned in sick, then went to bed.

'What I like about the Kama Sutra,' said Jenny, gazing up at the gold stars on the ceiling as she and Sanjay lay entwined one lunch hour, 'is the idea that familiarity is erotic. It's only when you get to know someone really well that true closeness can grow. That's when you can overcome your inhibitions and really learn how to please each other. And then you fancy each other in a more lasting way. Don't you think? I think I could quite take to being a Buddhist. One day, when I've got time.' Sanjay wasn't listening. He was absorbed in running his finger up and down her calf. It was two days since Janice had returned from Swansea.

'I mean,' she went on, 'in this country, sex has become an industry. It's got to be quick, frantic, and preferably with someone you fancy like mad but don't know. No emotions, just plenty of raw lust. It's the difference between eating fast-food junk, or really learning to cook.'

'Mmm,' murmured Sanjay. His ears had picked up the word 'sex' and he was ready to go again. Raw lust sounded fine to him. He began putting warm little kisses on her, all the way up from knee to breast, but when he got to the nipple she brushed him off absently. Her mind had moved on to what to cook for tea. She was beginning to find his lack of conversation and endless physical appetite just a tiny bit of a bore. They had done everything once, and several things lots of times, but she wasn't getting to know him. She was gradually realising that she liked talking just as much as she liked going to bed, if not more, and that it was an important part of intimacy. You can't get close to someone simply by locking your bodies together, she thought, feeling suddenly rather depressed.

She got up, walked through the sitting room and kitchen with nothing on, and disappeared into the shower. He found the ease with which she wandered around the house naked really exciting and liberating. He and Nita couldn't do that; they were too overlooked and Nita couldn't stand net curtains, said they were so suburban. She wouldn't do it anyway, he thought. She kept her fawn's body hidden from him. He had not seen her fully unclothed since their wedding night. Even though Jenny was fattish (which he found surprisingly luscious and desirable – he had always thought he preferred slim women) she was completely at ease with her body. He tried to follow her into the bathroom but the door was locked. It was a signal for him to go. She had several of these and he was getting better at reading them. At first he had had to be positively told to leave. When she came out, pink and steamy in a towel, he was smart in his suit again. She was casual and light in her goodbye, the surest way of making him want to see her again. 'Shut the door after you,' she said.

CHAPTER 7

Dear Jenny
Illinois excellent – as you predicted,
very friendly and social.
All bright sun and snow.
Hope you are well.
Regards – Henry. xxx

A picture of some supposedly famous high-rise block that Jenny had never heard of. An enormous concrete erection rising out of an impossibly green park. Very phallic, she thought bitterly. He must be having a good time. And 'Love Henry' had become 'Regards' – the cold-blooded toad. But still three kisses. Well, you can keep your kisses, Henry Proctor, for Miss Sunny Illinois. Jenny bit savagely into a piece of toast.

It was a terrible January morning, heavy, dirty rain and you knew it would not get light all day. In three days, the first dreary month of the year would be over. But winter would still be here for another two months, at least. Jenny loathed this feeling of wishing her life away. Henry was obviously enjoying himself in Illinois (she could imagine all the sunshine and brilliant snow all too easily – it was enough to make you spit) and meeting lots of long-haired, white-teethed all-American girls who would be only too eager to hear about Arctic Char. Sanjay was coming at lunchtime, at least that was something to look forward to. She had deliberately put him off for a couple of weeks, like a naughty treat that is all the better for being deferred, but she felt like seeing him today. Those calf's eyes gazing adoringly at her, that lovely way his hair grew upwards at the front – a real cow's lick – his uninhibited pleasure in pleasing, now that she had taught him how to do so. He might bring some tasty, curried morsel to eat, wrapped in brown paper and still warm as he sometimes did, if he had called in to his uncle's shop on the way here. Jenny brushed toast crumbs off her front, shouted to Josh to hurry up, and wondered which she was looking forward to most – delicious curry or delicious sex. She suspected it was the curry.

Janice was scooting round like a fly.

'Leave all that 'til tonight, it'll still be there,' Jenny said as Janice started on the breakfast dishes.

'You know I can't do that,' said Janice. 'Leave all those germs to breed all day?'

Jenny laughed. 'Doesn't sound too bad a way to spend a dreary day like this to me.'

'If I don't do them now I'll have to come back at lunchtime. I hate coming home to a pig sty.'

'This isn't a pig sty,' retorted Jenny, offended. Whatever was wrong with the girl? Her hands were all cracked from the detergents she used, at least she ought to wear rubber gloves. She was becoming obsessive.

'You're very touchy today. You don't need to do them, honestly. All right, do them if you must be a martyr, but I'd rather you didn't. Josh can do them tonight, it's his turn, but he never has to do a turn because you've always done them.'

Josh grinned gratefully at Janice. 'I don't mind if she really wants to do them – honest. Mum, can I have a pet mouse?' Janice gave an involuntary shudder. 'And can I stay at James's tonight?'

'Come on, Josh, have you done your teeth? Good, your packed lunch is on the bench. What about your swimming stuff? Got it? No, you can't stay the night at James's tonight, it's a school night. Well, maybe at the weekend, *if* they ask you. You're not to ask them again. Let's go, or you'll miss the bus. Have you brushed your hair?' She scruffed lovingly at his rough, scrubby head. 'No, I thought not. And *no* to a mouse. They stink. Anyway, Geoffrey would eat it for breakfast.'

'I could keep it in my room.'

'*No.*'

A typical naggy, fractious morning. Bet they don't have those in sunny Illinois. I'm getting worried about that girl, thought Jenny. She's had a total personality change since wet-wipes Roger gave her the elbow. That was months ago. I didn't think she liked him *that* much. Perhaps it was that weird weekend, something obviously happened then. But what? It wasn't like Janice to go in for a one-night – or two-nights, to be accurate – fling. She was much too concerned about the health hazards. And too sensible, anyway, too reserved. It was just not in her character. She doesn't seem that interested in sex, either, to bother with some seedy fling. She would find it much too unhygienic. As would I, Jenny reminded herself guiltily, thinking of Sanjay. He's not a fling, she thought, he's a luxury item. Then Janice's trip to Swansea to see her mother had been a complete disaster. She hadn't talked about it very much, but Jenny gathered it had not worked out as Janice had hoped. Poor girl, thought Jenny, I must make time to chat to her. Maybe I'll ask Kate's advice, she's good at this sort of thing, and it might take her mind off her own troubles. All these people in love, it causes nothing but pain and trouble. I curse you, Henry, for leaving us, for preferring a fish to me. Much better to have a beautiful boy for sex and fun, and friends for everything else. They left Janice scrubbing scourer round the sink, prior to doing the washing up.

Janice looked down at her hands. The skin was cracked and peeling, Jenny was right about the rubber gloves. But this was part of her punishment. The skin around the cuticles was red and inflamed, coming away from the nails. She would ask for some stuff to rub into them at work. Out of the kitchen window she could see Astrid in her flowery cleaning outfit, dimly visible behind her own lace curtain. Gavin was smashing at the end wall of her yard with a sledge hammer, oblivious of the rain. He liked to knock it down and rebuild it every year, Astrid said, it kept him happy, gave him something to aim for. It was his New Year's resolution every year, to piece it back together better than he did last year. Janice watched Astrid open the back door, pull at a bit of flaky paint as if it would make a difference to the door's state of neglect, then brave the rain in her slippers to put the rubbish out.

She waved brightly to Janice and crowed out something about the weather. Her eyelids were a dashing shade of purple today, with some glittery stuff just beneath the painted line of her eyebrows. She seemed to have painted on a new beauty spot, too, that she hadn't had before. She was clearly feeling very perky, despite the weather. She made a splash of colour on the grimy morning. Oh yes, it was bin day. Janice would have to rush to do that before work. She'd better get a move on. She turned the hot tap on full so that the water bounced off the dirty dishes and splashed her front. The phone rang. Blast. She turned the tap off. But she didn't go to pick it up. If she waited long enough, it would stop. The tone seemed more insistent each time, then more resigned, as if it knew it would not be answered, until after about twelve rings it stopped. Janice sighed with relief. Nothing would interrupt her.

That evening the phone rang again, just as they had sat down to eat a rather congealed bought chicken pie. Jenny had not had time to do anything at lunchtime, she had been rather busy, she said. She had come home with a glowing bloom on her, like a peach, Janice noticed, she must have had a good day. It was Josh who picked up the phone. 'For you,' he said, handing it to Janice.

To the other two, sitting at the table, Janice's already pale face went whiter still and clenched into a tightness. She didn't speak, just clutched the receiver with a white-knuckled hand, nodding and breathing noisily. Finally the other person had clearly finished, for Janice muttered, 'Thanks, yes, I'll come. Thanks.' Even Josh stopped chewing. Janice walked back to the table with the stiff, jerky movements of a puppet manipulated by an inept puppeteer. She sat down hard. 'My mother. She died today. A massive CVA.' The professional term crept in inadvertently, distancing her from the event.

Josh, with the nervousness children show when they do not know how to react, burst out laughing. It is strange, thought Jenny, how often this is our first reaction, even as adults – although by then we are trained to suppress it – when we are told of death. It is as if laughter is the only defence that can keep death at bay. She got up, went round the table, and held Janice very tightly. Her shoulder blades were shockingly near the surface. 'It's OK,' said

Janice in a funny, dry little voice. 'I can't cry, it's OK, I'm not going to cry.'

Jenny mentioned the death to Kate. She had never discussed her home life with her before, other than the odd comment about Josh in response to Kate's occasional friendly inquiry. Mostly they talked about work, seriously, and in between they carried on a light, jokey banter. For some reason, although they were friendly enough, they had never become friends. Jenny had always had the impression that Kate liked to keep herself to herself. But Jenny needed to discuss Janice with someone in confidence, someone who was wise and sensible and outside the situation, someone whose advice she would respect. So she confided in Kate.

'Oh God, poor girl,' said Kate, with a vehemence that surprised Jenny. Kate was usually calm and unflappable, even here in the hospital, where even the calmest nerves got shaken. 'How is she? Who's comforting her?'

This struck Jenny as a little odd. 'Well, me, I suppose. She's got me and Josh to keep her company.'

'No one else? No – boyfriend, or whatever?'

'Oh, no,' said Jenny. 'She's been in a state of decline since she disappeared for two days in November. Very strange, that was, she's never discussed it at all. But she hasn't been the same since. I think she met someone – well, I know she did – but nothing came of it. She was very secretive about it, though. There's been no sign of anyone since then. She's just been really miserable and practically stopped eating. And that's not easy to do in our house, I can tell you. Perhaps she got whisked away by aliens for a couple of days, and didn't like to say.'

If Jenny had been a little more aware, she would have noticed that Kate had gone pink. She did seem a little more agitated than usual. But the new social worker, a tall young man called Steve – quite attractive if you liked that type, personally Jenny didn't, too skinny and diffident, but some people might call it sensitivity, not diffidence – had just walked in. She thought it must be he who had made Kate go quiet. Jenny didn't think he was her type, she was much better-looking than he was. It just went to show, you never could tell. Taste is such an unpredictable thing, she thought. Look at me with Sanjay. Or Henry, for that matter. Why love a man who prefers fish to people?

'When's the funeral?' Kate asked casually, when Steve had gone.

'Next Friday. Down in Swansea. Poor Janice, it's even worse when you haven't got on. All that guilt. At least with mine I see her often enough to make it up each time. Falling out's a hobby for her, she enjoys it. I think I'll offer to go down with her.'

Kate didn't say anything.

Janice got through the week on autopilot, a feeling that was becoming familiar. It was lucky that she had perfected the technique beforehand, she thought. She was going to catch the early train on Friday. They had offered her the week off work but she had refused politely, saying it was better to work, she was better if she kept herself occupied. She did not tell them that she was worried less by the death than by the fact that she was not prostrated by grief. Surely she ought to feel more than this strange numbness that was itself a kind of death. On Thursday night there was a knock at the door. It was Kate. 'Come in,' said Jenny with enthusiasm, while thinking, how odd but how nice, a friendly gesture. She invited Kate to lead the way into the sitting room. Josh had gone to James's for the weekend after all (James now had the added attraction for Josh of a computer of his own in his bedroom) and Janice was putting a few things together for the morning. She was holding some clean washing, just about to take it upstairs, when she saw Kate.

Jenny was suddenly embarrassed. She had no idea what was happening, she had not realised even that Kate and Janice knew each other, but there was a feeling in the room that made her want to be somewhere else. The electricity was tangible. The two women were staring at each other, frozen, Janice clutching the pile of washing to her chest, her eyes bright and wide above the greyish vests. Looking from one to the other, Jenny realised it had never occurred to her before that they looked rather alike. Kate was tall and athletic, while Janice had the physique and grooming of a starved starling, but their colouring, their general demeanour and most of all, their eyes, were startlingly similar. There was some bond here that she had never imagined, that she did not understand, and from which she was most definitely excluded. Jenny was not one to be easily embarrassed, but now she wished most ardently that she was elsewhere. The other two were locked into a strange, intense silence as they stared at one another. Janice let out a huge sigh of release. It's like some awful tacky novel, Jenny thought, as the two women moved towards each other as if pulled by a cord, and fused together in a tight, oblivious embrace. She mumbled something inaudible and scuttled upstairs.

Upstairs was not her territory. She only came up here occasionally, to change Josh's sheets and make some vague and usually abortive effort to tidy his room. His bedroom had an alien smell of boy. The blue fish curtains were looped up over the foot of the bed and two days' dirty washing lay strewn around the floor. My God, Jenny said aloud, who would have thought it. Kate's a lesbian. And so is Janice! The word was inadequate, it did not convey the intensity, the energy she had felt between them in that room. She had peered over a precipice into another land. And they've fallen for each other! She wanted to laugh out loud, it was so preposterous. What ever was the point? I mean, both of them are attractive enough, at least Kate is, but how can they fancy each other? And what is it like in bed? Isn't it just all foreplay without the actual sex? What's the point of that? It wasn't that she couldn't imagine it, nor that she found it distasteful, indeed, some of her own fantasies ran along that theme. But that was the whole point of fantasies – they stayed safely in your mind. It was just that this had been happening, for goodness knows how long, right under her very nose, so close to home – *in* her home, in fact, and she had known nothing about it. How could I have thought I knew Janice, she thought, when such an important part of her life was completely hidden? How much do you ever know about anyone, even when you live with them? And what was all that with Roger, then?

This was like an echo, faint and dim, but an echo nevertheless of something that had happened long ago, another time when something else had been going on under her nose and she had not noticed. Then, as now, she felt, among other, more complex feelings, a fool for not having noticed anything sooner. She was pulled up short once again, by the recognition that she could not take anything for granted. Many things, she reflected sadly, are not as they seem. How blindly we muddle on, always negotiating with circumstances for something we can be content with in our lives. The only person you ever really knew, and only then if you were unusually brave and lucky, was yourself. She felt depressed and profoundly alone. She thought of all the people around her, all those she had contact with in daily life. Astrid, Mrs Dimmock at the paper shop, the Patels who ran the late shop. Margaret, Steve, Dr Bulgy, all the other staff at the hospital. Josh, Maggie, her mother and her chronically blocked drains. Perhaps they were all secretly enacting fantasies that satisfied part of themselves, whether it was some sexual quirk, or a desire to play rugby for England, or simply, in the case of her mother, to be young, clear-headed and slim again. Perhaps the only difference between those who were patients at the hospital and those who walked the streets, supposedly 'normal', was their ability to distinguish between fantasy and reality. Maggie, with her fantasy of being arty and in-tellectual – different – always chasing after the image of an ideal that existed only in her head, when what she was really good at was being a healthy, devious young animal with the sexual magnetism of a bitch on heat. For the first time ever she actually felt a little sorry for Maggie. Whatever she had found on her travels and in all her sexual escapades and dramas, it was not happiness. Perhaps Kate and Janice, in the unlikely shape of each other, had found exactly that. They were negotiating their own happiness. Jenny almost envied them. They were so together, they were like two images of the same person, superimposed one on top of the other to form a complete three-dimensional picture of a whole person. They had found something together, a private something from which the whole outside world was excluded. Yes, she did envy them at that moment.

After Jenny had made her tactful exit, Kate and Janice held on to each other in a long, silent embrace. Janice's face was buried in Kate's neck. Kate wanted to look into her eyes, to see what she could read there, to understand. Perhaps she had made a mistake in coming. She had stood at the corner of the street for long enough, thinking about it. She thought that the long hug told her what she needed to know. Janice's fingers were digging uncomfortably into the flesh on her back. She took that as a good sign. But she needed to be sure. Eventually she tilted Janice's face up gently so that they were looking intently at each other again, their faces only inches apart.

'You've come back, you've come back,' said Janice. 'I can't believe you've come back.'

'Yep,' said Kate, awkwardly brisk. 'It's me all right. You didn't think I'd leave you to cope with your troubles on your own, did you? As soon as I knew – you know, about your mother – I came.' Then, in case this sounded too dramatic, as if her visit were prompted only by pity for a friend in distress, she added, 'I'd have come anyway, only – I didn't know – I mean, you know – ' For once it was she who could not find the right words to express herself.

'I – didn't know what to think,' faltered Janice. 'It was all so – weird. Like a dream. I didn't know anything any more. I feel as if I've been – stranded in the desert.' Suddenly she was fluent, words rushed freely from her as her feelings, dammed up for so long, flooded out.

When the wave of her own shock had broken over her and she had given them sufficient time to do whatever it was they wanted to do, Jenny went back downstairs. The two of them were in the kitchen, one dark head bent close to the other, as they chatted and laughed. There was a real sense of merriment and fun in the house suddenly, as if someone had switched an extra light on, a magic light that brought out the brilliant colours of everything. This wasn't just foreplay without the sex. Jenny felt ashamed at even thinking that it might be. This was a real togetherness, real sharing, a genuine understanding and giving. Maybe, she began to have a glimmering understanding, maybe it is the person, not what sex they are, that matters. It doesn't really matter what you call it, she thought, love is a brave thing, it puts you out on a limb and there are many ways of loving.

'I'm just making Kate something to eat,' Janice explained rather over-fussily, it seemed to Jenny. She felt like a mother when her

144

teenage daughter brings the first unprepossessing boyfriend home for tea.

'You do what you like,' she said breezily, 'you do live here.'

Janice paused, awkwardly, her hands slightly raised as if she was about to introduce them.

'Yes, we do already know each other,' Jenny pre-empted her. She shook Kate's hand in mock formality. 'Pleased to meet you. Looks like I'm your future mother-in-law.'

What am I saying? Shut up, you fool. Embarrassment is making you say even more asinine things than usual. The other two laughed in delight, as they seemed to be doing about everything. Jenny looked from one to the other, their smiles, their shining eyes. 'Don't let her buy any bleach,' she told Kate. 'And get her to put some hand cream on those hands.'

'I don't think I'll need to, now, somehow,' Janice said. Then she looked at Jenny gratefully. 'Thanks for understanding,' she said.

Jenny smiled. I'm not sure I do, though maybe I'm learning, she thought, but really, what does it matter?

The funeral was a sad, reluctant affair as these things always are, the chill February drizzle a reminder of the chill that had set into her mother's bones and heavy, hardened flesh. Janice was familiar with bodies, dead and dying, but she couldn't believe that the actual body, the living flesh that she had come from – the body that, no matter what had come after, had grown her, nourished her, protected her, and pushed her out with pain and blood and crying into the world – was a lump of greying meat in that wooden box. The clean newness of the coffin seemed grotesque in view of its contents. It was surprisingly small, almost like that of a child. Our parents are the buffers between us and death, she thought. When they die it is we, until now the younger generation, who are suddenly the buffers, now we are the ones who are left, marching next in line towards death. She glanced at Kate, inexpressibly glad that she had come. She looked solemn and smart in a well-cut black suit. She had never seen Kate dressed smartly before and the effect was magnetic. She inspired confidence. Janice wondered what Kate was thinking as she held a large black umbrella over them both. The formidable blackness of the massive Victorian chapel reared menacingly over the few bedraggled mourners as the minister spoke small, shrunken words over the gaping hole, a hopelessly inadequate attempt to confront the enormity of death. There was no love in that death, no reassurance of an afterlife as they peered in turn over the edge to drop a few flowers, already withering in the cold damp air, onto the coffin. They were each peering over the precipice to catch a glimpse of their own death.

Reg was there, smart in a black suit, which strained slightly across the front and had shiny patches on the cuffs and lapels. Irene's ironing, presumably, thought Janice. It seemed more natural now to refer to her mother by her first name. She had not been a mother, Janice felt, in any sense that the word conveyed, for a long time. Reg's ginger hair was slicked back, fifties-style. He had a plumpish girl with him, thirty-something but trying to look younger, in a very tight black mini dress, more suitable for a disco than a funeral. She had the same gingerish hair, only fluffed out and back combed in a rakish mop. Her lipstick was like a gash in her face and her tights made her legs look like raw sausages, her face the colour of a corpse. So Reg had a daughter too. My stepsister, Janice thought strangely. Thank goodness we never met. Cathy and Frank were there, the only ones she recognised among the dozen or so figures with bowed heads at the graveside. The others looked as though they were mostly a contingent from the Legion, who attended every death of one of their members. One woman was wearing a hat with an untidy bunch of speckled feathers on the front. Kate peered closer and was surprised to see that it was a dead starling, its eyes all sunken and closed as if a cat had just caught it that morning. She hoped it was stuffed, and not quite as fresh as it looked. Janice looked round at them all, dressed in their funereal best, all thinking no doubt, about their own death, or the last funeral they attended, or what would be on offer at the funeral tea. Even one or two, perhaps, thinking that however much you disliked someone in life, you cannot speak ill of the dead. So this is how it all ends, she thought. In a windswept graveyard on a scrubby hillside, where only a handful of people know you and only one or two of those have ever really cared, under the shadow of an ugly, pompous, architectural monstrosity, a symbol of man's massive self-regard. What an indictment on a life. She shivered, and Kate put her arm around her shoulders and squeezed. That moment was the best part of the miserable day.

Reg came up as they were leaving the chapel. The daughter, it turned out, was called Lavinia. A combination of extreme hunger and a glimpse of black stocking-top, peeping out from beneath the minuscule skirt, gave Janice a bizarre feeling that nothing was real. Lavinia, unlike Reg, spoke with a far back, plummy accent and said she was an actress. And I'm Mother Theresa, thought Kate.

'I would ask you back,' began Reg, 'but after last time . . . ' he trailed off.

Well, it should be peaceful enough this time, now my mother's not here, thought Janice.

'As a matter of fact,' he continued, reddening, 'I think you having a go at her like that didn't help her heart. She had high blood pressure as it was, and – well, you turning up out of the blue and going for 'er like you did, it didn't help her nerves. You could 'ave made more effort to get on with her. She's been through a lot, you know.' He spoke as if she were still there, listening from another room. Perhaps in a sense she was, thought Janice. But that was just a fanciful idea. She tried to feel an awareness of her mother, tried to conjure up her spirit as Reg was speaking. But she could not. She felt the blood rising in her own face. How dare this – this smelly, greasy man, this – how *dare* he imply that she had anything to do with her mother's death. She would have slapped him if it hadn't meant touching that pitted, shiny complexion. Kate was with her, watching her, Kate's own natural stillness giving Janice the strength to stay calm. She was part of something now that Reg, even in a million lifetimes, would never understand. She took a deep breath and spoke in her nursey voice. 'I think forty cigarettes a day for thirty years had more to do with it, don't you? With high blood pressure she could have gone at any time.'

Her words were icy, sharp little splinters of sound. Reg shrank visibly. 'I'm not saying nothing,' he back-tracked rapidly. 'You're welcome to come back for a bit of spam and beetroot. Lavinia's got some sherry in.'

'Very kind of you,' put in Kate quickly, 'but we really have to get back.'

Janice sighed. 'Look, Reg, I don't want to part on bad terms. I know you loved my mother and it's very hard for you now, and I'm sorry. But I've known my mother a lot longer than you, and maybe there are some things about her that I understand, that have nothing to do with your life with her.' She realised suddenly that she, too, was speaking in the present tense as if Irene were still alive. 'I'm glad you made her happy, Reg. I will probably never see you again. I just hope you get on better with your own daughter than she and I did. I hope you can show some – understanding.'

They both looked across at Lavinia, who was sidling up to the minister, a youngish bearded man, totally inept at deflecting her feminine wiles. The sausagey legs with the tight skirt stretched over them were well in evidence. You'd think she'd get chapped legs in this weather, thought Janice as they watched her preparing to envelope the minister like a huge amoeba.

Jenny and Sanjay were lying entwined on the bed. She was gazing up at the gold stars on the ceiling, her mind drifting among them. She felt a cold, sad shiver of something not quite glimpsed. Something had flitted through her mind like the silver flick of a fish in murky water, so brief that she was not sure if it had been anything at all. She came quickly back down from the stars on the ceiling and turned lazily towards Sanjay. 'Will your parents make you have an arranged marriage?'

'What?' Sanjay looked up startled from the piece of thigh he was nibbling.

'An arranged marriage. Will you have to have one?'

Sanjay's eyes were muddy with lust, he did not immediately focus on what she was saying. Why was it not enough to bask in the warmth of each other's bodies, float on a tide of pleasant sensations? Why did she always want to talk? He gave her a long kiss to shut her up in the best way he knew. She giggled with pleasure, surprising him as she often did with the girlishness of her responses. If he shut his eyes she could be eighteen. He began to make love to her with absorption. But later she broached it again.

'How come a lovely, attractive, wealthy young man like you

148

hasn't been married off to a fine young woman from a good family?'

He felt she was mocking him, ridiculing his culture. His pride rose in him. 'As a matter of fact, there is someone lined up for me. I don't know if I want to marry her, though. But she is very beautiful. And clever.'

'Oh, who?' asked Jenny delightedly. She was surprised and pleased to find she did not feel a shred of jealousy. Sanjay had always been on loan, a special treat. It was in the order of things that he should marry a beautiful girl of his own background.

He made a decision. He would be as truthful as he could, without risking losing Jenny. She had taught him so much – they shared an intimate world, a bubble of privacy and pleasure where anything was possible. It was not just Jenny that he did not want to lose, it was the person he became when he was with her. For that version of himself only existed when Jenny brought it out. She created him, made him complete – a proper, primitive man. She unlocked him, and he did not want to have the door clanged shut again, the key thrown away.

'She is called Nita. Nita Patel.' He used Nita's maiden name. He tried to describe her, but the words at his disposal could not convey the elusive essence of her. He could not bring her to life, here in this room with Jenny. It felt strange, this meeting of his two worlds, trying to describe his wife to his lover. He felt he was betraying them both, without either of them knowing.

'And how do you feel about her?' Jenny asked.

Sanjay exhaled slowly. How *did* he feel about her? How did he feel about anything? He was not used to thinking like this, no one had ever asked him this kind of question.

'Well – ' How do you describe someone you are so used to that they feel like part of yourself? How can your own eye see itself? 'She's just – I don't know. She is small – petite, I suppose you would say – stern, serious. She frightens me a bit, she's clever with words and she can fly into a temper sometimes. I never know what to say, so usually I say nothing and just wait until it passes. I'm not sure if she likes me, she never shows it, but – ' He was stuck. He just could not go on.

'But what?' Jenny prompted him gently. This was obviously

difficult for him, his words were coming out stilted and faltering. She had stumbled on something. Something about Nita's flaring into a temper did not quite fit. It did not seem quite right for a betrothed couple. Displays of temper usually came after the wedding, not before. She was intrigued as to what it was he could not say. He rolled abruptly off the bed and started pulling on his clothes. This was a bit drastic. She had touched a raw nerve.

'Sanjay –' she tried to touch his hand, but he pulled away. She felt rejected, old. He had never been like this before. At the door he turned. He was scowling like a hurt boy who will not cry. Really, he was pathetic sometimes.

'I don't think I will come any more,' he said, sounding lordly and dismissive. Jenny was astounded. Five minutes ago they had been making love with gentle tenderness. Suddenly the mood had changed. He was the haughty prince with the ranks of his ancestors massed behind him, she the ageing concubine. She leaped up and stood tall, her creamy nakedness giving her a vulnerable dignity. He wanted to rush to her and hold her, squeeze his hands into the soft flesh on her ribs.

'You don't think you will come any more, do you? I see. Leave the money on the table as you leave, then. Is that how it is?' She was breathing heavily, angrily.

'Don't be cheap and ridiculous.'

But something shameful crossed his face as he spoke. Something guilty and revealing. She pulled on a shirt and her voice went quiet with the chill of realisation. 'So that's it. I was right.'

He darted her a look, with the white rolling eyes of a dog.

'You're already married. That's it, I am right, aren't I?'

He nodded.

'How long?'

'Three years.'

'Happily?'

'No.'

His vehemence stopped her. She went slowly towards him. 'I don't believe you.'

His eyes were wide, alarmed – he hated it when women got angry with him. It had not happened often enough for him to handle it smoothly or let it go over his head, as more hardened miscreants might do. She took his silence to be further evidence that he was lying.

'You lying, cheating, slimy piece of – of *stinking, rotting dog meat.*' Her face seemed to have flattened like a cat with its ears back. He backed away from her and knocked an open bottle of body lotion over, so that the pink cream flowed out into a large blob on the carpet. He trod in it with his sock. 'What's this been for you? You just wanted a quick, easy, convenient screw, didn't you?' she hissed. 'A nice, convenient "fancy woman", isn't that the term? Someone to teach you how to do it. God knows you didn't have a fucking clue to start with.' Get him where it will hurt him, make him feel something, get a reaction. God I'm being horrible, she thought, looking down on herself from above, as if watching a play from the lighting platform. I'm being a horrible, jealous cow. So let me give him some more. He deserves it. He has deceived and humiliated me. She picked up a copy of *Yoga Weekly* and started batting him about the head with it. He ducked and dodged, putting his hands up to shield himself. 'How's *that* then, slime ball?' she growled, smacking the rolled-up magazine harder on his head, then jabbing him in the stomach with it like a sword. He twitched and dodged, trying to escape the blows. 'Or *that*?' as she poked him in the groin with it. He stepped backwards again and bumped his head on the edge of the open door. Still she thwacked and bashed at him, driving him further and further back.

'That's it,' she snarled as he turned to make his escape, 'Piss off now, shit, while you can still walk,' and with a mighty shove she sent him headlong down the hallway so that he stumbled against the front door. He brushed himself down and straightened his tie in an effort to regain some composure before opening the door. He did not want anyone to witness such an ignominious exit. As he bent to tie his shoelaces a pile of dirty washing landed on his head and he stood up with a pair of last week's knickers hooked over one ear. He just managed to dodge a flying container of talcum powder as he fiddled with the catch, and a heavy pot of cold cream caught him neatly on the temple as he darted out. Perhaps not surprisingly, he left without saying goodbye.

★

'I wish we could have a dog. A Labrador.'

Jenny looked at her son. Perhaps this preoccupation with a pet was a sign that she wasn't giving him enough love. She gave herself a few lashes of guilt and resolved to hug him more often.

'We haven't got room for a dog. They need endless walking. And we can't afford to feed one. I couldn't be doing with it, all that pooing in the back yard.'

'Can't you get ones that don't poo?'

Jenny laughed. 'Unfortunately not.'

Josh adjusted his sights. 'What about a gerbil, then?'

'Too like a rat. Horrible, ratty tails.'

'That's a good idea – a white rat. I could take it to school in my pocket.'

'You'll do no such thing. Anyway, who's going to clean out the cage of this possible pet, and feed it? They need a lot of looking after, you know. It's a commitment – you can't just not do it because you don't feel like it that day. And you certainly couldn't leave it to me, I've got more than enough to do.'

'I'll do it. I promise.'

'Even on rugby days? On cricket days? On days when you stay with James?'

Josh thought for a moment. 'Well then, what about a goldfish?'

Jenny was driving home from work the first week in March. She had not heard from Sanjay since that last lunchtime, five weeks ago, which was not entirely unexpected. It was just another messy, inadequate ending. The first chafing winds of spring were whipping through the streets like a pack of invisible dogs, racing for their lives. A few grimy snowdrops struggled for survival in the park. Pedestrians had the grey, flaky look of the deadened end of winter before the sap begins to rise. It was only six weeks to Easter, which was in mid-April this year, when Henry would be home. She had not heard from him for over a month now. She thought that he had probably only bothered to keep in touch until then because he had not yet made any new friends. Now that he was having a sociable time in Illinois, doubtless the wish to maintain any sort of friendship had ebbed away. With sadness, she reflected that with everything new and interesting around him to stimulate his senses he had probably forgotten all about her and grey, dreary Britain. She never really believed those people who claimed to have been in love, but were now just good friends. Perhaps they stayed 'friends' to assuage some sort of guilt, or because secretly they were hoping for another chance. Perhaps they desperately needed to be liked by everyone, even those they have hurt, or who have hurt them. You could only be friends if your heart was not raw with aching loss, and if you were not full of pain at losing someone, how could you say you had loved them? 'Just good friends' was for the cool-hearted, those who pride themselves on being civilised. It was not in Jenny's nature to be cool-hearted or civilised. Perhaps it was just as well that Henry had stopped writing.

As she drove the car and listened to the radio, she realised she was starving hungry. She had been feeling queasy for the last few days. She pulled in at the corner shop and as Mrs Patel greeted her with a smile, she considered asking if she was any relation to Nita Patel – now Nita Baljekar. She might even bump into her here without realising it, she thought, if Nita came to visit her relatives. Perhaps Jenny had even met her already, helping out behind the counter. That was a strange and horrible thought. There was a pleasant girl here on Saturdays, perhaps it was her. But then Jenny told herself that she was getting carried away. After all, Patel was a very common name. Her eyes raked the shelves hungrily. There, that was exactly what she needed – a jar of pickled gherkins. She knew instinctively that they, and only they, would quell this hungry, sickly feeling. It was only when she was eating the sixth gherkin in the car outside the shop, that the implication struck her.

She was pregnant. A test the next day confirmed it. With this positive result the world as she knew it came tumbling round her ears. Her mind went racing back over every time with Sanjay. She knew the exact occasion – it would be branded in her memory for the rest of her life. She had a strange feeling at the time, but in retrospect she had put it down to some sort of premonition that he was married. Now she knew it had been a premonition of a more important nature. She could recall the moment, the strange, suspended second up among the golden stars, when something had changed inside her and this life had begun. There was only one thing to do.

CHAPTER 8

Dear Jenny
Char research looking good.
Illinois still great. Body and
soul being catered for!
Henry.

A picture of some sort of military plane – the pointy sort that take off vertically from aircraft carriers. Jenny didn't even have the heart to read the small writing to see what type it was. She simply put it aside with the red telephone bill, to be given attention later. Not even a 'Regards' this time, or a single, solitary, measly kiss. Oh Henry, she thought, where are you? I've lost you. You've really gone now. I can't even reach you in my head any more.

The GP was a desiccated man with rimless spectacles. He exuded stale pipe tobacco and a jaundiced view of humanity. Jenny felt like a victim, perched awkwardly on the edge of the padded chair – his concession to the notion that the patient should be treated as a fellow, though not an equal, human being. He himself sat in a large, leather-buttoned affair and pressed the tips of his fingers together. But she was determined not to behave as a victim. She told him why she had come. With the experience of many years and a diverse knowledge of human strangeness, he showed no reaction when she told him she was pregnant. He always waited for the patient to go on before he showed congratulations or commiseration. In fact, he felt neither. His medical training just after the Second World War had consisted of a process whereby his feelings had been surgically removed without anaesthetic. He had a certificate on the wall proclaiming his achievement in the study of a hundred stomachectomies between 1945 and 1947. But patients always expected you to show a reaction, so you gave them what they wanted. Commiseration, clearly, in this case was required. Of course a termination could be arranged. If she could pay for it privately, which he strongly recommended, he could telephone to arrange it here and now. She baulked slightly. It was a bit quick, she hadn't really had time to take it in. But yes, she could pay for it, and she wanted it as soon as possible. The quicker the better, she said, wincing at the neatness of the words. Naturally, he assured her, he would be able to tick all three boxes on the form saying that a termination would be in the best interests of the mother, the unborn child, and the existing children. Are there any existing children? he asked, not having had time to look at the notes. They would be computerised soon, he wasn't relishing the upheaval, he'd managed perfectly well for forty years, but he would be retiring in July anyway, so it wouldn't matter to him. The junior partners were clashing antlers in a struggle for dominance. He had said at the time that they shouldn't have taken on that pushy little new man, he was a bit too clever by half, but he himself was old and on the way out, and nobody listened to his opinions. He would be glad to be out of it to concentrate on his golf and prize fuchsias.

With an effort he tuned in again to this woman who was talking to him. She told him about Josh (what sort of name was that, he wondered. They went in for such weird and wonderful ones these days) and explained a little of her circumstances – as little as she felt she could reasonably get away with. He glanced surreptitiously at his watch. If he got rid of this one quickly, he would have time to squeeze in a coffee before his home visits. But then he'd only need to use the lavatory at a patient's house. Thankfully this woman didn't appear to be upset. He hardly ever saw anyone for this sort of thing nowadays, they all went to the younger doctors. He got the arthritics and elderly depressives who have been on sleeping tablets for twenty years and wonder why they no longer have any effect. He picked up the phone. As he dialled the number of the private clinic he heard her say she was an occupational therapist. Really, he thought, he had no time for these people who could not run their own lives, let alone give advice on anyone else's. People like her, in the medical field – albeit not in the mainstream, but rather in the backwater of basket-work therapy, a notion he had no truck with – ought to know better.

The unborn child. His use of that phrase had hurt. He had used it quite unthinkingly, automatically, but Jenny wished he could have said 'foetus' or 'embryo'. That was what it was, after all, just a collection of cells, dividing and dividing as cells are programmed to do. It was no different from having your appendix out. But an unborn child was different, Jenny thought. An unborn child is alive. She would not judge anyone else for thinking differently, but she, Jenny, felt deep inside her that this was true. This unborn child, this brother or sister for Josh, this brown-skinned child, was due to be born in the autumn. But she couldn't afford to think like this, she *had* to shut it out. It was an emotional indulgence. She had to have this bunch of cells, this growth, this product of an accident, removed. And that was what she was going to do, on Tuesday 17 March. It was a suitably dull, anonymous date in ten days' time. Nothing ominous-sounding, like the Ides of March. Just an ordinary, dull day, no different from any other. She had never liked the sound of the word Tuesday, for some reason. It smacked of duty, dreariness, of being sensible. Last weekend has disappeared, the next one with its promised pleasures is still far away, and Tuesday is stuck there, not quite in the middle, grey-suited and drab. It was her least favourite day of the week. At least Wednesday is more than halfway through. They might even be able to call her earlier, the doctor had said, if they had a cancellation. It was so early on, he said, she would hardly notice it. He knew, did he? Been through it himself, had he? It will be just like a period afterwards, he told her. So you know all about those too, do you, Doctor? You do surprise me, she thought.

Jenny was desperately isolated, locked in alone inside her prison cell of stress. Henry's last postcard had just aggravated her still further. *Body and soul being catered for* – that could only mean one thing. She had obviously interpreted his previous card correctly, the one with the tall skyscraper. The bastard. Still, naturally he would want a girlfriend after all those months in the ice. There were some needs even the biggest and best Arctic Char could not satisfy.

Although she had booked the date at the hospital, she was still, as the days trickled inexorably away – just as the blood would afterwards, the life blood of her baby – she was still in an agony of indecision. She tried to picture the future, both with and without the baby, in an effort to help herself decide. Without was easier of course, it would be much the same as now. Living alone with Josh to look after and work to occupy her and mark the days, punctuated by holidays, Christmas, Josh's birthdays, visits to her mother, the occasional fleeting love affair, only those would be even fewer and farther between from now on. She could picture that life all too easily; it was what she had known for the years before Henry had come along. She did not know what to do about Sanjay. Perhaps she should tell him, but then he had disappeared before this current predicament, and she knew that this was her problem to be shouldered alone. A married boyfriend ten years younger than herself, who had vanished from the scene even before the pregnancy had made itself known. Really Jenny Burdge, she told herself, how could you be so *insanely, incredibly* stupid.

Suddenly, irrationally and belatedly, since it had already happened, she had a terrible fear of being abandoned. Usually quick to cast off any relationship that was hitting a rough patch or looked as if it was getting messy, she now longed for security, for the comfort of knowing you are loved, for the snug, safe togetherness of cuddling up to the same familiar back each night. It must be her hormones that were giving her this terrible yearning. A mortage, a nine-year-old son, and a string of disappearing men. She had made the right decision, there was no choice. And yet . . .

A delicate, black-eyed, fine-boned girl playing in a garden (not this scrap of yard filled with rubble), all enthusiasm and small huffs. Dark, shiny hair, heavy and straight. Josh would adore her – or perhaps he would be hatefully jealous, try to poke her when Jenny wasn't looking. It wouldn't be kind to Josh, he had had her to himself for far too long. He would feel pushed out, rejected, and he'd had enough of that with his father disappearing. She and Josh were a team, they understood each other. They were always there for each other. They went back a long way. All the way, of course, for Josh. Then there was the practical consideration of money. She could barely keep the house going as it was, and certainly could not do so without Janice's contribution. And Janice might not be around for much longer; already she spent a lot of time at Kate's. All those broken nights, she would not be able to function at work. But then, other people did it and managed pretty well, and even if it is a struggle for the first few years, that's only a relatively short time to get through, compared to a lifetime . . . Right until the day she was due to go in, she did not know what she was going to do.

When Janice was on early shifts, Kate often came home to find the tempting smell of dinner wafting through the flat. Washing would be neatly arranged along the radiator to dry, the breakfast things would be clean and put away.

'You don't need to do this, you know,' she would say, coming up behind Janice at the sink and kissing her neck, slipping her hands round the small breasts, enjoying the clean, now familiar smell of soap and lemon shampoo.

'I know,' Janice would say. 'I just want to.'

Kate liked this atmosphere of domestic cosiness and harmony. Janice seemed happy to cast herself in the role of housewife, and this put Kate in the dominant position of the main worker (although Janice worked just as many hours, and probably harder, but many of those hours were during the nights, and she did not seem to need a lot of sleep.) This gave Kate the feeling of power and control that she supposed most men must have when they have a home-making wife. No wonder they are so loath to give it up, she reflected as she watched Janice stacking up a pile of newly ironed clothes.

Janice still lived officially at Jenny's and spent two or three nights a week at Kate's. When she was there, Kate noticed that there was no housework left to be done. No piles of dirty washing or old magazines were allowed to sprout in corners as they used to, there was never the sour smell of a rubbish bag that needed taking out. It was curiously restful. She frequently offered to do her share, but Janice would not let her. She genuinely seemed to get pleasure from housework. It was almost as though she needed it. So, sensing that this was conveniently the case, Kate let her get on with it.

'Wouldn't you like to – be here all the time?' she asked one evening over supper. They drank a considerable amount of wine, so most evenings had a rosy glow over them. Janice looked up. The skin on her hands was healed now, and her cheeks had a touch of colour in them. She was silent for a minute, her eyes bright.

'You do want to, don't you?' Kate felt a moment's doubt. 'Because I want you to. I want us to be – a proper couple. To share everything, to be together all the time.'

A few weeks ago this would have sounded rather a tall order, a remote dream on the horizon, but now, after such a short time, it seemed to her the most easily attainable thing in the world. Stability, security, were things she had only ever known when she was alone. She had shared plenty of other things with different people, like excitement, variety, laughs, lust, but never, even with Nita, had she felt this strong conviction of being on solid ground. This was not the grand passion of her life, this was not fireworks and the vigorous, exhausting drama of constant jealous rows and falling out, then passionate making up and vowing that it will not happen again. She had known all that before, once long ago. This was just – real, solid, relaxed contentment, where the practicalities of life provide the stepping stones towards greater understanding, and shared experience builds the bond of love. Where mundane tasks, such as going to the supermarket together, planning meals and outings, had pleasure in them because you were doing them together, and for each other. This was two people, predisposed to please each other, involved in total, mutual giving and sharing. This may not be the grand passion, but it was, Kate knew, the enduring one.

Janice was naturally quiet and gentle, generally happy to go along with what somebody else wanted, having no pressing alternative of her own. They communicated just enough, Kate thought – not constantly, intensely, often painfully, as lovers sometimes do – but just enough. Paradoxically, although they did almost everything except work together – although they were so close that she could now hardly perceive Janice as a separate entity, so bound up with her was she – she had more space and privacy in her own head than she had ever known in a relationship before. Janice did not keep asking her what she was thinking, wondering if she was feeling all right, as Nita had done. Janice had a child's lack of surprise, a willingness to accept anything new, whatever came along. It was as if she had put her hand unquestioningly in Kate's and was happy to fit in with whatever was going to happen. It was close to what Kate imagined a marriage between a Western man and an Oriental woman to be. Sometimes this lack of a strong will of her own in Janice exasperated Kate, she sometimes offered her a choice and longed for her to have a strong preference for one alternative or another, even if it was only for semi-skimmed milk instead of skimmed. But on the whole, like many men who have accommodating women, she grew to like it, and enjoyed the restful lack of conflict it produced. But now, at this moment, she needed a strong statement of preference. She had asked Janice to make a choice.

'Well, I'd be letting Jenny down, I've been her lodger for a long time now. She's been good to me, we've had some good times.'

'She can find another lodger. She'll understand. She's probably expecting it. I'll speak to her if you like.'

Janice lifted her glass, studied the light shining through the red liquid, and hesitated.

'Look,' said Kate. 'It's simple. Forget the practicalities, we can sort them out. You've already paid your rent until the end of the month. That will do instead of notice. It couldn't be simpler. Do you want to live with me, or not?'

'Do you want me to?'

'Don't be so bloody stupid, of course I do. I wouldn't be asking you otherwise, would I?' Her tone was rough but affectionate. Janice looked hard at her for a minute, thinking.

'I'll tell her.'

'Fine. Whatever you like.'

'What if she's angry? What if she says I'm letting her down?'

'Well, you're not. She's not your mother, you don't owe her anything, she's a friend. She'll understand. She probably assumes you'll be moving in with me. And anyway, who cares? We don't have to answer to anyone, we please ourselves. We just want to be together, don't we? What more is there to it than that?'

Janice still hesitated. 'I feel – embarrassed.'

'What for? Nobody's out there looking at you. Just live the life you want to. You do want to, don't you?' Kate asked again.

Janice smiled. 'Of course I do,' she said. 'I just find happiness rather a difficult habit. Haven't had enough of it to practise, I suppose. Or having what I want. This definitely *is* what I want,' she reassured her. 'I'm just not used to it.'

Kate reached across the table and enclosed Janice's hand in hers. 'Well, you'd better get used to it,' she said firmly, 'because it's here to stay. And so are you.'

Janice told Jenny the following evening. It was the Thursday before the hospital appointment.

'I've got some news,' she began, with suppressed pleasure. It felt bizarre, like announcing an engagement, only not.

'So have I,' Jenny stated bleakly.

'You first,' Janice egged her on, wanting to make maximum impact herself. Jenny would be so pleased for her she had finally managed to find something good, and had the courage to go for it. Jenny liked that kind of thing in people. She looked so unbearably smug and coy that Jenny said, 'No, you first. I can see you're bursting with it. Mine can wait. I insist.'

Janice told her. She waited for expressions, if not of congratulation, at least of good wishes. None came. Jenny just heaved a sigh.

'Well, at least you won't be hanging around here like a lovesick cow any more. To be quite honest, it was embarrassing. When Kate was here I felt like a gooseberry. It seemed so ridiculous, I didn't know what to say. All that fooling around, endlessly laughing over nothing. It was sickening. At least you'll be fooling around somewhere else from now on.'

Janice was offended. 'I thought you'd be pleased. You could at least have pretended.'

'Why? Pleased because I've got to find a new lodger, or sell the house? Pleased to see two of my friends come out of the wardrobe or whatever, and "declare their sexuality"? Pleased because you're happy and in love, and you want to tell the world? Been there, sorry, got the T-shirt. And the scars, as a matter of fact. Pleased because I'm pregnant?'

She sat down hard and began to cry. Janice put her arm round her heaving shoulders. 'God, I'm sorry, I've been so selfish and thoughtless. I never even thought. I haven't even noticed what's been going on with you. I've been so preoccupied, what with Mum dying and Kate coming back, trying to work out what I wanted – who I am – I haven't known whether I'm coming or going, things have been changing so fast. We haven't had a proper conversation for weeks, have we? I'm really sorry.' The truth of the situation sank in. 'Oh my God, how awful, that's terrible.'

'Thanks a lot, that's a bloody lot of help. I'm sorry, I shouldn't burden you with this. I'm happy for you, honestly, I really am. Part of me almost envies you. Not that I fancy women at all,' she added hastily. 'At least you'll never get pregnant by accident,' she laughed through gusty sobs. 'It was the last time. I was really careful up to then. It makes me sick. The last bloody time. People take stupid risks every day and get away with it, I take one small one and this has to happen to me. Oh Jan,' she pleaded hopelessly. 'What am I going to do?'

Janice took charge straight away. 'You're going to keep that appointment,' she told her. 'It's the only sensible thing to do, you've got more than enough on your plate already. I'll find you another lodger, there's bound to be someone at the hospital needing accommodation, they are always desperate to get out of the nurses' home. But I won't go until we find one, I'll tell Kate I can't go yet. I'll look after Josh, get him his tea and what have you, and I'll come and pick you up from the hospital. Where are you going, St Margaret's?' Jenny shook her head, and named the private clinic thirty miles away.

'No problem,' Janice said, 'I'll be there.'

And she was. When Jenny emerged into the windy car park, the small blue Fiesta was there like a glossy-backed insect at the kerb, waiting to fly her away. If only she could, Jenny thought as she lowered herself into the car. She sat down carefully. Janice peered at her. 'You look fine,' she said, although Jenny did look very pale. 'How are you feeling?'

Jenny smiled at her as the car turned and Janice put some music on loud.

'I'm absolutely fine,' she shouted above the din, which was presumably an effort to distract her from the pain. 'I didn't let them do it.'

'What?' Janice shouted. Jenny turned the music off. In the resounding silence that followed, she repeated, 'I didn't let them do it. I'm keeping the baby. My child's coming home with me. She's still safe.' Then she howled out loud all the way home, while Janice drove on, unable to say anything.

'What made you change your mind?' she asked her later. Jenny shrugged. 'Intuition, gut feeling, whatever you want to call it. I just couldn't go through with it. It didn't feel right. I just knew I was doing the wrong thing.' She laughed. 'If only that instinct worked more often. Also, it was the thought of some cold, sharp metal instrument poking about inside me, gouging stuff out. I just couldn't stand it. Revolting and – wrong for me. I'm not squeamish, I just don't want anything fiddling about in there.' She patted her stomach protectively and looked at Janice's doubtful face. 'I know all the problems are still there, it will be a shock for Josh, I'll be desperately short of money; but I've got seven months to sort all that out. Now,' she said, starting to bustle round tidying up the kitchen. 'It's getting late, you get off to your lady friend. You've been great today, thanks a lot.'

When Janice had gone Jenny went upstairs and pushed Josh's door ajar. He had kicked the covers off and was lying spread-eagled across the bed, sleeping the even sleep of the innocent. She tucked the covers in again and kissed him gently on the forehead. He smacked his lips in his sleep, as though he was tasting something delicious. She looked out of his window onto the backs of the terraced houses for a while. The orange sky, marked by the dots of red and green of a small plane moving silently across it, the cramped yards and shabby back gates in the brick walls, the occasional shadow moving behind a bathroom blind, all these things steadied her. Life, in its undiscerning, indiscriminate wisdom, embraced all this, and a multitude of other things, of which she could only ever have a glimpse. She watched the black cat she could see weaving its way along the top of a fence, intent on its own purpose. As she watched it pour itself down the side of the wall like thick, dark liquid into the pool of blackness which was the yard beyond, a stooping figure in a pale raincoat came out of Astrid's back door. It picked its way along her path to the back gate and, peering surreptitiously around, let itself out and disappeared into the alley. As it looked right and left before slipping away into the shadows, Jenny recognised the shrivelled features of the rimless doctor.

'How was the meals on wheels?'

Her mother had perked up noticeably in the last few weeks. She had started painting her eyebrows in with a thick, black eye pencil. The effect was a little severe, not to say startling, but Jenny thought it best not to say so.

'Very nice, thank you dear. I've got them coming twice a week now, permanently. Well, 'til Easter, anyhow.' Her mother coloured slightly and looked pleased with herself. Perhaps she had got them to deliver free gin with the dinners.

'You've done your hair differently. It's a different colour.'

This sparked off a tirade against the feckless Sylvia, who, it appeared, had taken it into her much-perfumed and artificially augmented head to retire to the south coast. 'Airs and graces, I call it. 'It be*hoves* me to live in *Hove*.' Where did she get that sort of money, that's what I'd like to know. Not doing hair, that's for sure.'

'I'll pop in on Friday after work.'

Her mother patted her newly browned crowning glory. 'Rich Burgundy', it had said on the bottle. She'd left it on half an hour longer than it said, to get value for money.

'Don't bother, dear, I won't be here. I'm going to my club.'

'What club?'

'Never you mind. I have got a life of my own, you know. Anyhow, I won't be in. So I'll see you next week.'

Jenny left mildly amused. If her mother preferred playing bingo or singing songs with old folks, it was all the same to her. She wondered if it was compulsory suddenly to enjoy community singing after the age of sixty, or whether it just happened to you naturally – you wake up one morning thinking, Oh, I just fancy a good burst of 'You Are My Sunshine' with a bunch of senior citizens today. She certainly did not intend to be doing that herself at sixty-four, but then she was not her mother. It was a good thing that she had a new interest. It might take her mind off her ailments and her drink.

Sanjay had been paralysed for weeks. He was completely at a loss what to do next. Even Moira said he was looking peaky, and recommended some horrible-sounding tonic that she had given to Mr Moira when he had gone down with the flu. Being at a loss was not a feeling with which Sanjay was at all familiar, and he did not like it. He dreamed of Jenny every night, and when he awoke at four in the morning in a raging sweat and tossed uneasily through the long, small hours, it was Jenny who filled his mind. He would throw his weight around the bed, unable to find a position for his limbs to rest where they did not feel cumbersome and uncomfortable. Nita would end up with six inches of cold bed in which to sleep, and a dog end of the duvet. He had let Jenny down. He had betrayed Nita. He had betrayed himself. In short, he had messed everything up. But most of all, he had destroyed his secret world with Jenny – his dream, his private joy. He had walked into a warm room where he had been welcomed in, then through his own crassness, as he saw it, he had wilfully smashed it all up and left, slamming the door behind him. This was the gist of the repellent dream that haunted his sleep and distracted his waking hours.

There were variations on this theme, where he and Jenny were making love and he was ripped away from her by a black and icy wind, his body dragged across the floor and out of the door as if he were nothing but a bunch of rags. Or another time, Jenny would turn away from him as Nita always did, and then she would become Nita, crying and accusing him of stabbing her. He would deny it with horror, but then he would see the black blood oozing from her nightie, the long baggy T-shirt that Nita always wore in bed. He would put his fingers to the wound, a small hole, to try to stop the blood, and it would turn into the ignition on his motor bike, the narrow metal hole where he put the key. He would be flying, tearing along a bleak road, the bike lifting off at every bump, racing for his life, his freedom, willing the bike to take off properly into the air and join the racing clouds. But it never would, for somewhere in the distance, far away, he would hear Jenny calling. In the end he began to wonder if he was going mad.

One night he had even hung about outside the house in Hazel Terrace, hoping to get a glimpse of her. It had not been a great succcess. He had felt pretty stupid when anyone walked past and he had tried to look as if he was waiting for someone. At one point a fat cocker spaniel had almost taken him for a lamp post. The only event of the evening was when the door of the house next to Jenny's was opened and a small man with large, high-heeled cowboy boots on and spectacles as thick as the bottoms of bottles had emerged, and given him a hostile stare before strutting into the shadows.

Nita and he were more distant than ever. He got a twitchy feeling of anxiousness and annoyance whenever they were in a room together, and he felt how far from each other they had become. He wondered if they had ever been close. Thinking about it, he realised he had never been really close to anyone, not even Jenny. The thought depressed him. Nita was sad too, she had a new downward droop to her mouth. He chose to assume it was work, and she chose to let him assume this. She hardly ever talked now, except on the phone to her mother, or one or other of her friends. She seemed to have more friends these days, she was always on the phone, or popping out in the evening with somebody. Nobody in particular, though, no single friend stood out from the others, it was always just 'the gang'. Sanjay never established who 'the gang' was, but they seemed to be a bunch of the sort of women she met through work, the sort of women he instinctively did not like, sensible women, tough-looking some of them, unfeminine women to his conservative eyes. Women with big personalities and sensible shoes who laughed at a lot of 'in' jokes that he was not meant to understand, and that he somehow felt were aimed unkindly at him. He could not see what on earth Nita found interesting about these women. What a lot of unkindness there is in the world, he thought, seeing this for the first time.

And he thought again of Jenny.

He considered talking things over in a man-to-man way with Paul during one of their Friday night drinks, only those had rather gone by the board since Nita had given up going to the refuge. Paul was completely besotted at the moment with some young air-head called Hayley, who was a beautician, and Sanjay was not sure he would get much sense out of him even if he did confide his troubles. Paul would think him a complete idiot for getting himself in such a state – and the thought of appearing an idiot to Paul filled Sanjay with horror. He would have to sort it out himself.

He must go and see Jenny, he decided. He had not been as clever over this business as he could have been – as some other men might have been, he thought. He realised that leading a double life required a degree of deviousness and detachment that he did not possess. He was essentially an open, straightforward character and it always bewildered him when he came across people who were not so. But for the last few months he had been living the life of a cunning plotter, a layer of plans. Much of the time, he now realised, he had simply been in a daze of sexual satisfaction. He had not been thinking clearly – if at all.

In a way he was glad that his being married had come out into the open, although he would not have wished Jenny to have guessed it. He would have preferred to pick the time to tell her himself and to gain the moral high ground. He would have explained the whole situation, the arranged marriage, even the sad little details of his sexual deprivation, and Jenny would have pitied him. He was convinced that she would have understood. It did not occur to him that, if she had not guessed, he would have been unlikely ever to have told her, but would have been content to keep up the lie as long as possible. He still thought of himself as a good man, a man with honour, and although he knew that what he had shared with Jenny had been wrong by his own standards, he could not *feel* that it had been wrong. It had felt as right and natural as the dawn. He needed to see her, to put it all right. He was fairly vague in his mind as to what he meant by putting it right, but he felt that as soon as he saw Jenny, everything would become clear. His path would be laid out for him. It was eating him alive, he had to see her, if only to put an end to unfinished business, he told himself. One more time, he promised himself too, one more time in bed with her in order to say goodbye for good. She would make him feel fine about himself and everything else, as she always did. She would give him the strength to do what he knew was right, and attend to his marriage.

He had no one to confide in, no training to negotiate this assault course that his personal life was turning out to be. None of his expensive education had equipped him for this kind of problem. If only there were just one problem, but there appeared to be dozens, massing up on top of each other like storm clouds, waiting to discharge their menacing load. Everyone was eager enough to see you embark on it, this journey of marriage, but no one would give you a hand if the going got tough along the way. Of course, they told you it would get tough, mentioned it just at the last minute, when it was too late to turn back. They told you that almost with gloating, as if having suffered themselves along the married path they got pleasure from seeing someone else in difficulties, although he had not seen it like that at the time. The comments of his father and uncles, even his mother, had seemed like jokes; he had certainly taken them as such, just part of the general spirit of good humour and festivity that had attended the wedding arrangements. How could anyone not be happy, with a wife as beautiful and obedient as Nita had seemed? There must be something wrong with him, they would say. Was he not a proper man? Everyone had envied him, winning her as his prize. But once you had started, when you had won the competition, taken home your prize and the daily working part began, you were on your own. The illusion of perfect contentment, if illusion it was, must be maintained at all cost. The two of them were trapped, two alien creatures who could not recognise each other, could not even offer each other any sustenance or help, trapped in a cage that was becoming ever more cramped and claustrophobic.

Spring was in the air. Nita decided she must do something to put an end to this wintry existence with Sanjay. The need to act was becoming more and more urgent in her, like an alien, uncomfortable thing swelling inside her, pressing harder and harder against her ribcage, desperate to get out. She had tried to talk things over with him, to tell him how she felt, to try to find out whether their mutual isolation was as unbearable to him as it was to her – for she really could not tell, he seemed so adept at ignoring it that she wondered if he even noticed it at all. But this kind of conversation was a kind they had never learned to have. Communication between them had always been on a practical level, with occasional efforts on his part to be sentimental (as she saw it) that simply irritated her. So now, when they really needed to talk, they could not. Whenever she said, 'Sanjay, I think we need to talk,' he took this as an ominous sign that she had been reading a women's magazine again, with titles on the cover such as, 'When his friends mean more to him than you', and 'Can you trust him? Real women tell', or 'Single Power – why being single is better than ever'. He took this as his cue to disappear to the local shop, or to tinker with his motorbike.

One Saturday morning in March she was scanning the jobs section of the newspaper as usual, more out of habit than anything. One job caught her eye. The job specification fitted her exactly, and it was the natural next step for her, a promotion that would put her in charge of a team. She had known for a while that this was what she wanted, to move up the ladder, to take on new responsibilities and stretch herself. In the absence of some other things in her life, increased job satisfaction and a good salary would, she felt, make up for a lot. She tore out the advertisement and tucked it into her purse. She would apply, and if the job had her name on it, she told herself, she would get it. She did not admit to herself the decision she had already taken on a deeper level – that if she got the job, she would go without Sanjay. There would be time to tackle that if she were actually offered the post. It was in London.

It was not easy for Jenny to find a replacement for Janice. Feeling partly responsible because she had left Jenny in the lurch, Janice paraded a selection of young nurses and nursing students in front of her, hoping each time that Jenny would like the girl, the girl would like Jenny, and the girl would like the house. Each one was unsuitable for different reasons. Josh was getting fed up with it, and the constant presence of strangers in the house poking about and commenting that the bathroom was a bit small was making them irritable. The cat had registered his protest by leaving home. They saw him curling round Astrid's legs and being given chicken skins. 'They're all the same,' she said to Jenny, 'cupboard love, that's all it is.'

'My lodger leaves to live with another woman, my son wants to live with the neighbours up the street, and my cat moves in next door,' said Jenny. 'What am I doing wrong? Was it something I said?'

So one way and another the lodger idea was shelved temporarily. The peace and privacy were definitely worth it, and she would just have to make economies instead. She would be all right for a while, and when things got tight she would have to think again. But for now, solitude was what she needed.

Henry would be home in April if he stuck to his original plans (and he usually did). It would take a pretty amazing and determined woman to deflect him from a chosen course, thought Jenny. It was nine months since he had gone – the irony of it struck her – nine months is all it takes to grow a life, and the baby's was not the only life that had grown in that time. With a mixture of sadness and surprise she realised the unthinkable had happened, and she and Henry had truly lost each other. He might have travelled (or at least flown over) many countries since they had parted, but she had travelled many worlds. She wondered if he would turn up on the doorstep as he had done before.

The memory of that evening still made her cringe, she had so mismanaged it, thanks to Maggie. How pathetically full of self-doubt she had been then. How little it all mattered now. She still missed him, but his loss had become more the dull grieving for a lost ideal than for a real, living, warm-blooded person. She grieved too for the years with him, when everything had appeared simple and straightforward. Now, because she had chosen to have the baby, nothing else was at stake. The primitive dictates of her hormones had been dredged and sifted down through thousands of generations. She realised with the reluctant willingness of all mothers, just how much she was giving up for this child.

It was Monday evening, the supermarket run. The last chill, blustery day of March. Jenny did most of her thinking in the car. As she sat stuck in the traffic jam, alongside the city walls, she noticed that the drifts of daffodils that crowded the grassy banks were all in pale green bud, just starting to change colour. Soon they would be a glorious mass of yellow. The new leaves would soon be bursting from the trees, all crumpled and shiny. The sap was rising as the baby was growing inside her. It was all in the natural order of things. She would manage. Astrid had asked her to get three jars of mussels because she had read an article saying that most British women are short of zinc in their diet. Zinc, apparently, improves your libido, and Astrid was worrying about hers. She had looked a little less perky than usual when she had popped her head in through the back door earlier.

'Don't you mean oysters?' Jenny asked.

'Well, them's got it in too, but mussels is cheaper. In vinegar if you can, I'm not keen on the briny ones.'

It would take a miracle to resuscitate my libido, thought Jenny, it gave up the ghost so long ago, I've forgotten it ever existed. In fact I rather wish it never had, life would certainly be so much simpler. Now I'd much rather have a box of chocolates and a hot water bottle any day of the week.

'Must be the time of year,' Astrid said. 'Spring takes so long to come. Even I gets tired some days, and can hardly be bothered. Not often, though.' It was beyond her understanding that some people managed to live long, fulfilling lives without ever discovering wonderful, exciting passion. To Astrid, lack of passion meant you must be seriously off colour.

'You looks like you could do with a bit of sunshine yourself, get rid of that puffy, pasty look. Can't you find yourself some young man to take you away for a few days? That'd put some colour in your cheeks. Can you get me some of that special chocolate drink they shows on the telly, too? That's supposed to do the same thing.'

Sadly, Jenny reflected that sex and sunshine are not the universal panacea Astrid seemed to believe, and that she herself might have believed they were until a few weeks ago, but she did not have the heart to say so. Still, perhaps in Astrid's line of work losing your libido is like a ventriloquist mislaying his dummy. Jenny promised to get the mussels.

The sky blackened as they trundled slowly through the traffic, and with the capricious vagaries of spring weather, spikes of rain were now slashing across the windscreen. Josh was reading in the back as they waited for the traffic lights. Some woman on the radio was harping on about the effects of travellers on the peaceful life in some Sussex village. Bunch of complacent, rich stockbrokers, she thought, what do they know about life? Their only worry is some hairy recipient of unemployment benefit using their front garden as a lavatory. Not very nice, granted, she thought, but hardly a disaster of life-threatening importance. She felt angry just hearing the woman's blue-rinsed voice. She would have to get a baby seat for the car, she had long since got rid of all Josh's baby paraphernalia. Not that she was counting any chickens, she reminded herself.

'Can we get that new cereal on the adverts, Mum?'

'Mmm. We'll see.'

'James's Mum gets those chocolate ones. Can we have them?'

'Bad for your teeth,' she said automatically.

Jenny thought of Sanjay's wife, the lovely Nita she had unwittingly betrayed, and whom she would never meet. She wondered if Nita had known, as she had known, and never said anything. If she did know, Jenny could feel exactly what she must be feeling now, that sickening sense of being on shifting ground where you cannot tell whether the tufts of grass that look solid are really just as hollow and treacherous as the boggy areas that are clearly lies. The truth blends so easily with the lies, they look like each other and you have no safe place to put your foot. She could only hope, against her instinctive belief in openness, that Sanjay's wife did not know. Having been on the receiving end of that herself, she had vowed that she would never, ever be the cause of inflicting that kind of pain and sick feeling of life-shattering knowledge on any other woman.

She allowed herself to remember her brief marriage to Josh's father, Mark, which was over before it had really begun. Mark had always been one of those men with a radar permanently switched on, which beamed in on anything reasonably attractive in the vicinity. He was very attractive in a dark, moustachioed sort of way that Jenny now disliked whenever she saw it on men in the street. But he had something more than good looks. He had a magnetic attraction for women. What was more, he was aware of it – in the nicest possible way – and used it to the full. This had seemed an exciting quality· at first, a sign of worldliness and experience, of confidence that might rub off on her, and it had given her a strange new feeling when he used to cast his appraising, predatory eyes over her, taking in every detail appreciatively. But all too soon, only other women received this attention from him. It was a romance conducted at a heady speed, and before she knew it the honeymoon was over and she was pregnant. As her girth increased and a few stretch marks appeared, she could feel his interest waning. From then on, the most she saw of him was the back of his head as he eyed up every woman under thirty-five who walked past. If they were sitting in a café his eyes would travel up and down the bodies of every woman who came and went at the other tables. Every waitress was the recipient of a brief but concentrated glance. Jenny would have difficulty in gaining his attention. She did not know how to attract it away from these passing strangers and back to herself. She would say something bright and trivial, and reluctantly he would drag his eyes back to her for a moment before letting them scan the room again. Despite her size and blooming complexion, Jenny felt invisible. His behaviour made her feel as if she was absolutely nothing. Instead of just seeing Mark as immature and ill-equipped for parenthood, Jenny had allowed his behaviour to sap her confidence like the life blood slowly dripping from an internal wound. She took his attitude as a measure of her own self-worth, rather than a sign of his inadequacy. With hope born of naiveté, she thought things might be different after the baby came.

Maggie had been a schoolgirl then, sophisticated seventeen with all the bloom of youth upon her, and the sexual magnetism of a nubile young girl wanting to test her powers. Perhaps she had not been entirely to blame. A man who is on the lookout will find someone – anyone – to go off with eventually, if he is determined to do so. It wasn't Maggie who finally finished off the marriage, funnily enough, it was the one after that. Maggie had disappeared shortly afterwards and did not get in touch with her family at all for a while. But it was Maggie who finished it for Jenny. And Josh was not even born.

Maggie had been living at home then, in the house where their mother still lived. It was less dilapidated in those days, with her father there to make an occasional attempt at DIY, harangued constantly from the bottom of the ladder by her mother while he tottered at the top saying, 'Yes, dear, I do see what you mean, I just wish you'd said so before I started.' It was a glorious afternoon in June, Jenny remembered, because the heat was making her legs swell and she had spent the afternoon sitting in a deck chair, reading and drinking iced tea and eating grapes under the cherry tree. Mark had gone to fix her mother's drains, they had been dodgy even then – the essentials of life do not change – and in the heat the stench was terrible. Her father, hen-pecked as ever, had been dispatched to town on the bus to get some caustic soda. Maggie must have been sunbathing in her bikini in the back yard, in the sun trap between the end wall of the kitchen and the shed. Josh was due any day.

About four o'clock Jenny decided to wander over for a chat, she remembered, to see how Mark was getting on. The front door was open, and the house was dark and cool after the hot, bright street. She was about to call out when she saw her mother dozing in the chair. A fly was looping lazily around her head. Even now, almost ten years later, every detail was etched in her memory. She crept over to the window to look for the others. There was a slight sound from upstairs – a breathless, subdued giggle. Jenny's heart started pounding, she could feel the blood rushing in the side of her neck. Slowly, trying not to step on the two creaky steps, she went upstairs. They were in the spare room. The door was half open, and she peered furtively through the crack, feeling as if she were the guilty one for spying. She was punished for it instantly. There, on the spare bed, on the pink candlewick bedspread her parents had been given as a wedding present, was her husband shoving himself into the tight, elastic young body of her sister. Maggie was as firm, creamy and sweet as a white chocolate. Mark was a slavering beast, his clenched buttocks (never his best feature) almost green in the dimness. The bikini hung over the side of the bed like a piece of string. All Jenny could do was watch, horrified. Yet transfixed. Time hung poised, not moving on the gloomy landing. There was a horrible old picture of a child holding a puppy, Jenny remembered. A fat, glycerine tear oozed down the child's cheek as it stared down impassively at her misery and shock. Her brain, presumably overloaded by the trauma in hand, took a few moments out to wonder where and why her mother had acquired such an awful picture.

Jenny went downstairs, almost overbalancing as she did so, crept past her sleeping mother, went out into the baking concrete of the yard, with its chalky walls and few, ailing annuals in tubs, and was sick. Again, her tortured brain took in the interesting detail that the grape skins seemed to have gone down whole, and were not digested at all. They clearly did not dissolve in tea. It is strange what flashes of insight flit through the mind in moments of extreme stress. She stood there for a while, bent over the tub with its drooping pansies and marigolds (a flower she had never liked) gripping it on either side as if it were a toilet seat. Then she felt a sudden rush of hot water between her legs, and looking down she saw that the concrete where she was standing was a darker grey than elsewhere in the yard. For a second she thought that the second-worst humiliation had befallen her, after the first one upstairs, and she had wet her pants. Then she realised that Josh was on his way.

She thought of Henry. It had been sweet of him to send the postcards, a typical Henry gesture (like the time he had sent flowers for her birthday but had got the wrong month, mixing her up with some other girl, she had always suspected, and thereby totally spoiling the effect), sweet, but pointless. She rubbed her stomach gently. She was feeling very sick and had a slight pain on one side. Work had been particularly draining today, they had had to deal with an attempted suicide. The girl, Jackie, a pleasant, quiet schizophrenic, had a constant voice in her head telling her she was useless, stupid, a waste of space, that she should jump from the window and do everyone a favour. Having managed to resist it for five years, for some reason today she had decided to obey the voice, but one of the nurses had happened to see her climbing out. Jenny wondered idly if the voice was like that of 'Outraged from Sussex' on the radio. If so, she could sympathise with Jackie. They could have done without it, however. Jenny was tired, Josh would have to push the trolley. She must get some of those cheesy biscuits with poppy seeds on, plenty of them. And a large tub of chocolate ice-cream. For some reason they suddenly seemed the most desirable food in the world.

A letter plopped through the neo-Georgian-style front door and onto the doormat. Nita opened it. It was a letter inviting her to attend an interview in London, in two days' time. She phoned the station to book her train ticket. As she glanced around the hall with its neat telephone table and bentwood umbrella stand, she wondered how many more times she would do this. Despite her efforts with a few pictures and a vase of tulips, the tidiness had a sterility about it. A blankness filled the house, flowing into every room as soon as she left it. Somehow, even with the benefits of immaculate, expensive furnishings and up-to-the-minute central heating, including a real coal effect gas fire, they had never managed to bring the house to life. This was probably because to turn a house into a home you actually have to live in it, thought Nita sadly, not just use it as a base from which to conduct completely separate lives. The 'Welcome' doormat did not in fact offer any kind of welcome, warm or otherwise, to the few visitors who called. She had her friends at work, he had his, presumably – she had only once had the dubious pleasure of meeting his friend Paul – but she realised that she and Sanjay had no shared social life. It was as if they had both been unconsciously shutting down their joint life and developing individual lives for quite a while now, as if secretly they both knew what must happen. She pulled the door shut with desolation in her heart, and let the house return to its silence.

CHAPTER 9

Dear Jenny
2 weeks in California –
my paper v. well received,
weather not as warm as this picture
but beaches & people v. pleasant.
Trust all same as ever with you.
Hang loose (as they say here)
Henry.

It is difficult to hang any other way when you have cut slits in the sides of your leggings at the waist, and you have to wear your jeans with the zip undone, thought Jenny. She wasn't really showing yet, but she had put on some weight. It was the third of April, so he would be home any time now, he could even be home already – not that it mattered when he came, the result would be hopeless whenever it was. The postcards were getting more telegraphic and casual – or perhaps she was simply reading them more casually, giving them less attention. She wondered why he was still bothering to send them at all. Nobody except Janice knew about the pregnancy yet, and Jenny wanted to keep it like that as long as possible. She was feeling foul and bad-tempered and Henry's jaunty card with its talk of hanging around on beaches, and its assumption (which sounded arrogant to her in her jaundiced mood) that everything was still the same, only irritated her more. What does he think we've done while he's been away – stuck ourselves in a cardboard box to wait for him? This time at least he had splashed out on a picture of a palm tree and a glorious stretch of white, sandy beach. The water was turquoise; you could feel the heat in the bright white light. She'd have preferred another Boeing 747; it would have been less depressing. She felt lumpen and sick.

She was starting to worry about money, too, because although Janice never said anything, Jenny knew she was eager to leave. There was still no sign of a suitable tenant.

One evening when Jenny was tucking into her third round of tomato and mayonnaise sandwiches (with cheesy corn snacks on the side) and Josh was struggling at the table with the intricacies of multiplication, the phone rang.

'Jenny, is that you?'

Jenny took a deep breath as she recognised her sister's voice. She let Maggie speak while her own breath calmed down. For once, Maggie sounded subdued and uncertain. 'Jenny, please can we be friends? I think you may have misunderstood – there was nothing wrong with what I was doing, honest. It wasn't what you thought.' Still Jenny kept silent and let her talk, quite curious as to what might emerge. 'Anyway,' Maggie went on, getting a fraction more belligerent, 'I don't need to justify myself to you, you're not my mother. And don't you think you're being just a touch inconsistent, judging me, but having no problem being friendly to your neighbour, Astrid?'

'So there is something in it, then?' Jenny permitted herself at last. 'You are like Astrid? Anyway, how did you know about Astrid?'

'I got chatting to her out the back one day last summer. And no, there's no similarity. I was just pointing out that you judge me, but not her.'

Yes, thought Jenny, I do. 'You're my sister.'

'That's why I want us to be friends,' said Maggie, seizing on this and misunderstanding it.

There was a pause which Jenny chose not to fill, but let her thoughts flow into it instead. 'All right,' she said at last. It is only in families where the skin can grow over the most terrible injuries, without anything being said. 'But don't expect miracles.' Then a splinter of old distrust slipped in. 'What made you ring now?'

Maggie laughed. 'You know me too well,' she said, as if that was a good thing. 'I don't suppose you could put me up, could you? For proper rent this time?'

Maggie flowed into the house like water, changing everything.

She wore a particularly pervasive scent that seemed to make even the curtains smell of her, and her possessions, though few, changed the feel of every room they inhabited. There was a large wooden Janus head (particularly apt, thought Jenny) whose features were enlarged to grotesque proportions, the smiling face grimacing and imbecile, the evil face contorted into an expression of real malevolence. This charming object lurked in the hall to unnerve any visitors of a nervous disposition. It was a job to get anything past it. Apparently, it was a present from some grateful Arab businessman. Ill-gotten gains, thought Jenny drily. Odd details like this slipped out about Maggie's life and gave Jenny a most lurid picture of a life that she could barely imagine. She never asked where Maggie had been since she last saw her, and Maggie never said. It seemed better that way. Janice left with thinly disguised relief, and Maggie was to stay for six months. Until the baby arrives, Jenny calculated, then we will have to think again. But she did not say anything to Maggie about the baby. She felt as if all of them – herself, Janice, Maggie, were moving into their own bizarre new phases. Most of the things she had taken for granted, her old values, were changing. They had left the old normality with its relative security and daily bickering far behind them, and were occupying a strange hinterland of life where anything was possible. It was disorientating but interesting, and she was learning to trust in the unknown.

It was six o'clock one morning and Jenny was surfacing from the depths of a dream in which she was comfortably lying in a boat, looking up at the sky while Henry wielded a pair of oars. He seemed to be making heavy weather of it, and kept complaining that someone was trying to shoot at them from the shore. The bangs were certainly loud and frequent. She felt frustrated with Henry and wondered why they were making no progress. The bangs became louder and more obtrusive, and gradually she surfaced to realise that someone was hammering on the front door. She peered at her clock, groaned, then twitched back the curtain. A shiny black motorbike was parked proudly at the curb, the spring morning sunshine glinting on the petrol tank. She saw the dull silken sheen of the leather seat.

'Oh my God.' She dived out of bed, then sagged back down again because she saw stars. Frantically she grabbed a shirt and jeans and scraped a reluctant comb through her hair. She peered in the mirror. Awful. What the hell. 'All right, all right,' she called as she staggered out into the hallway. She opened the door onto an evil spring draught that whistled through her clothes, and Sanjay.

'What the hell do you want? Funny time to come round, what the hell are you thinking of, knocking on people's doors at six in the morning?' She looked more closely. He had been crying, his eyes were puffy. They only looked like that if you had been crying all night. Jenny knew. 'What's happened?'

He shook his head in reply, unable to speak. She put her arms out to him, she sensed that he was an injured animal in need. They hugged on the doorstep, his head against her breast. Then, seeing the milkman turn into the street, Jenny said, 'You'd better come in.'

'Nita's gone, she's left me,' he blurted as soon as they were in the sitting room.

'So at least *somebody* around here's got some sense,' she said, then added, 'sorry, didn't mean it. Tactless of me.'

'This was the first place I –' he could not finish.

'Excuse me,' said Jenny quickly. 'Nothing personal, I just have to be sick.' She dashed for the bathroom. This had become a daily occurrence just lately. Sanjay, submerged in his own anguish, did not give it a thought. Thank goodness he's too upset to notice, Jenny thought, without meaning to be callous. It meant the poor boy's shocks could at least be spread out a little.

'I'm sorry,' she said, thinking, how inadequate, how ordinary a thing to say, but what else could you say? What else, really, given his own behaviour in the last few months, had he expected? But that, of course, could never be said. Words could not help him until he had started to recover. 'You're in shock. Let me make you some tea.'

When he had calmed down a little, Jenny asked him gently, 'Why did she go? I mean – what reason did she give? It wasn't because of – us, was it?'

Sanjay shook his head again. The tea had revived him a little, but a tear spilled out from under his eyelid and landed on the tablecloth. He swallowed hard.

'I'm sorry. Don't talk about it yet if you don't want to.'

He looked at her for the first time. 'It's not that. I want to – it's just – such a shock.' Jenny stroked his hand as it lay limply on the table. 'I know. It must be terrible.' But not *that* terrible, surely, she thought. After all, you were happily fooling around with me until a few weeks ago. But she knew that there was nothing rational about this kind of pain.

'I mean – she talked about going – she often talked about it – but I thought she was just trying to – to get at me. Because she was angry with me, you see.'

'Why?' asked Jenny quickly, thinking, so she did know, after all.

'She was angry because she was – disappointed. I disappointed her. I was too –' he searched for the word. 'Too – ordinary for her.'

'*I* don't think you're the least bit ordinary. You're fine, Sanjay, there's nothing wrong with you.'

'But she was – special. Different, not like you or me.'

Thanks a lot, thought Jenny. Still, what's wrong with being ordinary? Being extraordinary seems to bring no better chance of happiness, she reflected.

Sanjay was still talking, almost oblivious of her now. 'I can't put it into words – if you met her you'd know what I mean. I never learned how to please her. Not that she ever said anything. She was just sort of – switched off. She had something about her – a kind of secret. You felt like she always knew something you didn't, and you were always at a disadvantage because of it.'

Jenny had never heard him expressing himself so clearly and articulately before. Despite the constant charm and friendliness he had always shown her, she realised now that a part of him had always been kept hidden – of course it had, she thought, he was married. A huge part had been hidden. Now it was torn open and he was raw and exposed. Even though he was distraught at the loss of another woman, she found his new vulnerability touching. It made him more likeable.

'Where has she gone? Did she say?'

'She's got a new job. A promotion, of course.' For the first time he sounded a little bitter. That's a good sign, noted Jenny professionally. 'In London. She did try to tell me about it, a week or so ago, but I didn't listen. I didn't think she'd really take it. She's staying with a cousin while she gets things sorted out. She says she's quite willing to see me, to talk about things, but what is there to say? She's decided.'

'Did you have any idea this was coming?'

Surely he must have done. He said himself that they were not happy. He just shrugged and gazed out of the window into the back yard. The ivy on Astrid's wall was waving erratically in the rain-laden April wind. Each dark leaf was spotted with droplets of rain that showered down with every gust. A few sparrows dipped and flitted amongst the ivy like dead leaves on the wind.

'Oh, Jenny, if only I hadn't been so stupid. You were so good to me – if only I had been honest from the start – then I could have been with you. You were so good for me, too, you gave me so much. It could have been so different – couldn't it? I've thought about you such a lot – I wanted to see you. I didn't know what to do.' He seized her hand and kissed it. Jenny sighed. She felt so much older and more experienced than he was. He was still so young, so untried. And at the moment, she could see, so bewildered.

'I don't think so, Sanjay.' She studied his dark eyes and felt a rush of affection for this lost boy. But even as she looked at him, she found it difficult to believe that she had ever seen him as anything other than a beautiful boy. Perhaps he had never been more than that. Perhaps that was what Nita had discovered, she thought. Everything else had been inside her own head. She smiled at his anxious expression. 'It was great,' she said kindly. 'It was a wonderful bubble, quite unlike anything else I've ever experienced.' He looked gratified at this. 'But it was just for fun – lovely fun that did us both good, but – just that. It could never have turned into anything more.' Suddenly she remembered the baby. 'Oh God. Oh God, oh God.'

'What is it?' asked Sanjay, alarmed.

'Nothing – I mean – well, not nothing, but it's OK.' The time was all wrong, he could not bear it, she wanted to protect him from another shock. She also realised suddenly that she did not want to share the baby with anyone. Not even Sanjay. She just laid her head across her arm on the table.

'Are you all right?' he asked, stroking her hair. They were treating each other like invalids who each needed looking after.

She did her best to smile. 'Yes, Sanjay, I'm fine. Really. It's just – the shock, yes the shock of seeing you again.'

'I'm sorry.' But she could see he was easily reassured, only too glad to dwell upon his own miseries.

'Hey, look, we've both done more than enough of being sorry. How about some toast, and I'll make another pot of tea?'

Half an hour later, thinking she was up before everyone and would have time to hog the bathroom, Maggie came down to see her frumpy older sister sitting cosily having tea and toast with the best looking man she had seen in a long time. Jenny had the pleasure of seeing her sinuous, sexy sister for the first time ever with her mouth hanging open, totally lost for words.

Sanjay rang in sick and slept on the sofa most of the day. Maggie assured her sister that she would look after him. 'I bet you will,' said Jenny, but she said it with a smile. Sanjay was too distraught to appreciate what Maggie could (and probably would) offer him. As for Jenny, the news that Nita had left made no difference. Although she felt sorry for Sanjay, in a way she was relieved. After all, he had been cheating on his wife. It gave her a sense that there was still some justice in the world to think that Nita had left him. She wondered if she *had* found out about his infidelity. He was still naive enough to think that she had known nothing about it, but Jenny knew that a clever woman, a woman of the sort that Nita appeared to be, might not confront him like a screaming banshee, waving his infidelity in his face and beating him with it. She might be more subtle and leave him still wanting her back, believing himself still safe from discovery. Jenny realised that she would probably never know the truth about Nita. She would always be a mysterious, intriguing figure, beautiful and wronged. Jenny was beginning to wish she had met her, if only to satisfy her curiosity. Now she knew she never would.

What Jenny had shared with Sanjay had never been more than an illusion, a beautiful bubble, a shimmering tissue of lies. But the baby – justice for herself, perhaps, she thought – was real enough. There was nothing illusory about that. The notion of living life on your own terms, as she had tried to do, was a complete nonsense. Just when you think you are calling all the shots and you have every angle covered, no chink unprotected, life throws down a hand-grenade to make you see that you have very little control at all. You may be sitting in the driver's seat, but someone else has their feet on the pedals. You can take what you want, if you must, but there is always a price. Jenny had learned that painfully in the last few weeks. Perhaps Sanjay was learning it now, and would begin to grow a little.

Maggie got most of the story. Jenny heard it for the second time over tea, while Josh was out of earshot in the bath with the radio on. He was just getting to the stage when he liked his own music on. Loud. Maggie, it appeared, had extracted more of the nitty gritty, juicy details that Jenny had been too sensitive to ask about. They had made Sanjay go home to his empty house with the promise that he could come round to talk about it again tomorrow.

Apparently Sanjay had come back from his kung-fu class the night before (I never knew he did that, Jenny exclaimed) to find a note on the table. She'd just left, no warning, it seemed, no reason, apart from the job. They had not been getting on particularly well, but that was nothing new; they certainly had not fallen out. They hardly saw enough of each other to fall out. No, he really had no idea why she had gone, he told Maggie and Maggie told Jenny. Jenny's heart sank. Was he really so obtuse? He had not tried to ring the London cousin and he was too mortified to tell his parents, let alone phone Nita's family, who would be horrified and accuse him of mistreating their daughter. All hell would be let loose, he had led Maggie to believe. This was a terrible scandal for him and his family. Jenny felt sure that Maggie must be distorting the picture, because from what she said it sounded as if Sanjay had recovered amazingly quickly and was more concerned about avoiding a scandal than about the loss of his wife. Surely that could not be right. He had certainly been upset enough this morning. Maggie must have had a remarkable effect on him.

'Didn't they get on?' asked Maggie, curiously. 'There must be something wrong with a woman who can't appreciate a man like that. How did *you* get to know such a gorgeous specimen, anyway?' Jenny ignored this and the barb behind it.

'You never know what goes on behind closed doors in a marriage,' Jenny said, thinking, you should know.

'That's true,' Maggie agreed. 'Look at your Mark.'

Jenny went scarlet. 'What do you mean?'

Maggie was shameless. 'Well, nothing really,' she said coolly, covering herself. 'Just that you didn't always get on, did you? I mean, you parted, so you can't have done, can you?'

Jenny nearly choked on her pilchard rissole. When she had recovered with a glass of water she sat and studied the neat, pointed features of her sister while they ate. She had never noticed before how like a weasel she was. She stared hard into those flat dark eyes but could make out nothing except her own reflection in their murky depths. Both women kept a stiff silence. Peace, of a sort, was maintained.

Josh's music stopped and he padded through on wet feet into the pool of quietness. He was pink and damp from the bath, his hair stood up in tufts. 'Listen to this, Mum,' he said. He made a noise with his lips. 'Do I sound like an exhaust pipe?'

'Yes, you do, love. Very good.'

'What's the matter?' he asked, sensing something and looking anxiously from one to the other. Jenny grabbed him and gave him a kiss. 'Yuck, get off, that's sissy,' he said affectionately.

Jenny laughed. 'Nothing's the matter. Get ready for bed and I'll be up in a minute.' When he had gone the silence flooded back into the vacuum.

'By the way,' Jenny said eventually as she got up to clear the table, 'I'd prefer it if you didn't move in on poor Sanjay. He doesn't know it yet, but I'm expecting his child.'

For the second time in one day, surely a world record, Maggie was stunned into gaping silence while Jenny glided calmly upstairs to say goodnight to Josh.

Bridlington is not the place to be on a freezing day on the fifth of

April. It was impossible to believe that this was officially supposed to be spring. Kate hoped they had not come here on a fool's errand. The wind came off the Urals, everybody said, and Janice could believe it. She had no idea where the Urals were, or even what they were, but they sounded so cold, hard and distant, it was natural for such a vicious wind to come from them. She and Kate walked arm in arm along the promenade, hunched against the relentless blast. The long concrete arm that curved around the bay might be a pleasant place to stroll in summer, but now it was bleak, chill and desolate. Crisp packets chased each other round in circles and flurries of sand were whipped up off the beach to shot blast any unfortunate fools who dared to brave the elements. All the amusement arcades were still boarded up, although they would be open any day now for the start of the season. The sea was iron grey and far away. It grew blacker towards its furthest rim, indicating that rain would soon be squalling in. A few hardy specimens shrouded in scarves and woolly hats walked stout, reluctant dogs just far enough for Fido to do his stuff (usually right in the middle of the promenade), then turned with their backs into the wind to be blown home to tea and crumpets by the fire. It was Sunday, and only a paper shop and one dreary café was open, its window staring bleakly out to sea, the grey net curtains seeming to mourn its lost dead. Inside it smelled of chip fat and a blackboard propped against the counter bore the inspiring words: Today's special – Tripe and onions, bread and butter, mug of tea, £2.50.

'Are you sure this is a good idea?' Kate asked for the ninth time since they had got off the train. She warmed her hands around the greasy mug of strong tea. They had been through it all before. 'You've still got time to change your mind.'

Janice was unusually resolute. 'I won't change my mind. I have to see him. Just to know. Just so I can put it aside and get on with my life. With you.'

'It may not be how you hope it will be.'

'I don't hope anything.'

'Yes you do. You hope he'll be overjoyed to see you, that he's thought about you all this time, and that you'll regain a father and he'll regain a daughter.'

Janice's eyes began to fill. 'You can be very cruel,' she said, sounding far away.

'I'm just trying to warn you. Protect you from disappointment, that's all. Because I care about you.'

Janice stared at her. Her cheeks were raw and red from the wind, and anger made them flame even more. 'No you're not, you're jealous. You're afraid if I find him again, I won't want you. You think I'll have a new family and won't want you any more. That's it, isn't it?'

'No. Don't be ridiculous. It's you I'm thinking of.'

'That's what people always say when they're thinking about themselves.'

Oh dear, not a quarrel, not here, not now, when we need each other more than ever, thought Kate. 'You're right,' she said. 'Of course that's what I'm frightened of. I'd be stupid not to be. It might be all hunky-dory for you, they'll put you off me, and I'll be out in the cold. It *is* bloody cold, isn't it? I'm freezing in this draught.'

Janice reached across to her and smiled. Her thin cheeks were shiny and cherry-like now in the steamy atmosphere. Kate was usually the stronger one, the driving energy, yet she had odd, surprising moments of weakness and self-doubt. There are advantages in not thinking about things too much, Janice thought. She found these glimpses of vulnerability intensely touching in someone otherwise so forceful and competent. 'They won't put me off you,' she said. 'It'll be OK. Have a bit of faith.'

A little faith goes a long way, thought Kate. She drank her tea.

The Shangri-La was dreary in the extreme. It was one of a row of decayed Georgian seaside houses in a street at right angles to the promenade. The Shangri-La was one of the more dilapidated. Some had bravely put out window boxes of winter-flowering pansies, and here and there the odd daffodil was in bloom and an occasional purple crocus had stuck its head up just to have it battered down again by the wind. All the houses had iron railings across the front, and a little iron gate leading down some stone steps to the basement doorway.

'I've always liked the idea of basement steps,' said Kate, trying to put some brightness on the grim scene. 'You can paint them white and have pots of geraniums and whatnot.'

The Shangri-La looked like a DSS Bed-and-Breakfast place, and grey paint peeled off the front door. There were six doorbells. 'Flats,' said Janice. 'Which one shall I try?'

'Well, not Braithwaite,' Kate said unnecessarily. None of the others were named. Janice's finger hovered over the bells, encased in its knitted glove. A horrible feeling was dragging at her stomach. The clouds were racing overhead like torn grey cloths flapping on a washing line. A few sleety drops whipped down the street. 'Hurry up, it's going to start chucking it down.' Janice stabbed randomly at a button. They heard a distant farting sound deep inside the building. Eventually some heavy feet thudded down the stairs and the door was opened a crack. The nose which appeared in the gap was large, freckled and male. A few whiskers twitched. 'What?'

Janice made her enquiry. The door opened a little further to show a tall young man with a long face and a moustache to match. He was wearing a heavily studded leather jacket and a pair of ripped jeans. 'Sorry love,' he said pleasantly in a strong London accent. 'I don't know no one. I'm only here for the weekend. I only know Hatchet.' He shouted upstairs. They heard a distant reply. 'Nope. Hatchet's never heard of them. Sorry. There's a girl called Sheila lives downstairs,' he offered helpfully. 'No? OK. Ta-ra.' Janice wilted against the shut door.

'Maybe we've got the wrong place. Perhaps that address was out of date. It was a few years ago your auntie saw them, wasn't it?' Janice nodded. 'What do you want to do, then?' Kate asked her.

Janice shrugged, at a loss. 'I was stupid, I should have phoned or written first. I wanted to surprise him. I should have looked him up in the phone book, at least.'

It seemed so obvious now, in the face of failure, that there were so many better ways to look for someone than just to turn up on the doorstep of a strange house in a strange town, on the basis of an address from years ago.

'What now, then?' Kate repeated. 'Do you want to look him up, if we can find a phone box?'

Janice looked up at the rushing clouds for a few moments and blinked hard. Those clouds were whipping away whatever intention she had come with. They were scouring the sky. 'No. I think I've made a mistake. I've changed my mind, you were right, it was a stupid idea. A kid's fantasy. I feel like a stupid idiot. Sorry I dragged you along. Come on, let's go home.'

They trudged back to the station, Kate trying to give her silent comfort by holding her hand inside her jacket pocket. Janice didn't cry, she practically never cried, she said. Well, hardly ever. Secretly Kate was relieved. She had had enough. 'Maybe it's for the best,' she ventured when they reached the station. The next train they could catch was in half an hour. Just time for a plastic sandwich and a cup of tea. 'Maybe,' Janice said.

'What happened to your fish man – that Henry?'

'*That* Henry wasn't a fish man, he was a researcher doing a PhD. And he went off to the Arctic, remember? Last time you were here. Well, Greenland. That's the Arctic, isn't it?'

'Ah yes, I'd forgotten that.'

'You've forgotten? I wish I could. That evening was terrible.'

Maggie laughed. 'You know how to pick them, don't you? Is he playing hard to get, or what? Is he ever coming back?'

'To Britain, do you mean, or to me?'

'Both.'

'I wouldn't have the faintest idea. He's probably back in the country already, for all I know. Now which of your rich and famous clientele is taking you out tonight?'

Maggie gave a wide, languorous yawn. 'It's another Arab businessman tonight. What a bore. Dressing up and being the ornament on some man's arm for business dinners – really, it's such a drag.'

'My heart bleeds for you. Is that – all you do?' asked Jenny curiously. 'Go to dinners and look decorative?'

Maggie gave her a very straight look. 'Of course. It's a very upmarket escort agency. Mostly it's business dinners for foreign businessmen. The occasional ball or posh company do, with some poor sad sap who hasn't got anyone of his own to go with. You just have to look good and be pleasant to all the boring farts he wants to impress. And make appropriate conversation when required, though they don't usually want you to talk – opinions are not decorative, my dear. Anything else is strictly forbidden. Officially, that is, although I must admit I bend the rules just a little, for the occasional one.' She flashed a naughty smile. 'What else did you think?'

'Isn't that a bit silly? To bend the rules? And dangerous?'

Maggie shrugged. 'I suppose so. I like to live on the edge a little. You might think that stupid. But then, we're not all the same, are we? It's important to know what you're good at,' she smiled. 'Since talking to Astrid, I'm even thinking of branching out a bit. Extend my repertoire. And let's face it,' she laughed, 'I've had plenty of practice.'

'You're not, are you?'

'Oh Jenny, you take me so seriously. No, I'm not. I don't think slapping elderly gents about with carpet slippers or belts and telling them what naughty boys they are is quite up my street, do you? Boarding schools have got a lot to answer for. She's good company, though, to talk to, isn't she? Did you know she's got a room upstairs that's completely lined with red nylon fur? Yes, honestly, bed cover, walls, cushions, furry blind across the window, the lot. Fake fun fur, she calls it. Says her regulars like it. That's her working room, though – not her bedroom. She's got enough stuff in her wardrobe to kit out a theatre company.'

'Talking of which, have you given up the idea of going to drama college?'

'You don't forget, do you? Mum told you that, I suppose.'

No, I don't forget, thought Jenny. I wish I did.

'Well, I have applied, and I've got a place to start next autumn. Here, locally.'

'That's great,' said Jenny, 'well done.' She was genuinely pleased. Then an idea struck her. 'You wouldn't want to lodge her permanently, would you, while you're at college? If I could stand it, I mean?'

Maggie laughed. 'I don't think *I* could stand it – no offence, Jen. But big sister watching over me and disapproving isn't exactly what I had in mind. I'll still be working for the agency. That way I'll be able to supplement my grant. Not a bad existence.' She blew out a slow plume of smoke and they both watched it float up to the ceiling and disappear. 'I didn't like you much until recently,' Jenny said thoughtfully.

'I didn't like you much, either.'

'I was jealous – Mum always seemed to like you best.'

'I was jealous of you. You were the oldest, and brainy – you know those stupid labels Mum insisted on sticking on us – you always got to do things first. I hated having to wear your clothes. You always got them new.'

'Did I? I don't remember that. We were too far apart. I never knew you, you were just a bratty little kid who hung around with my friends and played up to Mum and Dad. You were a scheming little madam. It used to drive me mad, the way they never saw how you manipulated them.'

'Still am a "scheming little madam", as you so kindly put it. It's important to have a talent. You were a fat, boring goody two-shoes, who always passed your exams. I just longed to see you fail, or do something badly. I could never understand how you could be happy being fat. I couldn't bear it. It used to annoy me, just to see your fat behind bulging over your jeans. It used to sort of stick out in wedges at the side. You used to have this habit of trying to tuck it in. And holding your breath when you looked in the mirror. That used to crease me up.'

'I still do that. Doesn't everybody? Anyway, I wasn't fat. Just pleasantly rounded. I was jealous of your skinniness, and the way the boys were round you like flies.'

Maggie lit a cigarette, her silky dark hair flopping forward. She looked young and tired. 'Poor Mum,' she said. 'She did her best.'

'And who can do more than that?' She was thinking of Josh and this unknown one who was coming.

They sat in silence and pondered this for a minute. Then Maggie said, 'What do you think of this new bloke of hers?'

'What bloke?'

'This Bernard. From Alcoholics Anonymous. Wears a cravat.'

'What?'

'I know. I didn't think anyone still wore cravats.'

'Not that – Alcoholics Anonymous. You mean – '

'Yes. That's her club she's always on about. Didn't you know? Apparently he came round with meals on wheels just after Christmas. He's into Alcoholics Anonymous, spotted a kindred spirit in Mum and dragged her along.'

Jenny just sat back, taking this in. After a minute she said, 'That explains the hair. Well, at least there'll be someone else to do the drains for her.' There was a long, peaceful pause. A police car went past the end of the road, the siren blaring then dying away. Jenny looked across at her sister, lying back in the comfy chair, her thin arm hanging over the side. She should eat more, she was too thin, she thought protectively. Something warm flooded into her, something suspiciously like affection. Whatever else came and went, you were always blessed – or cursed – with your family. 'This is the first proper conversation we have ever had.'

Maggie blew another blue stream of cigarette smoke out slowly. 'Yes,' she said. 'Yes, I guess it is.'

Bridlington station did not improve with further acquaintance. The train was twenty minutes late, so Janice and Kate huddled together on the platform with one or two other unfortunates who had no better means of transport. Janice's cheeks were blue. She slid her hands round Kate's waist under her jacket to warm them up, but Kate winced because they felt like blocks of ice and pushed them grumpily away. On the opposite platform a man was remonstrating with a small child who would not sit in the pushchair and was grizzling with the cold. 'Mummy will be here in a minute, Mummy will be out of the loo in a minute, she won't be long.' The words seemed more for his own benefit than for the child's, as he seemed incapable of supervising his own son for more than a few minutes. The child was hell-bent on smashing the front of the chocolate machine in the hope that it would spew out a chocolate bar by mistake, since his father had given a weak and beleaguered 'No, we'll have to wait and see what Mummy says' to his repeated requests. He didn't appear to know how to operate the fastening on the pushchair to keep the child in. Kate watched them without interest. Today had been a complete waste of time, and there had been a good film on television that they could have cuddled up and watched instead. Janice seemed almost relieved that her mission had failed. She skipped around the platform in a light-hearted way, to keep warm she said, puffing and jumping up and down, until Kate felt really irritated. Why did she have to be so jolly all of a sudden? This had not been one of their better days.

At last the train pulled in, and they climbed on board to be greeted by the familiar smell of brake fluid and burning rubber that always seems to pervade high-speed trains. Idly, and as she always did when she got on a train, Kate wondered why this was. Perhaps it was some sort of design fault. Presumably it is quite difficult to eliminate a smell. As the train pulled away and the platform began to slide smoothly backwards, they saw a man standing still, back a little from the train so that he was moving more slowly away from them. He wore a brown mac and a cap over his lean, stooping figure. He was waving to someone on the train, saying goodbye. Janice saw him and leaned forward, and as their window passed him, he saw Janice. He was a small, grey man, the sort you would not notice in a crowd, but the likeness was unmistakable. The same pinched cheeks either side of the same beaky nose, blue eyes, watery in his case, but the real giveaway was that tender, timid half-smile that was so characteristic of Janice. Kate knew she could not be mistaken. No two people could have that smile unless they were related. There was so much expressed in that smile, it lit up an otherwise plain and unremarkable face, just as it did with Janice. He and Janice locked eyes for an instant as strangers sometimes do, just by chance, in a fleeting moment with no significance attached to it except a momentary passing flicker of interest in another human being. They could not have been within each other's sight for more than ten seconds, fifteen at the most, Kate calculated. But he saw Janice, Janice saw him, and with a flash of shock, then doubt, and then a beam of recognition, he smiled. His hand came up almost automatically, and he waved to Janice. The train was speeding up and there was nothing else to do. Janice leaped up to the window and dragged frantically at it to open the small sliding panel at the top. He was out of sight now, the platform had given way to the backs of terraced houses and a car park, but she put her face to the icy gap and screamed, '*Dad*!' Then, '*I'll be back! I'm coming back!*'.

She flopped down breathless onto the seat. 'Do you think he heard me?'

'I should think the whole of Bridlington heard you. You should have shouted your phone number. But I guess he wouldn't have been able to remember it like that, bellowed from a train window,' she added, seeing Janice's stricken face. 'And whatever your mother said, Janice, that man is definitely your father. There can't be two faces so alike anywhere else in Britain. It doesn't look as though your mother's genes got a look in. No wonder you're so small. Petite, I mean. I can see it all now.'

Janice's face was glowing as if it was flooded with a brilliant light from the inside. Her whole being was shining. 'Do you really think I look like him?'

'Yes, I do.'

'So you think my mother – ' Janice hesitated, weighing the charge – 'Lied. To get rid of my father.'

Kate shrugged. 'It's possible. People do the strangest things. Especially when lust or money are involved. Who knows? We'll never know now, will we? Not for sure.'

'But how could he be so pathetic, not to fight for me, just to let her throw him out like that? He can't have cared that much – maybe she was right.'

Kate reached across the narrow table and took Janice's hand. A man in a dark raincoat gave her a funny look and scuttled behind the safety of his newspaper.

'Look, Jan, please, let's try, really try, to put it behind us. We all had terrible things happen to us in our childhood – some more awful than others, true enough, but really, does it matter any more? Now is all there is – the future is the only thing we can control, not the past. Please, Janice, let's live for now. For each other. I'm not being heartless, but you've got to put it behind you and get on with living. You're twenty-four years old. It's not about how many times you fall down – we all fall down – it's about how you pick yourself up.'

Janice closed herself up like a fan and gazed out of the window with faraway eyes. 'I never even got to read his letters,' she said in a distant voice.

'I shouldn't worry. At least you know he wrote them.'

Janice failed to look mollified. Her whole body seemed to contract and occupy a smaller space than ever.

'Anyway, the news would be a bit out of date by now, wouldn't it?'

Janice flashed her a filthy look as if to say, 'How could you be so callous?' Then seeing Kate's eyes twinkling, she relented and allowed a small, pinched smile.

'You can be a right cow, Kate Marsh, you know that?'

'I know,' said Kate, and blew her a kiss.

Sanjay had not been entirely honest when talking to Maggie. For some reason her presence had made his shock and grief fade miraculously into the background. He could not say he was recovering – that would be too much to hope – but certainly the person of Nita and the pain she had caused him were already receding. He could even glimpse the possibility of a day – in the distant future, of course – when he might actually get over his loss. With women like Maggie and Jenny in his world, anything was possible. He found, during his day alone with Maggie, that by lunchtime he had said all he wanted to say on the subject of his marriage. He wanted to talk about other, more interesting things with Maggie. He wanted to discover things about her. He wondered why Jenny had never mentioned the existence of a stunningly beautiful sister. Nita, with utter reasonableness, had even left a phone number for him to call her to talk things over. In the morning he had intended to call her when he felt a little better. By the afternoon he had changed his mind. If she wanted to come home he would not stop her, but he would not beg her either. She'd be back soon enough, when she'd come to her senses. They were married, after all. They weren't close it was true, but they never quarrelled either, and for all he knew perhaps all married couples were like this – coexisting without touching, where passion, excitement and lust were part of an underworld he had stepped into with Jenny. Nita would be back any day. But he had not said any of this to Maggie. Blinded with grief as he assured himself he was, he had still registered that she was a fine-looking woman, beautiful in fact, a sort of willowy, darker, honed-down version of Jenny. It was as if Jenny had been put in a pot-boiler and condensed, and the best essence of her poured into a mould of perfection, cooled and polished, and the result had been Maggie. She was young, too, young and – what was the word Paul liked to use – nubile. Yes, nubile fitted her exactly. All these qualities and their effect on him had made him, for some reason which he did not analyse, economical with the truth.

He had not come round on impulse that morning with any intention of reviving things with Jenny. It was just that in his moment of need he had felt an overwhelming need to have her motherly arms enfold him in their plump, white embrace, to smell her comforting bodily smell of bread and talcum powder, to have his face squashed kindly between those doughy breasts, and to receive some succour. She would understand and be sympathetic like a mother and most of all, unlike his own doting mother she would make no demands on him, she would not judge, she would just listen. And early in the morning, over the pots of jam and the large brown teapot, she had done just that. But during the day as he slept on the sofa while Maggie padded gracefully round him, and afterwards, when Maggie had sat next to him on the sofa listening quietly while he talked, their knees touching casually, each of them pretending to be unaware of it, yet neither of them moving away, he had grown up all over again. With Jenny in the early morning he had been a needy little boy. Gradually, through the day with Maggie, he became a man again.

The house was a morgue to him without Nita in it. He had been sleeping on Paul's floor for two nights, but Paul was kicking him out tonight because Hayley was staying. Sanjay said he didn't mind. Paul said *he* did. Sanjay said well then, he might as well go home. Paul said good idea. Change your socks. Sanjay said what if she rings? Paul said what if she does? Act tough, they respect you if you act tough. Act like you don't care if she comes back or not. It might make her sit up a bit and realise she's made a mistake and come back. Sanjay looked doubtful. Paul said, you do want her back, don't you? Of course, Sanjay said, wondering if he did. Well then, Paul said, there you are.

At home there were two flashes on the answer machine, but no messages had been left. Whoever had phoned had just hung up. Sanjay wondered if it had been Nita. He hoped it might have been Maggie. He looked in the fridge, but all he could find was a tube of tomato paste and some ham he had forgotten to wrap up so it had gone all stiff and curly at the edges. Some milk had gone off so he poured it down the sink. The sour smell hit the back of his throat as he rinsed the soft, lumpy bits away. There was some hard bread in the bread bin. He scraped off the few spots of green, cracked the bread in half and stuck the ham between the two hunks. It was like eating a couple of pieces of wood with something vaguely salty in the middle. He washed it down with tea.

Upstairs, a few small things in the bedroom had been rearranged. Two pictures were missing – Nita's pictures, the arty sort he never could understand, with bits of bodies here and there, bright colours and you couldn't tell which way up they were supposed to be. Nita liked this type of thing, she called it Art. He never could see the attraction, himself. Anyway, two of them were missing, a large blue affair with splodges of white, and a yellowy one with big pink bosoms in the middle. He had quite liked that one, at least you could see what they were supposed to be, although he couldn't make out the rest of the woman who Nita assured him was in the picture. The rest of it looked like an arrangement of tree trunks and oyster shells. Weird. He looked in the wardrobe. All Nita's things were gone. She must have phoned to check he was out, then come to take her possessions. She must be back in York. Either that, or she had instructed someone, some friend or relation, to come and fetch her things. That meant she had confided in someone. Perhaps she had told her family by now. 'The gang' probably knew all about it – for all he knew they had probably gone to the station to wave her off. He felt suddenly angry. He felt she had no right to go telling people that their marriage was over before consulting him. He did not see that she had been trying, in her own way, to consult him for the last two years. Those sorts of conversation seemed boring and pointless, and he had never listened. But no, he decided, she must have come herself. No one else would have known exactly what to take. No one else, however close to Nita, would have thought of taking the pictures. She could have told him she was coming. He did not consider that she might have been trying to contact him, but that he had not been here.

He pulled another picture off the wall, a fishy thing in liquid blues and greens, and stamped on the glass. It splintered into a cobweb pattern of cracks. He picked it up and flung it at the wardrobe. Swearing under his breath, he grabbed a few clothes and stuffed them into a carrier bag. He could not sleep here, it was polluted. He felt as if the house had been burgled. She hadn't even had the courtesy to do the washing up before she went. It was all piled up and crusty, just as he had left it. He was livid with Nita, the way she had always excluded him, pushed him away, but he was angry too with himself. Paul was right. If he had been tougher with her earlier in their marriage, shown her how it was going to be, instead of trying to be kind and understanding, letting her keep him at arm's length, hoping like a fool that one day she would warm to him and let him in, none of this would have happened. She was a frigid, brittle little prick-teaser (one of Paul's expressions). He wouldn't have her back now if she begged him on bended knee. *She* had left *him*, he was not the guilty one, he had nothing to reproach himself for. She could not possibly have known about Jenny, and by some bizarre twist of logic he felt entirely justified now in looking for solace with Jenny. What red-blooded male would not? Because Nita had left him, abandoned him, deserted him, all his guilt was absolved. He would spend the night on the sofa in Jenny's cluttered sitting room, and let the warmth of the two women wash over him.

He knocked on the door and Josh opened it. He stood back to let Sanjay in without speaking. His silence was a gesture of taking him for granted as a friend, that touched Sanjay. His presence here was accepted, even by Josh. Ever since the motorbike incident, Josh had tolerated Sanjay with careful interest. Sanjay walked down the darkened narrow hall, pleasantly anticipating surprising the two women in a scene of cosy feminine domestic harmony. He could see it in his mind's eye even before he pushed open the door. Jenny would be sewing, as she sometimes did, and Maggie would be looking beautiful, combing her long, dark hair. They would be chatting comfortably about who knows what – himself, hopefully.

What he saw did not quite coincide with his mental picture. The television was on, blaring out some nonsense that Josh must have been watching. Jenny was standing in the kitchen doorway and he could tell by the set of her shoulders that she was tense. Her cheeks were flaming and she had clearly just said something to Maggie, who was lounging back in the one comfortable chair, and was the only one who appeared to be relaxed. The remains of their meal was still on the table, and Josh's homework book was perched on the edge next to a flat dish with some scrapings of meat in it. Jenny glanced briefly at Sanjay. He could not read her expression beyond receiving a signal that he was not welcome. He had picked a bad moment, they were clearly in the middle of an argument.

'Sorry,' he began, backing out politely, 'I didn't mean to intrude.'

Jenny flashed him a look that he could only describe as tortured. He interpreted this as her wanting him to stay.

'Not at all,' said Maggie calmly. She was as cool and white as Jenny was hot and pink. That summed up their different characters quite well, he thought, the neatness of his observation pleasing him. 'Do stay,' Maggie went on sweetly. 'We were just talking about you, weren't we, Jen?'

So his mental picture had not been too inaccurate. He cheered up and looked brightly from one to the other. Jenny's eyes were stretched wide open, staring at her sister, saying, shut up, shut up, shut up. She was too agitated to speak. There was another knock on the door. Josh answered it again. Oh no, thought Jenny, horror-stricken. It'll be Henry, arrived home and calling to surprise me.

'Mum. Can I go out on bikes with James?'

Thank God. 'Yes, love, you go. Mind the road, and be home by half past seven. Only up and down the street and the back alley, remember.'

Josh grabbed his cycle helmet and slammed the door. There was a sudden, heavy silence.

'Well,' said Maggie in a soft, sinuous tone. 'I think he has a right to know. He is the father, after all. Are you going to tell him about the baby, Jenny, or shall I?'

CHAPTER 10

Henry had always liked travelling by air, ever since he first went in an aeroplane at the age of eight on a trip to Paris with his father. He was the first boy in the class to go in an aeroplane and the teacher, Mrs Bold, had asked him to stand up and describe it to the rest of the class. Of course, it would not be like that nowadays, some children probably travelled by air more often than they went by train. But it must still be exciting, he thought, the first time you feel that thrill of acceleration pushing you back in your seat, and that moment when the bumpy runway gives way to smooth air beneath you and you realise you are airborne. That surely must be a thrill, even to the sophisticated youngsters of today.

Now as an adult, it was the passivity of it he enjoyed. Whatever your cares and responsibilities (not that he had many, he reminded himself – he was as free as a bird), whatever pressures you had at work, problems to solve, decisions screaming to be made (and Henry generally waited until dilemmas were at screaming point before he made a decision), while you were in the air, everything had to wait. He would never be one of these businessmen he often saw, muttering frantically into a tape recorder so that they could throw it onto the secretary's desk as they strode through the door, saying, 'Type that lot, please, as soon as possible, Miss Flake.' A lap-top computer would never crowd his knees as he juggled with sales figures or extrapolated annual profits. Henry pitied these people, running like crazy just to keep up with themselves. For Henry, air travel meant complete relaxation. He particularly enjoyed the arrival of the first gin and tonic. He liked the way immaculate air stewardesses (or flight attendants, as they were called in these days of non-gender-specific terms) wove their way evenly down the aisles, trailing a cloud of efficiency and corporate perfume behind them. 'Tea or coffee, Sir? Madam, tea or coffee?' He liked the even, impersonal repetition of every attendance. Every passenger was treated with identical de-humanised, sanitised pleasantness. He liked the neat trays of food, as sanitised and pleasant as the stewardesses, served at God knew what time of day or night, and the neat, individual sized bottles of wine. He was interested to note on this flight from Los Angeles that the stewardesses, all American and past their first youth (he'd heard somewhere that they put the older ones on the long haul flights – he wondered why) all had something else in common too. They all appeared to have been to the same plastic surgeon who had removed the folds of skin that naturally develop beneath the lower eyelid – what Jenny would cheerfully describe as laughter lines. All these women had the same pleasant, wide-eyed, de-humanised stare, showing slightly more white of the eye than is natural. The skin around the eyes, naturally crêpey and expressive of character by the age of forty-something, on these women was smooth and taut, almost shiny with tightness. It gave them all a resemblance to the stars of the American soap operas he had seen occasionally during his stay. To him, they too were almost indistinguishable from one another. How strange and interesting and faintly distasteful, thought Henry. Why on earth do they do it? But after three months in America he had a pretty fair idea.

He was flying in the evening. The spring sunshine filtered golden-brown through the layers of Los Angeles smog and the sea made a deep blue, white-rimmed sheet, shifting but solid-looking, all along the coastline. The famous beaches were a thin line of beige along the lacy rim. He thought of Jenny. He had thought of her quite frequently, although not as frequently as he hoped she had thought of him. Everything had been so busy and interesting, his mind had been so crammed and crowded out with stimulating new experiences, he had only just had time to miss her. He had missed her, though, especially during the dark days and nights in Greenland, he had missed her with a dragging pain during that time. But in sunny, snowy Illinois, and sweet, mild, crazy California in spring, she had become more of a vague, comforting sensation in his mind, something pleasant that he knew was there and that he intended to go back to, but that he did not feel the need to pull out and look at all the time. Her face had taken on a softer focus in his memory, her features were blurry even, so overlaid were they by the faces of new friends and acquaintances he had made. He felt guilty when he realised this, that he could not exactly conjure up her features, so he took out the photo of her that he kept in his wallet, just to remind himself. Dear girl. She would be there, loyal and loving, constant and caring, looking forward to hearing all his adventures. He had deliberately not told her his exact date of arrival, he was looking forward to surprising her. He smiled to himself when he thought of that last postcard. She would not have received it yet, he had only posted it from the airport. It would follow him across the Atlantic. He wanted to be there with her when it arrived. It did not occur to him for one single, fleeting second that she might not have waited for him.

He was glad, in retrospect, that he had not asked her to marry him on that last night. It would not have been the right time. It would have made it harder, not easier to leave, and his circumstances would have been harder to explain to new acquaintances he had met on his travels. He felt uncomfortable with the word 'fiancée'. It sounded pretentious, and was neither one thing nor the other. It was easier not to have to mention a private life at all, then people took him at face value, a man alone without a present or a past. This fitted his idea of himself as a wanderer. What's more, it did not automatically cut off any possibility. He could choose afresh how to be with every new person he met, depending on what opportunities arose. Without, he believed, jeopardising his future with Jenny, he had left himself open to enjoy the present and make the most of every new encounter on his travels.

There had not, in fact, been any romantic encounters. Many women had flitted through his field of vision like bright, exotic fish through the beam of an underwater lamp. Many had been pleasant to talk to, some he had found attractive. He thought with particular fondness of Laura, a marine biologist at the university of Illinois. Laura was thin and brown with floppy hair and a voice like crackling beech leaves. She said her grandfather was Cherokee. They had drunk gallons of coffee together and had private chats covering every topic, which was more intimate to Henry and more of a disclosure of himself than sex. But Laura had a boyfriend in St Louis, Melv, whom Henry had taken care never to meet. They had exchanged addresses and promised to call and write, but Henry didn't think they would. Their brief closeness had the romantic aura of an encounter embedded in a time and place that cannot be recaptured.

The pilot informed them in a voice suggesting heavy sedation, that the plane was approaching Heathrow. They circled, stacked for half an hour because of thick cloud. The temperature and weather conditions sounded depressingly familiar for England at the beginning of April – dense cloud and drizzle, a mild twelve degrees. The dull green fields and acres of car park emerged beneath the smoky clouds. The pilot pointed out some of the features of London below them for the benefit of tourists and Henry saw the Thames lying like a twisted sheet of lead. Huge grey corrugated warehouses passed them, then the familiar sudden grinding of wheels on runway announced that they had landed. With a flat, sinking feeling Henry realised he was home. His feet were puffy and his mouth felt like an empty crisp packet. He wanted somewhere comfortable to sink into a hot bath, then slide between cool sheets and sleep. Rather surprisingly to him it was four in the afternoon here. It felt like midnight to his weary body. He booked into an expensive hotel with creamy decor and polite, faceless staff, and bathed, ate and slept. After some deliberation and several goes of picking up the phone and putting it down again, he phoned Laura just to say he had arrived safely. Her answering machine greeted him in Laura's husky American tones, and he put the phone down, half relieved. He would not call again. He considered phoning Jenny, but decided to surprise her as he had intended.

Now he was close to seeing her, all the feelings and dreams that had been put in cold storage during his travels began to thaw out and reawaken, warmth flowing painfully but pleasurably back into them, like blood into a frozen foot (a feeling he was familiar with after Greenland). He smiled at the thought of how delighted and amazed she would be to see him, how she would hug him till it hurt and he would gently, laughingly, prise her off him so that he could breathe. She would scold him light-heartedly for not letting her know so she could come and meet him at the airport, or at least have something in the oven for him. They would renew their love, and when they were back to where they had been before, he would propose to her and they would live happily after ever. Tomorrow he would go north and see her.

He spent the next morning in London browsing in bookshops, then over lunch in the Royal Academy tearoom he wrote a few post cards thanking his new American friends for all their hospitality. He hoped in his card to Laura that he had caught just the right tone of warmth and finality. The subtleties and shades of language were so difficult, especially as the American custom of spelling things out was alien to his nature. Laura had certainly liked to spell things out, nothing seemed to embarrass her. Talking to her had been like breathing purified, highly oxygenated air. With Henry, what was left unsaid was as important as what was said. He could not have coped with Laura's intense scrutiny of his psyche for long. Three months of her company had been excitingly foreign, but enough. He preferred his everyday benign detachment, where meanings floated in the air and were understood, as they were with Jenny. The closer he got to seeing her, the more he wanted to.

After lunch he caught the train. He arrived just after four. He caught a taxi, and he made himself call in to the University to check his mail and catch up with a few colleagues. He needed to arrange a room there for the night, if only to store his belongings. He hoped he would be staying at Jenny's. After a drink in the senior common room with Jake, a fellow doctorate student, Henry decided that he needed some fresh air and space before seeing Jenny. There was a leafy path running around the University lake and Henry strolled along it, adjusting himself mentally to being home. He sat and watched the ducks for a while in the late afternoon as they pottered about in the dark green water. The sight of a small boy throwing bread to them while his parents sat on a bench tugged at his heart for some strange reason and made Henry feel he was really home. You couldn't get a more ordinary, comfortable British sight, he reflected, than a small family throwing white sliced bread to overfed brown ducks. They made a wake in the still water as they swam around after the soggy pieces. A one-eyed goose, ostracised by the other geese, followed the ducks, hanging around on the outskirts of the group. Suddenly he felt lonely and his tiredness washed over him. He had saved his visit to Jenny until last. It was teatime. If he didn't go now, he would fall asleep where he was.

It was evening when Henry turned into Hazel Terrace. He had arrived on foot. The last rays of watery spring sunshine fell obliquely into the narrow street, so that the houses on one side were lit up, their windows aflame with reflected sunlight, while the other side of the street lay in a pool of darkness. Everything looked smaller than he remembered, the houses were more poky and cramped. He had an instant sense of claustrophobia at the sight of so many houses, all alike and joined to one another. It was an unpleasant contrast to the large, airy wooden houses of America, each on their own spacious plot, so unjustly described as a yard. Here the houses had real yards, mean scraps of concrete or grass, hemmed in by the crumbling red brick walls of the houses on either side. The huge, angular shape of the chocolate factory dominated the small street. He had forgotten how close it was. No wonder Jenny had bought the house for a good price. You would have to like chocolate to enjoy living here. She was all right on that score. He realised that America had spoilt him for this narrow existence. What on earth did people do here, he wondered, to give themselves that thrill of danger and adventure that he got from his travels? Sex, pubs and sport about summed it up, he thought. Unless you had a passion for medieval history and architecture. But perhaps it was just jet lag, he told himself, that was giving him such a jaundiced eye, and the inevitable feelings of depression that follow an exciting trip abroad.

He knocked on the door. While he waited for her to open it and after a gasp of delighted joy fall into his arms, he heard some sort of commotion within. A man (it sounded like a man – could it be?) was shouting. Someone else, someone who began to sound disturbingly like Jenny, was speaking in a raised, agitated voice. Words that he could not pick out were jabbing the air. Angry words are easy to recognise in any language, even through a closed door. After a few minutes he realised no one had heard his knock, so he knocked again. The voices stopped. Footsteps padded along the hall, and the door was opened not by Jenny, but by Maggie. He and Maggie stood in silence, staring at each other while the Cathedral clock in the distance chimed eight. Maggie eyed him coolly while removing a bit of food from a back tooth. She licked her finger with relish. He waited eagerly for a friendly greeting, possibly an ambiguous hug with a lingering trailing of the fingers in his collar. Instead, she turned back into the house and called out, 'Jenny, your fish man's back. It's Henry. What shall I say?'

Jenny came to the door, his lovely, warm, kind, funny, soothing Jenny.

'You've said more than enough already. Get out of my *sight*!' As she spat the last word her arm shot out like an arrow and she pointed to somewhere down the street indicating where Maggie should go to obey this instruction. Maggie melted away indoors. Jenny wiped her hands down her front as if they were sweaty, and focused on Henry. He held open his arms, but she did not fall into them. She just stood there, said 'Oh Henry!' and burst into tears. He climbed awkwardly up the step (there was not room for two) and hugged her in the doorway. The warm smell of her hair made a gush of love well up inside him, and he rubbed his face in the shininess of it. After a few minutes, instead of subsiding, the tears had gathered strength so that she was bawling into his shoulder rather alarmingly. It dawned on him that this was more than tears of joy at seeing him. He was vaguely aware of Maggie and a man talking quietly but urgently in the sitting room. 'It's not your fault,' he heard Maggie say. 'It was an accident. It could happen at any time. To anyone. You don't need to feel responsible.' He could not catch the man's reply, but the tone was unmistakably anxious. It must be something serious, for Jenny to be so angry with her sister and, it seemed, with the man inside the house. She was usually so easy-going and generous. Who was the man? He felt a stab of jealousy that he told himself was quite unreasonable. He banished idle speculation, it was always a waste of time. He had more urgent matters to attend to. The woman he loved, the woman he had come home to see, was crying in his arms. He stroked her shoulder lovingly. She just cried harder and wailed, 'Oh Henry, oh Henry,' over and over again.

'Hey,' he murmured, hoping to stem the flow of excessive emotion. 'It's all right, I'm home now.' Then, 'I missed you,' he added hopefully, thinking that this was what she was waiting to hear. He had noticed women liked you to say the obvious. But his words did not seem to help. She still clung sweatily to him, howling like a child. He was beginning to feel uncomfortable. He noticed the net curtain in the window of the house next door give a definite twitch, and a brightly coloured face like a child's play-school drawing moved across it in the dimness.

'Let's go inside.' He led Jenny in.

In the sitting room the lamp was on but the curtains were still open so that a shaft of late, pale evening light slid across the room, making the dust particles dance for a golden moment before vanishing. Maggie was handing a drink to a tall, elegant young man. This must be her latest flame. He had the look of obvious glamour that Henry assumed someone like Maggie would find attractive. He was much more aware of this kind of thing thanks to Laura. He had never realised, until his chats with her, how much was really going on in everyday transactions that, until now, he had taken in his innocence to be completely straightforward. The young man's eyes had moved away from Maggie to focus intently on Jenny the instant she walked into the room. Henry held out his hand. 'Henry Proctor,' he said.

'Pleased to meet you,' returned the man, without taking his eyes off Jenny.

'Oh – this is – Sanjay Baljekar,' Jenny managed. 'He's – he's – '

'An accountant,' put in Maggie smoothly. 'Henry has just come back from the United States. Haven't you, Henry?' She was speaking conversationally, adeptly steering things, just as she must do at the social functions she attended. Henry, after a doubtful glance at Jenny, began to tell Sanjay about his trip. Jenny looked at Maggie in surprise. She watched her remove Henry's coat without his noticing and place a drink in his hand, the consummate hostess. Having precipitated this crisis with Sanjay, apparently entirely for her own entertainment out of sheer spite, she was now in complete control, turning it into a social occasion. She's manipulating the whole thing, Jenny realised with horror. Why? Just because she can? These are people's lives, not some game with puppets to be jerked about for the fun of it. The shift in atmosphere was so sudden, Jenny felt as if the floor had moved beneath her feet and she was disorientated. Sanjay appeared to be listening politely, even putting in the odd question. My God, what on earth is going on? she thought wildly. Maggie glided over and pushed her gently into the kitchen. 'Leave it to me,' she whispered.

'*Leave it to you*? Do you think I'm completely insane? Everything you have ever touched in my life has turned to rubbish, and you say *leave it to you*?'

'Look,' said Maggie firmly, grasping her by the shoulders. 'Somebody's got to take control. What are you going to do? Trundle bravely on while it all collapses round your ears? For God's sake, pull yourself together while I explain.' Jenny sniffed. 'Listen,' Maggie went on, 'You're expecting Sanjay's child. He doesn't want to know. The best he's come up with is offering to pay for an abortion.'

'A true gentleman,' snarled Jenny.

'For Christ's sake, this is the nineteen-nineties, stop behaving like a victim, some sad Victorian housemaid who's got herself up the spout. Get a grip. Take control. That's what I'm doing *for* you – taking control.'

'But –'

'Shut up and listen. You don't want Sanjay, Sanjay doesn't really want you – no, he doesn't, Jen, I'm sorry, but there it is. You had a lovely time, an affair, whatever you want to call it, it was presumably fun at the time – I still can't see it, you and him, you're as different as chalk and cheese, and you know it. You wouldn't be satisfied, saddling yourself with a pretty boy like him, not for long. You'd be mothering him all the time, as you already have been, I can see it. Sanjay is sweet and lovely, and wonderful for someone, but not for you.'

'All right, all right, you don't have to hammer it home with a sledge hammer. I'm not stupid.'

'I'm sorry. I'm trying to help you.'

'But why? You've never wanted to do anything but wreck things for me before.'

Maggie ignored her and carried on. Now was not the time for that conversation. She doubted that there ever would be a time for the subject of Mark – at least, not if she could help it. They had to get on with the task in hand.

'You want more than just a body in a man. You want Henry, right?' Jenny nodded, her tears welling up again. God, what a mess, how had it all gone so wrong? 'And Henry wants you. Look at his face – he's alight just to see you. He wouldn't have come back, otherwise.'

'But he won't – not when he finds out,' she began to wail. Maggie shook her.

'Jenny Burdge,' she said firmly, '*Listen to me*. Just do as I say, and it will all work out. I promise. Well, at least if it doesn't, we'll have had a damn good try. And I owe you a few,' she added. The look between them conveyed more than Jenny had ever thought they would share – mutual knowledge. So she knows, Jenny thought, astounded. She has known all along that I knew. She knows I knew, and that I said nothing. I can't believe it. But as they looked at each other, with Maggie's hands still gripping her shoulders, Maggie's eyes looking into hers, she knew that it was true. Maggie pulled her close in a sudden, fierce hug. 'I'm sorry, Jen. You'll never know how sorry. I've spent years –'

'*You've* spent years. What do you think it's been like for me?' Jenny pushed her away. 'Now's not the time,' she muttered. 'And "sorry" is hardly an adequate word.'

Maggie gave her a look so tortured that it conveyed more than words could. Jenny put her arms around her sister. 'Hey, look,' she whispered into her hair. 'It's all right. It's all over long ago. It's all right. The poor bugger's dead now, anyway. Whatever stupid, cruel things he did – and he certainly did, so did you – it somehow doesn't seem to matter any more. He's not going to get any more out of life – but we're still here to make the best of it. Or cock it up, like I'm doing.'

They held onto each other for a long moment.

'You're amazing,' said Maggie. 'There's nobody like you.'

Jenny gave a blotchy grimace. 'Thank God.'

By the time Henry and Sanjay had bounced the balloon of small-talk between them for a while, just at the point when they were both beginning to fear that the balloon was running out of air and would sink onto the carpet leaving an awkward silence between them, Maggie and Jenny emerged from the kitchen. Jenny had obviously been to the bathroom, for her hair was brushed and her face was rather noticeably caked in 'natural beige' face powder. Henry noticed that there were blotches of pink still visible beneath the make-up, and he was touched.

'Now,' said Maggie in her smooth, hostessy voice. 'You two have had a little time to get to know each other? Good. Now we suggest – Jenny and I – that you, Henry, take Jenny out for a much-needed bite to eat, and have a *really good* chat – catch up on everything, and when you come back, Sanjay and I will have sorted things out –' Sanjay looked blankly at her, but she continued undaunted – 'and then we'll have a chatty hour or so all together. Get to know each other.'

'What about Josh?' said Jenny. He would be home any minute, it was almost half past seven. She could not allow him to walk into the middle of this adult drama. Everything must be normal for him, at all costs. She did not want him to see Henry, either. It would simply confuse and upset him to greet Henry as a long-lost friend today, only to be told tomorrow that he had disappeared again, this time for good. For that would surely be the outcome of this evening. God, she cried silently, what a mess. What a bloody, painful, stupid, agonising mess.

'I'll see to Josh,' offered Maggie, looking at her watch. 'I'll call him in when you've gone, and put him to bed. I'll tell him you've just gone out to see someone, and you'll be back soon.'

Jenny looked doubtful, but she was past making any sort of decision, however small. She realised that this was the first time that Maggie had ever offered to look after her nephew. Perhaps some sort of change was really taking place. Reluctantly, she accepted Maggie's offer.

Sanjay must definitely be Maggie's partner, thought Henry. He was just the sort of rich, glamorous young man, not too bright but highly ornamental, that Henry imagined Maggie would go for. Either that or a rich sugar-daddy, he thought wryly. Maggie always knew which side her bread was buttered. Henry was glad that he had had the sense to stick with Jenny. He was finding the atmosphere rather odd. Perhaps Jenny did not get on with Sanjay. Perhaps Sanjay had broken something of Jenny's, thought Henry, remembering the snatch of conversation he had overheard. Or maybe he had borrowed her car and had an accident in it. Jenny had always lent her car to friends with a freedom that Henry considered unwise. Maggie had said he was an accountant – perhaps she had trusted him with her savings and he had lost them. No, that could not be it – Jenny never had any savings. Still, no doubt he would get the full story at some stage. He was not all that interested in other people's love lives. He wanted to revive his own. At long last, Jenny was ready and they stepped out together into the gloomy street.

She has made it all sound so cosy and easy, Jenny thought, amazed at Maggie's nerve. She doesn't need to go to drama college, she's a consummate actress already.

'I hope Josh will be all right with Maggie,' said Jenny as they left the house.

'I'm sure he will,' Henry answered kindly, not giving it a moment's thought. He had his mind on other things, such as Jenny's nearness and distress. He had not anticipated such a violent reaction to his arrival. He was certainly flattered, if a little bemused. He was beginning to suspect that things might not have simply stayed placidly the same while he was away.

Henry and Jenny walked down the street in the gathering dusk, their arms around each other. His familiar, warm animal smell enveloped her. It was like the smell of horses, or warm hay – a primitive, reassuring smell. He had a rough, hairy jacket on that she had not seen before. It had a rugged, outdoorsy American look about it. There was something about the cut and the width of the shoulders. The sight of him in different clothes, clothes he had chosen by himself, or with someone else, seemed peculiarly to emphasise the time they had spent apart. They made him seem inaccessible and different from the version of him that she had held in her head all this time. For now that her memory of him was overlaid by his actual presence, she realised how faded and distorted the memory had become. He was harder, more attractive and more remote than the Henry who had left nine months before. His curly, wiry hair had been bleached by the sun. Alone with him at last, she suddenly felt quite shy.

At the end of the road they turned into a wide street lined with tall lime trees, now in bud. They made their way towards the city centre. The bright moon, almost full, was shining already and the shadows under the trees were purple. The sky was still washed with red in the west, where it showed between the tall houses. Lights were on and people were going about their usual evening activities in the Victorian houses with their high ceilings and elegant fireplaces. The people in the houses, thought Jenny, belonged to another world. She watched a few of them moving silently around. A woman in a dark dress handed a man a glass, then turned to speak to someone Jenny could not see. Her long dark hair was smoothed back into a bun. In another house a man sat alone in an apricot-coloured room, reading a newspaper. There was a large, spreading fern on a pedestal beside him. A ginger cat washed its face, peaceful on the windowsill. As Jenny watched, a hidden hand drew the curtains, enclosing the cat. The picture of serenity was hidden from the public gaze, to continue in private. Those lucky people, she reflected, who have their lives all tidy and sorted out. A black BMW was parked in the driveway of one house, a blue Volvo estate in the next. Who are they, she wondered, those people who clearly possess some vital piece of information about life that makes it all turn out right? How do they afford these lovely houses, with their large front gardens and a flight of steps up to the front door? How do they manage to have a solid, happy marriage, a couple of handsome, clever, well-adjusted children at one of the local private schools, a fulfilling part-time job that still leaves them enough time to look good and entertain a wide and interesting circle of friends? It all looked so easy from the outside, she thought. What is the secret to that kind of success? She wished she knew.

Jenny was still breathing gustily, but she had calmed down. Henry was relieved. Crying was a messy, snotty business, and women crying made him anxious. He was too full of love to talk – the strength of his feelings, suppressed for so long, overwhelmed him. He was so thankful nothing had developed with Laura to corrupt his love for Jenny. He kept planting dry, hot kisses on the top of Jenny's head. She looked in excellent health, he thought – blooming, in fact. He realised how much he preferred her peachy English roundedness to the lean, tanned American girls. Even to the brown and sinuous Laura. He gave her a tight squeeze. 'I'm glad to be back,' he said.

Jenny did not speak because she was busy rehearsing what she was going to say.

The cherry trees along the street by the Minster were dressed in their spring finery and appeared to hold light in their blossoms long after the sun had set. The Minster was floodlit and shone like bone. Tall horse chestnuts were coming into sticky bud, the fallen ones stuck to their shoes, giving off a piny scent.

'What would you like to eat?' Henry asked at last. 'Chinese?'

'Urgh, no,' said Jenny with a vehemence that was almost revulsion. He was surprised. She used to like Chinese food. 'Greek, then?'

They strolled, still fused together, down a narrow side street and into the Shambles, where a small taverna was run by a stout and friendly Greek couple – friendly to the clientele, that is, who were sometimes entertained to scorching, passionate rows between husband and wife among the stainless steel pans in the immaculate kitchen. Tonight, however, they appeared to be in harmony. The taverna was whitewashed brick inside, and green plants hung and trailed from every surface, so that the view from the street was of bright cleanliness and lush greenery. The glass door was slightly steamed up with cooking. Untwining their arms just to get through the door, Henry and Jenny went inside and the door closed behind them.

While they were out, Maggie treated Sanjay to the time of his life on the sitting room carpet. While he was in a vulnerable state of hazy astonishment, she lodged some key points firmly in his fuddled brain.

'So,' said Jenny when they had ordered. 'How's everything with you?' The words sounded so trite and casual, as if Henry were an acquaintance she had bumped into, whom she had not seen for a week or so. He sniffed his glass of wine.

'Hmm. Not a bad one. A lot of the Californian ones are quite good, but I do like a good French wine. Do you like this one?'

She couldn't even bring herself to choke down a mouthful. 'Mmm, I've not had this one before.' At the moment, she thought, I wouldn't know it from cat's wee. She toyed with the stem of her glass. 'So,' she tried again, 'what's been happening with you? Everything go well in the States? How were the fish?' It was like getting blood out of a stone.

He shrugged. 'Hard to know where to start, really. So much has happened.'

'You're not kidding,' said Jenny with feeling.

'How about yourself?'

Jenny put her glass down with a thump so that some of the wine spilled onto the cloth and made a purple stain that spread slowly across the pristine white cotton like venous blood. 'Come on, Henry, for Christ's sake. You've been away for nine months, with nothing but a couple of postcards to show you're even still on the planet. I torture myself with missing you, eventually I assume you've gone for good, then you waltz in again with a cool, "How about yourself?" as if I was your bloody granny.'

Henry shrank visibly and began dabbing at the wine stain with an ineffectual napkin. I'm getting it all wrong, she thought with despair. I'm backing him into a corner before we've even started. Jenny Burdge, she admonished herself, when will you ever learn? Give the man a breather.

'For God's sake, leave it alone,' Jenny snapped, then wished she had not. He never could stand conflict, she remembered. He gave her one swift glance, then a shield came down behind his eyes and they became flat and cold. Arctic blue, she thought stupidly. How appropriate. She had alienated him. She wanted to bite her tongue out. She had lost him now. He was hidden behind a mask of cool civility. He put the napkin down and called to the young waiter.

'Excuse me. My – friend – has spilt some wine. I'm very sorry. Could you change the cloth?' The boy moved swiftly round the table, moving cutlery and glasses with deftness, and shaking out a new, crisp cloth.

'Let's try not to make a mess of this one, shall we?' said Henry when he had finished.

Jenny was irritated by his patronising humour. Her heart sank like a stone. She knew she would not be able to eat a thing. The stress would be bad for the baby, she thought, instinctively feeling her stomach. It's OK, she said silently, calm down, it's OK. Although it would be another month before she would feel it move, for the first time she felt that the baby was a real, living person who was with her in this ordeal. She wanted to protect it, as she had on the day she went to the hospital, and the desire to protect something weaker than herself gave her strength.

'I'm sorry. This is disastrous. I've looked forward so much to you coming home,' she said. 'Only I thought – I didn't know whether you *were* coming home. Well, not to us, I mean – obviously you had to come back to York, to finish your research and what have you, but you left us so – '

'So what? I left you so what?'

Oh no, he's angry and defensive now, she thought. She struggled on. What did it matter, now? she reminded herself. It was all lost anyway. So she blurted out, 'You left us so casually, you hadn't been in touch that last week, then you were so – well offhand, I assumed you wanted to finish it, but didn't say so because I was so upset, you realised I'd already got the message.' He was staring at her. 'I mean – I know you never like to hurt people's feelings,' she added, hoping to retrieve herself a little. She wouldn't say anything about his not saying goodbye to Josh. Things were bad enough already. His eyes were colder than ever and his mouth was a thin line. Never had he seemed so remote. Never had she wanted him more. The waiter put two plates unobtrusively in front of them. Savoury smells wafted up from the food. Henry picked up his cutlery and appeared to give his dinner excessive attention. Jenny did not even glance at hers. She could not even remember what she had asked for.

'I see,' he said at last. 'Let me get this straight. You thought I stayed away in that last week because I wanted to avoid you. You thought I wanted to avoid you because I planned to dump you before I went away.'

Jenny nodded.

'You thought the only reason I didn't was because you were so upset and I didn't want to make it worse. You think I would have gone off cheerfully on my way, having dumped you but just omitted to tell you.'

Jenny nodded again, less certainly this time. Henry put his knife and fork down and finished his mouthful slowly. 'You stupid woman,' he said.

She waited in silence while he shovelled in a few mouthfuls of food. Nothing, it seemed, got in the way of his appetite. She nibbled on some dry bread – the food of penance, she reflected bitterly. When he had cleared his plate he sat back and looked at her. Your eyes are so beautiful, she wanted to say, your freckles move me almost to tears. But what came out was, 'Excuse me, I'm feeling a bit – ' With that, she dashed for the ladies' cloakroom.

When she came back he had ordered strong, black coffee, just as she used to like it. Now even the smell repelled her.

'Are you all right?' he asked kindly. 'You've been ages. I thought you'd done a runner. You don't look too well. You haven't eaten much, that's not like you.'

'I'm fine,' she assured him. He patted her hand and she smiled at him.

'That's better,' he said. 'More like old times.'

This was more than Jenny could take. Tears welled up and she fought them back. This would be a disastrous moment to cry again. He would think she had gone completely off the rails. In fact, she was beginning to feel rather close to it.

'No, not quite like old times, Henry. God, how I wish it was.'

'What do you mean?' he asked her, but before she could reply he went on, 'If you only knew why I stayed away that last week. What was going through my mind. Wondering how to say it.' Oh my God, she thought, panicking. Not some revelation of a sudden new love, I just couldn't stand it.

'It's OK,' she said quickly, 'I understand, you don't have to explain. It doesn't matter now, really.'

'You always did understand me,' he said, still holding her hand on the tablecloth. 'You've never needed me to spell things out. You just seem to know.'

Oh bloody great, she thought. He's complimenting me now for being bright enough to get the message when he wanted to ditch me. Well, I would have had to be a complete fool not to take the hint. Not phoning, not calling, never being at home, buggering off for nine months – those things might just have given me a clue. To her amazement, she saw that he had that old look in his eyes, a look in fact that she had rarely seen, even in the old days. His eyes were not cold and hard, but melting and warm. He squeezed her fingers so hard that the circulation almost stopped.

'So, then, since you can read my mind, and since you are my best friend, what do you say?'

Despite its bitter odour, she took a large gulp of coffee. It burnt her gullet as it went down. My God, she thought, he has opened out. He would never have told her she was his best friend before. Some American girl must have unlocked him in a way she never could. But what was he saying?

'Well, I – I – '

'It's OK, take your time. No rush. I know it might be a bit of a shock. Well, not a shock, I hope, but maybe a surprise.'

'Look, Henry. I seem to have lost the plot here for a moment. What exactly are you trying to tell me? What is it you want my opinion on? What's the surprise?' Her empty stomach shifted alarmingly. 'You're not – thinking of getting married, are you?' Please not that, she cried desperately. I don't think I could stand it. It's all too much. He burst out laughing.

'You are funny,' he said. 'I'm only getting married if you'll have me.'

Oh, Henry, she thought. My dear, kind, totally incomprehensible man. Whatever are the thought processes in that highly organised, rational mind, that you think you can come back after nine months of no contact except a few measly, hopelessly uncommunicative postcards, and say this to me? She looked at him in despair. His heartbreakingly softened expression was like a savage stab in her heart with a serrated knife. In two seconds, she thought with torturing pain, I am going to destroy that open, loving, vulnerable look for ever. I am about to jump off an emotional cliff. I will never see him like this again.

'You can't just come back and – well, I mean, we haven't seen each other for months. People can't just put themselves in the deep freeze while you are away. Life has been going on without you, you know.'

'I know that,' he said, his face darkening. In fact, it had not really occurred to him. When he had imagined anything, he had imagined that Jenny's life had been somehow static without him.

'Henry,' she said, with tears in her eyes, 'I love you more than anyone in the world – more than any other adult, anyway,' she added, strictly accurate.

He grinned. 'Well, that's all right, then.'

'No, it isn't all right. I do love you, but we can't just go from A to C without B, if you see what I mean.'

Henry didn't see. It all appeared perfectly simple to him.

'Henry,' she began carefully, 'I think there are a few things I need to explain.'

What Henry went through that night, over the stuffed vine leaves and a good red wine, will never be fully recorded except in the deepest recesses of his own very private mind. It is sufficient to say that in one evening he made up for thirty-eight years of emotional detachment and self-insulation. It was as if his heart had been ripped open and he was forced to examine some very bloody entrails. They were the last to leave the taverna. They had stood outside under the street light, stiff and far apart. She had pleaded with him, 'Please try to understand. I know you may not – *will* not – want me any more, but if you have any feelings at all – even as a friend – please just try to understand.'

'I think friendship will be out of the question.'

'But it was you who said – '

'That was before. You have hurt me. You are not the person I loved. That person would not have done what you have done.'

'Maybe you didn't know that person very well.'

'You're right there. I don't know you.' His face twisted into an expression of sheer contempt. 'I don't want to know you. You have made a mess of everything. I am confused, I don't know how I feel, but I do know I never want to see you again.'

He could not rid himself of those final words to her. Even in the darkness of his own pain, he wished he had not been so cruel. It had not been necessary. But she deserves it, he thought. She has destroyed it all. She has destroyed our future, our chance of happiness. She has paid a high price for a bit of cheap sex, he thought. But then, you often do, he added sanctimoniously. He had forgotten all about his own youthful follies.

'But how could I tell you anything, when you kept yourself deliberately out of touch? You could have given me an address, you could have phoned me, you could have tried actually fucking *talking* to me. Then none of this would have happened – wait, Henry, *wait.*'

He had always hated it when she swore. He couldn't take any more, so he began to walk away while she was still speaking. It was usually an effective way to cut people off. Jenny abandoned herself to rage and disappointment. She did not know who she was more disappointed with – herself or Henry.

'You're a cold fish, Henry Proctor. Why don't you try to understand, instead of judging, just for once?' She knew she was being unjust, and that desperation rarely produced good results. But she could not control the flood of love and pain that threatened to overwhelm her. 'You've always kept yourself deliberately out of touch, Henry. When are you going to reach out and touch somebody?'

Her desperate cries followed him down the empty street and echoed between the ancient houses that leaned together over the cobbles. This is just another drama these houses have observed, thought Henry numbly as he walked away. In his blackened mind he could see the wooden pallets being carried down the street, bearing away the dead after the plague, over six centuries before. He walked through a narrow gap between two houses where the wall had been worn away by the carts full of corpses. The streets would have been stinking then, he thought, with horse manure and raw sewage. The sound of horses' hooves would have accompanied his walk back to the university, not the passing scream of police cars under the orange lights. Only the university would not have been there. The sounds of distant revellers leaving a pub would have been the same. The river would have been flowing then, black and still with glittering columns of reflected light. These thoughts were a refuge from his messy emotions. He felt that where his heart had been, there was now just a bloody mass of gore. Suddenly, in his distress, his sensibilities were heightened so that he felt that only the thinnest veil separated him from some other night like this, centuries ago, when someone else walked home in despair to some lonely bed far outside the city walls, just as he was doing now. It was the weirdest sensation. It must just be the history of the place, he thought sensibly. Everything in America was so new, he had forgotten the oldness of York, and now it was pressing itself upon him.

'*You have always kept yourself deliberately out of touch, Henry. When are you going to reach out and touch somebody?*' Those last words had followed him down the street and ricocheted around inside his head long after he had left Jenny standing alone outside the taverna. He should have called a taxi for her, he thought mechanically. But matters like taxis seemed mundane and far away, far removed from this black and desolate place he had entered in his head. It was a fine night, she would be all right on her own. She had done enough other things on her own, without him, he reflected bitterly. She was a whore. He walked all the way home along the edges of the shadows, under the cold stars.

He returned to his monastic room at the university, one of the bare white cells normally used for first-year undergraduates who were all on vacation for Easter. Like a medieval knight undergoing an initiatory ritual, he stayed awake all night, trying to instil some calm and order into the raging riot of his mind.

Jenny stood staring up at the stars long after he had gone. The medieval roofs huddled together, leaning towards each other across the narrow street as if for comfort. Above them the new moon lay on its side, a thin sliver of pale shell trailing sparse threads of cloud, whose ragged edges shone blue in its cold, frail light.

Jenny wanted to throw her head back and howl up at the unfeeling moon. Instead she put her cold hands on her hot cheeks to cool them down and tried to steady her breath, and control the heaving sobs that were threatening to rise in her chest and burst. When she had steadied herself she looked up at the houses and down at the cobbles beneath her feet. The buildings were steady, solid and old. 'Bloody shambles is right,' she said, and set off in search of a taxi.

By six in the morning Henry was cold and stiff, and went into the tiny kitchen at the end of the corridor to make some strong coffee. A Portuguese cleaning lady was pleased to have some company when she came in at six-thirty, and he listened sadly to colourful stories in broken English about her lively and numerous relatives. At seven-thirty he telephoned America.

'Hello Agony Aunt,' he said when Laura picked up the phone. 'I need some advice.'

'Do you love her?' asked Laura when he had finished.

'I did. Well, yes, I think I still do. I'm just devastated. I'll never get over this.'

You will, thought Laura. 'Does she love you?'

'I think so – yes, she does.' A picture of Jenny floated up and melted his gloom. 'I really do love her, you know,' he said, feeling freer with Laura now that there were thousands of miles between them and he would never have her unnerving presence close to him again. 'But she's betrayed me. I can never trust her again.'

There was a long pause on the other end of the line.

'Has she, though? Did you tell her you loved her before you went?'

'No. I thought she knew.'

'Did you tell her you'd be faithful? Did you ask her to be?'

'No. I assumed . . .'

'It's never safe to assume anything, Henry.'

He said nothing.

'Did she know you'd want to be with her when you came back?'

'Well, I guess maybe not. I just sort of . . .'

'Assumed? Well, Henry, you're the cutest guy, but any woman who takes you on has got a job on her hands. Remember the three Cs?'

What were the three Cs? He had forgotten. Laura had always talked so much, sometimes he had simply enjoyed the soothing sound of her voice, rather than listening to the actual words.

'Commitment, Caring, and Communication. It sounds like you've got two out of three with this woman, Henry, from what you used to tell me, and that's not bad for starters. But how about working on the last one, honey?'

Henry iffed and butted a little longer. 'But a baby – some other man's bastard.'

Laura's feminist hackles rose. 'I think you're a little out of date, honey. It's her baby, Henry. She's having it on her own whatever, isn't she? I respect that. You should, too. No one takes that on lightly. She's a mother already, she knows what she's doing. If you choose to take it on, it will be yours too. A family can be all sorts of things. There are happy step-parents and step-kids all over the world. I'm going to become one, by the way. Melv and I are getting married.'

'Oh. Congratulations,' he said automatically. He vaguely recalled her mentioning some slobbish-sounding son of Melv's who liked computer games and had a weight problem. At least Josh was a boy after his own heart.

'Thanks. It's OK, this is about you. You like her son? Would you have preferred it if she'd had an abortion and not told you?'

'No, of course not. Yes. I don't know. I just wish it had never happened.'

'Not as much as she does, I'm sure. But she's been honest with you, Henry. And she loves you. Sounds like a gutsy lady to me. How many people can manage those two things? She might have said yes, then only told you later about the pregnancy. She could easily have misled you for a couple of months, and by then you might have been married, and it would be too late. At least you can't say she's tried to trap you. Or misled you. She might have let you think it was yours.'

Henry gave a barren laugh. 'Hardly. It'll be brown.'

Laura was losing interest, but managing not to show it. Henry still hovered in an agony of indecision.

'Well there you are, then,' she said, trying to terminate the call.

'If you love each other, you'll work it out,' as if that was all there was to it. And perhaps, when you came down to it, she was right, he thought. Perhaps that was all there was to it.

'Thanks, Laura. And – goodbye.'

Laura gave her husky laugh. 'Bye, Henry. You're sweet. I didn't know there were guys like you still left in the world. Good luck. Have a nice life. And by the way, that advice probably cost you sixty dollars. Hope it was worth it.'

'It was,' he said.

At eight thirty on Friday Jenny was just leaving for work when the post plopped onto the mat. Two brown bills and a postcard. This one was of a humpbacked whale blowing a plume of spray out of the blue, crispy water. The picture was so clear you could see a cluster of white barnacles on its dark, shiny wet skin. I shall be like a humpbacked whale soon, she thought. She turned it over. The postmark was dated a week ago, in California. There were only four words written on it in Henry's flowing hand, in thick black ink.

Jenny
Marry Me
Henry.

Her tears blurred the words until they were hardly legible.

On Saturday Josh went down to the river with James, his father and his little sister, Sarah. They were going to practise with their rollerboots, and Sarah was going to feed the ducks. Jenny gave Josh a stale loaf in a plastic bag to take with him. Sarah rode on her father's shoulders.

'Why haven't you got a dad?' she asked Josh as they walked down Alma Terrace to the water.

'Sarah, mind your own business,' said her father.

'I have,' Josh replied. 'He's dead.'

'Can you remember him?' asked James.

'James, Josh might not want to talk about this.'

'No, it's all right. I can't even remember him. Mum's cool. She

224

makes up for it. I don't mind not having a dad,' he lied, hoping he would be forgiven, if God was listening.

They reached the bottom of the narrow street and turned onto the tarmac path that led under the horse chestnut trees alongside the river. The path was covered with sticky buds.

'This is no good for rollerbooting,' said James. 'We'll get stuck on all the bits.'

His father sighed. He would have much preferred to stay in and watch the rugby. Ruth kept nagging him that he didn't spend enough time with the kids. 'Just get the damn things on and have a go,' he said.

'Actually,' said Josh suddenly, his head bent over his boots as he struggled with the laces, 'I have got a dad. He's an explorer.'

'Really?' said James, sounding impressed. 'Where does he go exploring?'

Josh could feel his status going up. He took a sudden, unconscious decision. 'In the Arctic,' he said. 'In Greenland. He studies fish. He's a world expert.'

It was James's father's turn to say, 'Really?' with pity in his voice.

'That's why he's not around very much. You don't get to come home much when you're an explorer. But he sends us postcards. My Mum's got them all up in the kitchen. You can see them if you like.'

'Mmm, that sounds interesting, Josh. Sarah, wait till we see some ducks. Don't eat it all yourself.'

Josh could tell James's father did not believe him. He desperately wanted to impress him. 'He's asked my Mum to marry him,' he said proudly. 'So he'll be my new dad. The card came yesterday, I saw it. "Marry Me", it said. Right soft. He's not soft, though. He's cool. It was all wet from the rain. Or from the Atlantic.' He loved that word. It conjured up images of wild seagulls, grey waves and salt spray. Josh stood up from tying the laces on his rollerboots and looked along the path under the trees. He could not believe his eyes. Fantasy was becoming reality, for there, walking along the path towards them, was Henry. Josh went very pink. 'There he is! I told you,' he said, and started skating furiously towards Henry's ambling figure. Much to Henry's amazement, they collided in a rugby tackle.

It was a long time since Henry had fed ducks. He remembered the family he had seen the day before. He and James's father chatted about work, and the improvements to the ring road that had been done while Henry was away. Josh wasn't very interested in ducks, but here on the river there were seagulls too, small, busy black-headed gulls – white-headed now – which had flown in from Scarborough and Whitby to escape the weather, and to enjoy the easy pickings of city life. There were large, cold-eyed herring gulls with sharp, devouring beaks.

'Look. If you throw it as high as you can, they'll take it from the air,' said Henry. Josh was proud of how far he could throw. After Easter they would be starting cricket in school and he and James had been practising in the back alley. Eager to impress Henry, he tossed the bread as high as he could. The gulls set up a shrill cackling as they swooped and dived for the food. Soon they were all engulfed in a cloud of screaming gulls. They could feel the draught from the wings as they flapped all around them in a mass of white screeches and rushing wings.

'I'm a bird man,' shouted Josh enthusiastically, remembering a book he had read. The closeness of the birds gave him a sense of wildness and excitement. When they opened their beaks he was close enough to see the wet, pale pink fleshy folds inside their throats, which was somehow shocking and unexpected.

'Watch this,' said Henry. He held a crust out in the tips of his fingers. Five gulls hovered in front of him, their wings beating fast, almost touching each other. Josh wondered how they managed not to clash wings and fall into the dark green water. Eventually the bravest bird came closer and snatched the bread from Henry's hand, then darted away, pursued by the others, chasing and dipping. Josh looked up at Henry, his face beaming with admiration.

'Cool,' he said.

'Yeah, cool,' echoed James.

Josh felt like a king. He gave Henry a hug around his waist. 'I think it's brill you're going to marry my mum. It's about time she got me a dad. She's a rubbish bowler. Listen to this. Do I sound like an exhaust pipe?'

'Yes, you do.'

'I can do that,' said James.

'No, you can't.'

James made a similar noise.

'Not as well as I can, anyway,' said Josh.

Henry felt terrible. He glanced at James's father, who just smiled.

Maggie was out for most of the next three days – 'sorting things out', she said mysteriously. Jenny floundered on with life as if she were wading through thick, damp sand. Sanjay did not come round again. Nor did Henry. On the fourth day he called. When Jenny came home from work she found him sitting at the table helping Josh with a cardboard model of the Statue of Liberty.

'Look, Mum, this is ace. Henry brought it back for me.'

Henry looked up sheepishly. His eyes were warm with the pleasure of sitting with Josh and helping him. He'd had a haircut so that there were little bands of white around his ears where untanned skin was newly exposed. The white bits touched Jenny, the skin looked soft and new against the weatherbeaten rest of him. She wanted to run her finger gently around his ear.

'You staying for tea?'

He grinned uncertainly. While she was chopping onions he came into the kitchen. He hovered awkwardly for a few minutes, taking up a huge amount of space in the small red room. Every time she reached to get something from a cupboard, he was there, filling the space between her and it. The kitchen had never felt so tiny before. Eventually he said, 'Did you get my card?'

She paused only for a split second, but long enough for him to notice. 'Oh yes,' she said lightly, 'All of them. I forgot to thank you. We did enjoy them, see, I've put them all up on the wall.' She pointed to them above the fridge.

'The last one, I mean. The whale.'

She had her back to him. 'Yes, that one came three days ago. Thank you. It was a nice thought.' She turned towards him, her eyes brimming over. 'It's just the onions,' she tried to laugh, wiping her nose on her apron. 'It was a lovely thought.' Her lip wavered despite her best efforts, and she began to cry. He put his arms round her. The smell of onions was very strong.

'Well?' he said, 'What do you say?'

She stood up straight and pulled herself away from him. 'You mean – it still stands? You still – I mean – even after –'

Spell it out, he remembered, they like you to spell it out. He was a man to persevere with a chosen course of action. Obstacles are not obstacles, they are challenges, he could hear Laura saying. She had often talked like a self-improvement text book. If you love each other, you'll work it out.

'Will you marry me, Jenny? Will you be my family? I've not had one, so I may take some teaching, but I'm sure we'll manage. You and me and Josh and – whoever?'

A few minutes later, thinking things had gone rather quiet, and wondering if there was any chance of a biscuit before tea, Josh put his head round the kitchen door.

'Urgh, yuck, soppy,' he said.

'How do you fancy a couple of years in Bangladesh?'

It was a Saturday in June, and Kate and Janice were sitting over coffee and croissants. All the trees in the city were fresh and green, making dapples on the old cream stone walls. Japanese tourists were starting to clog the streets, taking photographs of each other in front of every piece of old stone they could find. Kate pushed a letter towards her. 'It's a newsletter that comes twice a year, from the organisation I worked for in Zaire, World Health Plus. They're setting up a new hospital in Bangladesh, and they need staff to be involved at the setting-up stage, to get the whole thing off the ground.'

Janice read the letter, dropping crumbs on it. 'Are you serious? I thought you were happy here.'

'I am. It's just – well, I think a joint adventure would be a great idea, don't you? I mean, geriatrics is a bit of a dead end, isn't it?'

Janice gave her a wry look. 'In more ways than one.'

'You could be a theatre nurse in Bangladesh. Never mind theatre nurse, you'd probably be doing it all, from building the theatre to performing the ops. It's a fantastic country. Really interesting.'

Janice put a large dollop of jam on another croissant. The sun was beaming into the small wooden kitchen and a fly buzzed lazily against the glass of the open skylight. In a few minutes it would find its way out. 'It wouldn't be easy,' she said doubtfully.

'No, but you can't not do things just because they might be difficult at times. It would be a brilliant adventure. A "bonding experience", as they say. What do you think?'

That phrase decided the matter for Janice. 'Well, there's no harm in applying, is there?'

Kate kissed her forehead as she went to the fridge. 'That's my girl. More coffee?'

Just as Kate's hand grasped the coffee jug and poured the contents into Janice's cup, another hand was performing exactly the same task at exactly the same moment in another flat nearly three hundred miles away, in London. Nita had just spent her first night of passion in the arms of an arty, bearded photographer called Graham. As his lean, artistic hands (so dextrous and gentle, she recalled with a shudder of pleasure) poured the coffee, he spoke the words she had longed to hear, and that he had only spoken to two other women that year: 'You are the most beautiful woman I have ever met.' (Tender kiss.) 'You are the most incredible lover.' (Another, even more tender kiss.) She had her eyes closed so she missed his vulpine look as he said, 'would you let me take some artistic shots of you sometime?'

'See, what did I tell you?' gloated Maggie just before Jenny and Henry left. Jenny was trying to stuff yet another plastic carrier bag into the overloaded car. 'I knew it would all work out.'

It was August, and Jenny was feeling large and uncomfortable. Sensing the excitement perhaps, the baby was kicking her under the ribs with surprising vigour for one not yet born. The heat was making her itchy. 'I'm sure we've forgotten something. I'll remember what it is as soon as we get on the motorway. I'm so overheated, it's terrible. I want to wring my dress out.'

'If you think this is bad, be thankful you're not in Bangladesh,' said Maggie unsympathetically. 'Stop fussing, you're like an old mother hen. I must say, the thought of living in an old cottage in Wales for a year is very romantic. You'll turn into a real earth mother, wearing floral prints and baking your own bread. I can just see it. It'll suit you down to the ground. It would bore me rigid, of course.'

'Lucky it's not you who's going, then, isn't it? Do you think I can fit in that other casserole, the red one?'

'For God's sake, you've got enough stuff to set up a junk shop. Just get going. You're only going to Wales, you know, not Timbuktu. Think of Janice and Kate – they only took two bags each, and they're going to the back of beyond.'

Janice and Kate had come round a week before, to say goodbye.

'I never thought Janice had it in her to do something like that,' Maggie went on. 'But then,' she smirked, 'that girl was full of surprises, wasn't she?'

Henry had packed the car, which was so crammed with luggage that Josh had to sit almost doubled up in one corner of the back seat. He was already in, cheerfully ensconced with his cassette player, earphones and book.

Maggie and Sanjay stood in the doorway to see them off, the archetypal beautiful, successful couple.

'Sanjay and I will look after everything,' said Maggie, looking at Sanjay with a mixture of pride and wry amusement. 'We'll be good tenants – I promise. No wild parties – well, not many.'

'Just as long as that rent lands in my account every month,' said Jenny, calm and businesslike.

'Oh, Sanjay will see to that. Money's far too dull for me. Won't you, dear?' Maggie stroked his sleek and beautiful head.

'Look after mother.'

Maggie smiled. 'Oh, I think Bernard will do a reasonable job of that, don't you? Even if he is stupid enough to think her hair is naturally that colour, at her age. Love is blind, I suppose. Look at you two. Let us know if you do finally decide to tie the knot. We'll come and get drunk at your expense.'

'Not until I'm fit and trim again,' said Jenny. 'So it could be a very long wait.'

Astrid appeared in the doorway wearing some sort of long flowing robe with baggy red sleeves so that she looked as if she was dressed for a part in a Nativity play as one of the three wise men. Her hair was wilder than usual, and a brighter shade of pink. She thrust a large pineapple into Jenny's hands. 'I wanted to get you something to see you off with, but I didn't have time to get out. Hope you like pineapples – they plays havoc with my digestion.'

'Lake Gwynniad. It sounds so romantic,' said Jenny as they joined the roar of traffic on the motorway. 'A wonderful place for children. What a bit of luck they've got char there.'

'That means we can definitely get a dog, can't we?' said Josh.

'Hmm, we'll have to see. I think we'll have quite enough to do without that, to start off with, at least. If one's got our name on, it will probably come along. Things usually do, I find, don't they, Henry?' She reached across and patted his shoulder. Henry wasn't listening, he was concentrating on the traffic.

'My God, this seat belt's getting uncomfortable,' said Jenny near Birmingham. 'Let's open the chocolate biscuits. I'm going to have to stop for a wee soon. I hope that poor girl copes all right at work, my replacement. She was very young and quiet.'

'It's just that you're old and noisy,' said Henry affectionately, squeezing her knee.

They were renting a cottage close to the lake while Henry did the second year of his PhD. He had covered so much ground with Arctic Char the year before, it had been decided that he should move on to study the subgroup of landlocked char who only inhabited this particular lake in Wales. Apparently they had been left behind in glacial times, when the icy waters had receded and they had no longer been able to reach the sea. Amazing, when you thought of it, to last that long, stranded in a lake in Wales, reflected Jenny as the Welsh mountains began to rear up on either side of them, with their humped backs and soft, muted colours. In places the soil was so thin that the bare, grey rock jutted out in craggy lumps. Lean sheep cropped the short grass, looking from a distance like grey pebbles dotted all over the steep hillsides. Even a creature as humble as a fish can adjust to a different life pattern, she thought.

Change and growth are as natural and necessary as the rain on these wild and ancient hills. It's all a matter of adapting to survive, and finding a congenial life.

also available from

THE ORION PUBLISHING GROUP

☐ **Waiting for the Sea to be Blue** £5.99
PHILIPPA BLAKE
1 85799 875 8

☐ **The Normal Man** £5.99
SUSIE BOYT
1 85799 421 3

☐ **Mothers and Other Lovers** £5.99
JOANNA BRISCOE
1 85799 248 2

☐ **An Inheritance** £5.99
CARO FRASER
1 85799 964 9

☐ **Judicial Whispers** £5.99
CARO FRASER
1 85799 377 2

☐ **The Pupil** £5.99
CARO FRASER
1 85799 063 3

☐ **The Trustees** £5.99
CARO FRASER
1 85799 059 5

☐ **First Time** £5.99
LARA HARTE
1 85799 836 7

☐ **Wild Grapes** £5.99
GALLY MARCHMONT
1 85799 981 9

☐ **Ghost Music** £5.99
ALICE MCVEIGH
0 75280 920 2

☐ **While the Music Lasts** £5.99
ALICE MCVEIGH
1 85799 342 X

☐ **The Shrine** £5.99
CRISTINA ODONE
1 85799 429 9

☐ **The New Rector** £5.99
REBECCA SHAW
1 85799 731 X

☐ **Talk of the Village** £5.99
REBECCA SHAW
1 85799 732 8

☐ **Village Matters** £5.99
REBECCA SHAW
1 85799 851 0

☐ **The Beggar Bride** £6.99
GILLIAN WHITE
1 85799 844 8

☐ **Dogboy** £5.99
GILLIAN WHITE
1 85799 436 1

☐ **Grandfather's Footsteps** £5.99
GILLIAN WHITE
1 85799 337 3

☐ **Mothertime** £5.99
GILLIAN WHITE
1 85799 208 3

☐ **Rich Deceiver** £5.99
GILLIAN WHITE
1 85799 256 3

All Orion/Phoenix titles are available at your local bookshop or from the following address:

Littlehampton Book Services
Cash Sales Department L
14 Eldon Way, Lineside Industrial Estate
Littlehampton
West Sussex BN17 7HE
telephone 01903 721596, *facsimile* 01903 730914

Payment can either be made by credit card (Visa and Mastercard accepted) or by sending a cheque or postal order made payable to *Littlehampton Book Services*.
DO NOT SEND CASH OR CURRENCY.

Please add the following to cover postage and packing

UK and BFPO:
£1.50 for the first book, and 50P for each additional book to a maximum of £3.50

Overseas and Eire:
£2.50 for the first book plus £1.00 for the second book and 50p for each additional book ordered

---

BLOCK CAPITALS PLEASE

name of cardholder ....   *delivery address*
....   *(if different from cardholder)*

address of cardholder ....
....
....
....
postcode ....   *postcode* ....

[ ] I enclose my remittance for £..............................

[ ] please debit my Mastercard/Visa (delete as appropriate)

card number [ ][ ][ ][ ][ ][ ][ ][ ][ ][ ][ ][ ][ ][ ][ ][ ]

expiry date [ ][ ][ ][ ]

signature ....

prices and availability are subject to change without notice